KNIGHT HORSE

by

Bryce A Baker

W & B Publishers

USA

W & B Publishers

For information:
W & B Publishers, Inc.
9001 Ridge Hill Road
Kernersville, North Carolina 27285
www.a-argusbooks.com

ISBN: 9781942981077
ISBN:- 1942981074

Book Cover designed by Bryce Baker
Printed in the United States of America

Dedication

Dedicated to THOSE who walk in this world with a mind for justice and a heart that knows the difference.

And the woman that stands with me. My wife Rena.

Author's Note

Writing fictional books is like sailing through different worlds that may not be afforded us in real life. Authors command the adventure and realize the result without giving way to status quo. Putting the words to paper is scaling the impossible and immersing oneself in a dimension of imagination. It is a mind drug with incredible side effects.

Bryce A Baker

www.bryceabaker.com

The human brain is a complex, intricate combination of electrical and chemical interaction that miraculously controls thousands of thought patterns every day. Our ability to develop this control center is said to only function within a small potential. If we take what we already have and fully expand its capability we can accomplish incredible things.

Chapter One

The morning briefing is dragging out. My attention, along with my eyes, is wandering around the room. As my commander informs us of the day's objective, I focus on the U.S. Marshal crest directly behind him. Being a Marshal has been a weathering factor on my health over the last twenty two years and I am looking forward to retiring after twenty five, to spend my days out at my ranch full time.

This morning I have a simple solo assignment of securing an elusive felon that has been on the run for a few months. He has been located just miles away from my ranch in a wooded area I am quite familiar with. After briefing, I must drive out to the ranch and saddle up my four legged partner 'Image' and head out to the location.

Image has been my partner now going on three years. She is a gorgeous dark-brown and white, pure-bred Pinto with an attitude to match mine.

I will tend to this arrest on my own since it is close to home and should be an uncomplicated duty of the day.

This is the last assignment for the week and I am looking forward to the next two weeks of holidays to get some chores caught up around the ranch.

As I'm getting into my trusty old '89 Chevy pickup in the parking garage, I hear a voice yelling across from me.

"When are you going to park that beat-up old workhorse and get a new one?" It is Lance, another marshal. He snickers as he is unlocking the door to his shiny new ride.

"The beast is only just getting broke in, and she has never let me down. She doesn't give me a bad time like some of my old partners!" I smile back.

On my way home, the old girl did spring some attitude with the odd sputter, giving me second thoughts of maybe retiring her to a scrap yard.

I let the dirt cloud settle as I pull into the barn area of the ranch. The temperature is pushing over a hundred degrees today, so everything is dusty and hyper dry. Wearing body armor on the trail today will be out of the question, I would roast in it.

Getting my gear ready for the mission, Image is sending me her acknowledgment of my arrival home with a loud whinny.

***

Saddled and off we go. It is a great feeling enjoying the two things most in my life; my job and riding. Not many can say they get paid to have fun, even though things can get hairy. For me, corralling the bad guys and bringing them to the justice they deserve, fulfills my mental adrenaline addiction. Riding brings me back to the planet.

Image must be cooking in this heat like I am. She and I have been on some great adventures together and we interact on the job as though we are as one.

As we enter the general location, I pick up on a track that appears to be my target. We're about an hour out and in this sweltering heat, I want to make this a quick *snatch and cuff*. There's a cold beer waiting in my fridge that is begging me to drink it when all is done today. We are amongst a terrain covered in low bushes and thick trees. There are plenty of places to hide. My eyes share their attention between the ground and spotting for any sign of a threat.

The boot track is about a half an hour old and is the sole pattern shown on the file. He seems too stupid to change his boots after committing his last robbery. The boot prints on the liquor store floor are a strong match to the ones on the ground.

Image's ears are rotating like radar which alerts me to the fact that there is something in the area. I am giving her lead and her step is slowed. The breeze through the trees muffles any chance of me hearing anything other than something dramatically loud.

My mind is not focusing enough on my purpose, but is instead wandering into my next days of holiday mode. My training tells me to refocus but my complacency is overriding common sense.

They say you don't hear the shot that kills you, but the crack of a gunshot pierces my ears. A burning blast thunders against my shoulder and I am tossed out of my saddle to the ground. Through the pain I struggle to get my side arm from my holster but my hand is kicked clear of it. My assailant is now standing over me with a broad smile on his face.

He wipes his slobber from his mouth with his sleeve and gloats over me like I was a fresh deer killed by a hunter, "So this is the tough Marshal Bill Harden! You don't look so tough to me from where I stand."

Blood is saturating my shirt and my vision is getting hazy. The shock is wearing off and the pain is getting more intense. I raise my eyes to him and add, "So are you going to come *peacefully* or do I have to rough you up to bring you in?"

His sick laugh matches his demeanor, "Well, U.S. Marshall Bill Harden, I think I will just have to pass on that today. I can see you are in pain so you are in no shape to give me a bad time. I'm surprised they just sent one man after me. Guess they have too much confidence in you."

"Not to worry, I'm used to pain; I have been married two times!"

"You caught up to me on a bad day, Mr. U.S. Marshal Harden. You see, I have three strikes against me so if I go to jail this time, it will mean I won't get out 'til I'm an old man. As you can see, I have a lot at stake here, so I bid you farewell." He swings the butt end of his rifle and smashes the side of my head. All goes dark.

***

My consciousness wavers in and out briefly and Image is nudging me with her nose to get my attention. I have no idea how long I have been out, but she is with me. My wounds are now strangely numb, and my vision is double. Time is of no consequence now. The last I see is Image taking off at a full run.

Chapter Two

The beeps and buzzing of medical equipment brings me to semi-consciousness. I crack my eyes slightly to the bright light in my hospital room and see my commander next to my bed talking with my ex-wife.

Strangely, I notice a large ornate wall clock, and my stare becomes fixated on the second hand as it precisely changes position in measured movements. The wall around the time piece is covered in get well cards and letters. I must have been here for a long time to have enough to wallpaper. The ticking of the second hand is distinct in my ears and is reminding me that every second counts as a life time. It reverberates its movement to my awakening.

Waking to a state of disorientation is a substantial waver from sanity and triggers my body to defend itself, yet I am unable to physically move.

The tube down my throat has me on the brink of gagging. Aside from my mental convulsion, I have no feeling in any other part of my body.

They are not aware that I can hear them as my commander explains that Image came back to the ranch without me, and since I didn't report in, a team was sent to investigate. Image led them to where I was.

The doctor comes in and joins the conversation. He begins to explain to them the extent of my injuries, "The gun shot to his shoulder is surgically repaired and he will have no permanent dysfunction of his arm. However, he received severe trauma to his frontal brain lobe, and had massive cranial bleeding with two skull fractures. Like I said, his shoulder will heal, but he has no nerve response to any locations from his neck down. At this point we cannot determine if his nerve damage is permanent or the full extent he has suffered as far as permanent brain damage. We will have to wait until he comes out of his coma. We are keeping him heavily sedated because of his brain injury." The doctor goes on about lengths of coma without recovery and Jill, my ex-wife, begins to weep.

I want in the worst way to let them know I am awake, but I am locked in my own world without a key.

As Jill breaks down in tears, my commander wraps his arms around her to give comfort.

I slip back into my darkness.

Two weeks later.

I swing my head back and forth to shake the tube out of my throat as my eyes open to the blast of light. Jill was sitting next to my bed until my movement and goes calling for a nurse.

A rush of hospital staff barge in the room to my attendance. With them is the surgeon that I saw when I last woke. He tells them to take the breathing tube out of my throat and barks out more medical orders. The flurry of activity around my bed is making me unsettled. My mind has been in darkness and the activity shoots me with anger. Lost in a world isolated by my silence.

The doctor comes to my bedside and asks me some stupid questions; like if I know where I am, and what my name is. Of course I know! As he waits for my response, all I can do is mumble some unintelligible words. My lips can't form the words! No matter how hard I try, I can't say the words! I am in here. I can see you, but why is what I am thinking not transforming into speech? I can remember my life, I have memory. This should mean something! But I can't tell them! God! I can't feel my body! I can't move my body!

The doctor orders something for the nurse to give me and the shot slows my anxiety, but the anger is raging in my spirit. This is not like me to be so angry, but I have no control.

After the flurry of activity Jill moves her chair next to my bed and cradles my hand in hers. I can see her hold my hand, but there is no feeling.

Jill has warmth in her eyes, and that is all I can feel. I look into hers, but I can't say anything to her except a jumbled bunch of noises.

As I look at her, I can't see how our relationship ended in divorce. She is a good woman, but I neglected her to my mistress; my work. She didn't deserve what I gave her in return for her years of love and devotion. Now here she is sitting next to a vegetable and I can't tell her I am sorry. I close my eyes to darkness again.

***

The warmth of sunshine on my face raises my head upwards out of slumber. My eyes look about the room to gain awareness. I am home and looking out of my living room window! Of this I have no memory, coming home to be in this chair, in this spot. I last felt Jill's hand in mine in the hospital. All since has been blank.

A nurse is in the kitchen and sees me awake. Her smiling face welcomes me to the new morning and asks if I am ready for breakfast.

I remember being in the hospital with Jill, and now this. I want to *say* yes to the breakfast, but all that I can do is shake my head up and down. Understanding my emergence back into this world without memory evades me.

Any semblance of my time home is vacant. What a horrible isolation!

She comes over to me with a warm face cloth and wipes the drool from my chin.

As I look down I can see I rest in a wheelchair with a blanket covering my legs. My arms are cradled on the chair rails and as I attempt to move them, they lift only slightly. My fingers twitch, and the harder I try, the more I can lift my arms. It's hard to describe how elated I am to just twitch my fingers. There is pain in my shoulder and I have a brutal headache, but the sun is shining.

Out front, a car pulls up and out jumps Jill. As she comes to my side I get a hug and kiss on the cheek. She kneels in front of me and sees the tears in my eyes as I struggle again to raise my arms.

My eyes refocus on the barn and Image comes to mind. I try to talk, but give it up for a point with my finger toward the barn.

Jill says, "Oh, so you want to go see Image do you? Okay, let's go see her." She scoots around and wheels me toward the barn.

As we are approaching, Jill tells me that Image came home and led the search party to where I was. She saved my life because I was on the brink of death when they got to me.

My emotions are overwhelming. I want to say so much to my life saver, but all I can do is attempt to pet her. She gently rubs her head to the side of mine. She knows how I feel. She is my Guardian Angel.

Another vehicle pulls up and it is Commander Robert Dunham.

After my visit with Image, we go back to the house. Bob goes to the fridge as the nurse is feeding me breakfast and comes back with a couple of beer, "Well my good man, I'm sure you have been waiting a long time for a one of these. I know it is early, but this is a time to kick back and let the suds cool the throat."

My nurse protests, but considering my broad smile she gives in.

It feels demeaning to have to drink it with a straw, but it is the fourth highlight of my day.

Bob fills me in on my assailant, and advises that he was shot dead in a botched store robbery. It is good news that he got his in the end, but left me without thanking him before I returned his treatment. The Lord says, "Let vengeance be mine," but I'm sure He would let me loose on this one.

Bob speaks up again, "I see you are getting more mobile. That's great! Just don't get carried away rushing your recovery. The guys and gals at the office said to send their greetings. Now, I must get back, so behave and we will get together soon. Oh, that reminds me. The gang is throwing you a barbeque next week and we will come get you."

I didn't want them to see me like this, but there is no way to say how I feel.

My physiotherapy starts tomorrow and the sooner I can regain mobility the better. My legs are still in suspended animation, but hopefully they will return.

It feels good having Jill with me, but I know she has to get back to her job and will only be able to visit in the evening. The care nurses are here twenty four seven until I can gain more independence.

**

Jill is my mainstay at this barbeque. It has been a short time, but the use of my arms is getting somewhat improved. The nerve damage has deformed my hand positions like some monster from a horror movie, but at least I can hold my own beer now... sort of. Just feel silly drinking everything with a straw and having a constant wipe with a face cloth to keep my chin slobber from soaking my clothes. The other maintenance of body functions I would prefer not to describe. It is bad enough to experience the job Jill and the nurses have to endure along with my embarrassment.

The gang has thrown a big deal with this Q. The last time I had cake icing smeared all over my mouth was when I turned one. I can just see the pictures of it hanging at the Marshal's office bulletin board later. Jill is having a good time and is reviving some of the friendships she missed after our divorce. She doesn't have to be doing what she is for me now. It just shows what a wonderful person she is.

It has been a long day and I am tired. Jill asked to stay the night and sleep in the lounge chair in my room which I agreed. Having her here tonight is a blessing.

The doctor has me on some pretty radical medication for my brain injury which causes some strange dreams, sometimes with hallucinations during my daylight hours. They don't happen all the time, but can be rather entertaining.

Tonight in my dream, I wake up to have an old 1800's gun-slinging marshal come visit me. He has weathered cotton clothing and a dirty cowboy hat. He packs a Colt .45 like mine and has the demeanor of a hardcore shoot first; then shoot again lawman. His badge is tarnished and battle-scarred. He appears to be around my age, but through the dust covered exterior it is hard to be sure. Obviously he is, or should I say 'was' from Texas by his speech. He introduces himself as Longhorn because he once wrestled a longhorn steer to the ground in one of his drunken stupors. Now, being a rancher, I wouldn't consider giving a steer a dirty look let alone attempt to wrestle one. Our conversation lasts only a few minutes, but provides me with a good reason to get my meds changed.

Five weeks later.

My morning ritual of being fed is only highlighted by my visit to see Image. But at least now I can give her, her favorite treat by hand; carrots.

Friends from the Marshal's office have been excellent to volunteer their services to tend to the ranch responsibilities. The animals are well taken care of and the chores and repairs are all done.

Jill's visits are more spaced because of her work, but she gets out when she can.

It has been a long time since the incident and I'm getting bored out of my mind. This morning there is some tingling in my leg that is moving up into my arms. Now I don't know what this means, but if it gets more noticeable I may tell the doctor.

Longhorn has been a regular around here over the last week. Seems he likes the ranch and the nurses that take care of me. He's quite the ladies' man. I am sure to be careful when we converse that no one sees me talking to myself, but it is a break from my scheduled routine of boredom. Since I can write fairly legibly, I got Jill to research his name for me and found out he was a real figure in the later part of the nineteenth century. His no nonsense pursuit of justice shook the Marshal Service to the brink of insanity. He took a bullet to the back by a lowlife. Apparently he's buried in a cemetery just out of Houston. Jill is going to take me there on her day off. I told her that I'm thinking of filling my days with attempting to write a book on the old west. She thought that would be a great idea and would give me a hand with it when she could.

My nurse needs to head into town to do some grocery shopping and packs me into my wheelchair van and off we go for a great mobile adventure. I will have a coffee in a coffee shop while she does her thing. Such a plain excursion, but an adventure in my restricted world.

Here I sit with straw in hand and my third coffee in the coffee shop. If she doesn't get back soon, my diaper will overfloweth!

The coffee shop is new to me. Being slowed in life has given me a chance to discover new places; how be it mundane.

The theme is that of a fifties soda shop with old memorabilia all over the walls. I am visually entertained.

A young dad comes in with two young boys around eight or nine and they have a couple of superhero action figures in their hands. As their conversation continues, the one young boy expresses to the other that he is getting really bored with the same old heroes that have been around for too long. He expressed that the world needs a new super hero. Someone that battles bad guys other than the villains that are old now.

Now, as I guzzle my coffee through my trusty straw, I have a light bulb moment. That gives me an idea for my new book with my new western friend. Maybe my mouth and body don't work, but my mind is still relatively intact. I will write of an old marshal with super powers that travels through time to fight, *old school*. Simple in concept, but understandably as it is just in early stages being only two minutes old.

Just in my moment of excitement, a shooting pain shoots through my legs and up to my head. It throws me sideways and then to the floor. It felt like the day of the attack. The searing strike through my shell incapacitates any counter measure to regain myself. Most embarrassing.

First to give me a hand back into my wheelchair are the two boys. The pain subsides, but the consideration of the young men kindles my dedication to the new book. They intrigued me by their actions.

The nurse came in shortly after regaining my composure and asks how things were. I smile. But I am desperate for a pit stop.

***

This night my mind is not still; but alive with thought. There isn't much I can do about my physical dilemma, but my new purpose is to create a hero out of a long past gunfighter. As I lay mentally writing my story, Longhorn appears to pay me another visit.

He opens the conversation, "Well partner, how's the beef hangin' today?"

I write down my thoughts and experience of the day and pass it to him. He smiles and speaks out, "Why not *be* that hero yourself? Put your mind to it and heal yourself," he chuckles to himself and continues, "You know, I once seen a man take a shot that crippled him too. But he was so ornery that he just set out to make himself better. Before long, he was jumpin' on a horse and was twice the man he was."

I understand what he is saying to me, although my point of the book is to create a *real* new hero that the boys could look to other than me. It is obvious my crippled body will be lucky to ride again, let alone swashbuckle against the *bad dude villains*. Ah, it's only an idea anyway!

The next morning.

The events of the night rattle around in my head this morning. I ask the nurse to wheel me out to the barn for a visit with Image, and this she does. I request her to leave me alone and advise her that I will be alright.

As I spend time with Image, again, I have a shooting pain through my body that tosses me over. Image backs away a couple of feet and just stares at me. At first I feel abandoned by her, but as I struggle in the worst way to get back in my chair, the pain turns to a tingle. I fall back to the ground and lay on my back. I thought about the man who Longhorn told me about that recovered himself. I tell myself I am going to do the same. With all my strength, I focus on moving my toes. Over and over I tell myself I can do it. No matter how hard I try, nothing is functioning. There are two dead legs and a bruised attempt at an unrealistic concept; from my damaged being. There is no way my body will ever work again.

Longhorn is only a delusion. I can't fool myself to believe what some figment of my imagination is telling me to be true. I can't beat what has devastated my body.

My nurse comes out to check on me. She lets out a call to me asking if I am alright as she sees me on the ground. She scurries to check me out, then gets my dirt covered body back in my chair.

I tell her not to say anything about what happened; It wasn't her fault, but be prepared for me to be in the same position many times from now on. Stubbornness takes over. Now I plan on beating this condition. She swears to silence and gets me cleaned up.

Chapter Three

A month since my barn incident has passed. At night I press myself to my limit of endurance and as the days have passed, my ability to regain leg movement is substantial. The deformation of my arms and hands are straightening almost to normal. No one, other than Longhorn, is aware of my transformation and so it will remain. I will put an act on with everyone around me. I feel bad deceiving Jill but my plan involves continuing to have my injury as my cover. She will be told when the time is right. I cannot divulge my intentions to anyone.

Her help with my book is substantial. With my speech returning, I have been able to communicate better. My vocalization is one thing that I will expose to Jill. I have so much to tell her about how I appreciate her support and love. I can't even suggest her coming back to live on the ranch due to my plans. It is another cruel thing I do to her, but hopefully the end will justify the means.

My visits to Image have taken a big step. It is like she knows and has known all along what I am up to. She has a sense that is unbridled. I guess there are two holding my secret plans.

Jill finally got her free day, and our excursion includes my visit to Longhorn's grave. To Jill, this is to gather information along with a feel for him to put character to the subject.

As we follow directions to the grave site, I can see history of the people come to life around me. The epitaphs relay a brief understanding to whom these departed souls were. The stories that are literally buried here, are sad to be untold.

Marker by marker, Jill pushes me past. Thoughts of other book ideas are stacking and jostling for position in my head.

As we approach Longhorn's gravestone, he is standing next to it waiting my arrival.

I look at Jill to see if she is aware of my transient apparition, and her actions denote to me that I am the only medicated person with visions.

Longhorn just stands there without saying anything. As we read the epitaph, we both show our compassion.

It reads; *He took a bullet in the back from a coward. This is one bull he couldn't fight. His dying words were, "I have always said; Never turn your back to a coward. Guess I should have listened to my own advice."*

I am distraught for him. He died alone and for the wrong reason. I know how he must feel, having shared the same bullet of sorts.

I ask Jill for her indulgence and give me some time to myself. She is patient with my request and says she is going to read some of the other markers.

When she is out of earshot, I look at Longhorn to say how sorry I am to see how he died, "You were on the right side and got rewarded with a coward's bullet."

He breaks his silence and speaks, "When one lives the life that I did, and you are, we are all targets to the weak-minded evils of this earth. Now I see your lady and to lose such a treasure is the next greatest sacrifice to giving your life for another to live. You are embarking on a journey that you will not see reward other than the knowledge that you are, in a small way, cleansing this earth of evil. Like you were thinking in the hospital about letting God serve his vengeance on the bad; well, understand that there is a fine line between vengeance and justice. It is not vengeance when you seek justice. If you seek from your heart you will do your duty. But remember, if you cross the line, you jeopardize all you have and will accomplish. You may not be aware yet, but your senses are becoming more acute as the days pass. Your thought patterns and abilities are growing into areas of your brain that have been, until now, unused. Grow these gifts to understand, they are gifts not to be abused." He disappears before I can respond.

Jill is heading back and in good time. As she approaches me she can see I am entrenched in thought and she says nothing.

I just had a one sided conversation with my imagination and the scary part of it is, that it is true. My senses have been doing exactly what he told me. My hearing, sight, smell... everything is exploding. To tell Jill would be ludicrous. With my brain injury and meds, I am living in a world only I could understand; a world of delusional dysfunction. If what is happening is just my imagination, I don't want her to see me as a nut case.

Jill breaks our silence, "Let's go get something to eat!"

I agreed. At least I can eat without being fed now, along with drinking without a straw, though my malformation will be re-enacted.

Over lunch I'll need to clarify some matters with her. My mouth acts like I suffered a stroke, but my words are there, "Now that I can speak a little to you, I need to say all the things I have been meaning to tell you since my attack. There is no way to share with you the appreciation for your help and devotion, especially after what I have done to you in the past. One day I will make amends for the wrongs I have bestowed on you, with the hope you find it in your heart to forgive me. I have been thinking about asking you to come back, but there are some things that need to be done first. That's if you even would consider coming back. All I ask is that you be patient with me to let me finish what I need to do."

Jill looks rather taken back by all that is said and smiles, "Well Mr. Harden, I have slaved over your hot wheelchair all these weeks; all I ask is that you get better and this lady will remain with you as long as need be. As far as forgiving you for what happened to us; there is nothing to forgive. I want you to accomplish, what is said needs to get done and we will work on the rest later. I still love you and always will." She kisses me then says we need to finish eating.

***

My strength, with physical function is returning to my legs and arms, so I must be a good actor because no one is aware, not even my therapist. It remains hard to deceive, but again, there is a purpose to my madness.

As Longhorn said, my abilities are becoming astronomical.

I have spent many hours researching what is happening to me and learned that most people remain in the extreme low percentile of brain usage. Human capability as far as strength, senses and mental acuteness is commonly restrained behind social programming. The incidents of super strength and mental phenomenon is documented globally and referred to as such; phenomenon. I am tapping into this process, with the brain injury I suffered possibly triggering parts of my brain that have lain dormant.

Longhorn is right. A gift has presented itself and I fully plan on using it.

The meds the doctor prescribed for my brain trauma are still in my system to a certain degree, although I have been only pretending to take them, then disposing of the evidence. Since I have been doing this, Longhorn hasn't presented himself. I am rather disappointed in some ways because he was starting to grow on me.

At the breakfast table this morning I just want to straighten out and eat right but the act must continue.

After I finish eating, as per schedule, my nurse is helping push me out to my visit with Image. As I sit with her, my gaze wanders over to my beat up '89 4x4 truck. Now that things in my head are accelerating into overdrive, part of my plans include a radical modified set of wheels. Now, since my mechanical beast has served me well in the past, maybe it is time to give her the rebuild of all rebuilds. I can only work on it at night now since the night nurse is no longer required. It will mean long nights and little sleep, but the old girl is going to see new life. I can get parts delivered and tell the nurse that a friend is working on my truck to modify it to my disability. It can work; I know it can. I will start tonight!

Jill is here for supper and we plan on having a quiet night in front of the TV watching some movies. I have to be on my guard without fail to not expose my secret of healing.

My nerves are vibrating from the thought of getting started on the truck. Come to think of it, I have to name the old girl. My preoccupation away from focusing on the movie, and the lady next to me is causing suspicion with Jill. My spirit is in reckless abandon.

She pauses the movie and asks if I am ok.

I say I am and go back to planning the build, as well as coming up with a name. I toss a few super truck names around and finally decide on 'Knight Horse'. I giggle at my mental success and Jill looks back at me again.

"Okay, what's up with you? You have not been yourself all night. Are you taking your meds?" She isn't mad, but curious with my change of routine.

"I'm sorry, I was just thinking about putting a new character in my book. Only the character is going to be a vehicle. I'm done. Let's get back to the movie." I wasn't really lying to her, just a variation of the truth. I could write a vehicle into my story.

Toward the end of the movie, I again get that shooting pain through my body. I toss to the floor and my head starts to swim. I am having a convulsion and there is nothing I can do to stop it!

Jill gets to my side and keeps me from hurting myself. She grabs her phone and calls 911. She is calm in her actions, but has a look of terror in her eyes.

I black out.

***

Opening my eyes, and I'm back in the hospital. Jill is by my side and welcomes me back. She isn't all smiles though, apparently they did a blood test on me and it showed I was derelict in taking my meds.

Oh! Oh! I'm busted!

"Well Mr. Harden, you have now been pumped back up from your silly actions and from now on, the nurses and I will make sure the pills are sliding down your throat. You got that? Oh, and don't you dare pull another stunt like the other night ever again." She kisses me.

"Sorry. I just felt I was doing okay without them. Don't be mad at me. How long have I been in here?"

"Three long days, you slipped into another coma. They weren't sure if you would…" Jill can't finish her sentence.

"I am so sorry. It seems I just can't do the right thing around you. It's not you… It's me, I just seem to screw up."

She bends over and gives me a loving hug.

This is going to put a wrench into building Knight Horse! I have to be extra careful now. Just get me out of this hospital!

The doctor comes in to check me out and talks in private with Jill.

He leaves and she comes back over to me, "They are going to keep you in here for a couple more days, and if you don't behave they will strap you to the bed."

I almost get up to go to the bathroom, but click to stay still. This acting business is hard! I am hooked to a catheter anyway.

***

Home again!

My nurses are watching me like hawks now. I'm going to have to be sneakier. I guess I will have to take those bloody meds. As my thoughts are on them, Longhorn makes an appearance.

"So, Billy Bob, you have been shaking the tree, haven't you?!"

His gun hand is resting on his holstered Colt which makes me nervous. He may be a figment, but figments have been known to get out of hand too. Or so my delusions tell me.

It is actually refreshing having him back. Kinda missed his company. In my world, boredom is only surpassed by crazy. If I make it through this in one piece, I may not touch down to sanity again. Oh well, it's cheaper than drama on TV.

"You know, if you don't watch yourself, all that you have planned is going to sail out the window. Your lady Jill isn't lacking in the smarts department, so keep your medication up so I can keep you in line." Longhorn's hand relaxes away from his sidearm.

***

Having my preoccupation on building my 89 truck subdues the massive headache that has plagued me since the hospital.

I start to inform Longhorn what the doctor had told us, "The doctor explained to Jill and I that the gunshot wound is fine, but the crushing blow to my skull over manipulated my fifth and sixth neck vertebrae. This is what damaged my spinal cord, causing the paralysis. Also, from what the neural surgeon stated; my partial use return of my arms and speech is a surprise to him. The damage to my spinal cord is irreparable. It obviously is a good thing about my secret, but after the tests during my second stay in hospital, I should be, and remain paralyzed from the neck down. He also added that the trauma to my brain caused a swelling and permanent damage as far as motor functions. He meant that it is bad enough with the spinal damage; the brain trauma would have crippled me on its own."

Longhorn shifts to make himself more comfortable and lifts his eyes to mine. "Well, partner, the sawbones can be wrong sometimes. You can get yourself back out of the chair if you want. Just keep getting your brain to demand the damage is; pardon the misuse of a pun, but; *it's all in your head.*"

The nurse in the kitchen is making a nasty amount of noise. The piercing clatter and bang from that direction is making me more uncomfortable. I call for her to come over to me at the window. As she is approaching, her steps seem as though she is wearing army boots on a rough plank floor. I don't know if she is just unaware of the racket she is making or she just doesn't care. My temper is starting to escalate.

"Yes Mr. Harden. Do you need something?" She smiles and readjusts my lap blanket in an attempt to make me more comfortable.

"I have a bad headache and the noise from the kitchen is not helping!" I look down at her feet and realize she is only wearing running shoes.

"I'm truly sorry Mr. Harden, I am just wiping the counters. Maybe there is something from outside that is making a noise, I will go check for you. I'll be right back."

I don't understand. Her chores wouldn't create such an audible irritation and her steps would have been cushioned with her footwear. I am in worse shape than I thought. This injury is giving me an unstable mood. I am not that way! My anger is far beyond a reasonable rationale.

As my nurse returns, she has a confused look on her face, "Well, Mr. Harden, I can't see anything out there that would cause any noise."

My temper converts to frustration, "I'm sorry. This headache is throwing me for a loop. Is it time for my next cup full of medication?"

"Yes it is, I will go prepare it for you." She heads for the kitchen.

The thunder of her steps echoes in my ears. I turn my wheelchair slightly and confirm that it is her making the noise, but it doesn't compute.

Longhorn had zipped back into my cranial recesses' just at a time I needed to talk to him. I'm driving myself crazy in this chair and need to get out to the shop and get at it.

The nurse scoots over with my meds and hands them to me, "Now, Mr. Harden, I have strict instructions to watch you swallow these."

My look expresses my feelings on the matter.

As I toss them in my mouth, the extreme chemical content overreacts with my taste buds. They cringe my face like taking a cup of lemon juice.

I taste their particle makeup and could identify each ingredient. Since when did I become a chemical analysis machine? These meds are really screwing with my head! Maybe it would have been better that I just bought the bullet and died. I can see depression overwhelming me and this isn't a good thing. I am booked for a psychological evaluation next week. I'm sure this is to determine if I am a hazard to society so they can lock me up in some ward somewhere.

I need to get out and occupy myself in the shop!

It is almost supper time, with Jill coming over to make me dinner as well as keep me company until I retire to bed.

Tonight I plan on starting the long awaited project I've labeled *Knight Horse*. For what purpose I am building such a truck eludes a complete plan at this time, but I will at least have done something constructive with my negative disposition. No psychiatrist will make me feel better over giving my truck new life.

The floor below me must be engraving wear marks of my wheelchair from being in the same position by the window every day. But it does provide me with a view of the barn which also gives me a point to focus on as I flip through my thinking.

The site of Jill driving up is an emotional boost for me. She brightens my day and her company is warming to my soul.

My communication with her has improved since I first woke here, but even with my hidden development, I still talk as though I have had a stroke. The right side of my face has a mild deformity and my speech is still slurred.

These new developments are causing some distress. I feel like I should plug my ears and not eat anything. The hyperactivity with my senses is developing in ways beyond understanding. It seems as my body heals, my brain is overcompensating in other areas.

As Jill comes in, my temperament goes from anger and depression to enjoying the moment.

"So how is my sunshine this morning?" She bends over and gives me a warm kiss on my cheek, "I'll get started with supper and we can sit and have some *us* time after.

As she starts toward the kitchen I ask her to come back, "Can you pull up a chair so I can talk for a minute with you?"

Jill does as ask. While she settles to a comfortable position on her chair, her eyebrows tighten together. She moves her head for a better view of my ears, "Why do you have ear plugs in your ears?"

"That's what I need to talk to you about. My hearing is going nuts, or I mean it is driving me nuts. It's like someone is holding a bullhorn to my head and screaming into it. I can hear things in minute detail and that only I can. I don't know if it is my medication, or I'm just totally losing my mind. Whatever it is I'm going to have to see the doctor tomorrow. Brandon from the Marshal's office is coming to do some chores tomorrow, so I will get him to drive me in." My depression is now accompanied by frustration. I now know that working on the truck tonight is out of the question.

"Tell you what, I will stay the night and drive you in the morning. I could use a break from work anyway. Let's go together, we can have a nice lunch after," Jill smiles.

I smile back, "You are a wonderful person. That would be great if you would stay tonight."

"Okay, let me make supper now." Jill goes off to the kitchen.

My arms are gaining good strength and I am able to wheel myself rather well, considering. I'm not ready for the wheelchair Olympics, but can manage, "I'm going to see Image before supper, I shouldn't be long."

"Okay, but be careful. Take the whistle with you and just call if you need something."

The boys and girls from the office built a wheelchair ramp for me, and as I let the wheels loose on the down slope there is a rush of speed. Must have broken three miles an hour! *Should put a governor on this speed wagon before I get a speeding ticket.* The speed rush soon ends as I hit the packed gravel driveway. The physical exertion makes me think I should motorize this contraption.

There is sounds of Image shifting about in the barn. Her keen senses are picking up on my journey to visit her.

To get out of this chair right now is pressing on my patience. Although my legs are improving they are still rather shaky. Besides, that element of healing is still undisclosed information.

Image welcomes me as usual with a tongue slobber across my face and her head moving to find her treat. Amongst all of the struggle, both Image and Jill bring me hope that the future will have a lighter load.

I open her gate so she can walk with me to the '89 in the back of the barn.

As I rub my hand down the side of my metal steed, I picture the '89 standing proud as the Knight Horse. Thoughts of hers' and my purpose are yet to be drawn, but my quest has begun. Building the K Horse is throwing wrench's into my thoughts; a picture of her thundering horse power as we chase the villains through the dark night to do battle. Click; a light bulb moment again! *THAT* is my purpose! To chase villains and bring them to justice and become the dark avenger of the populous! Well... I will build the truck and see what happens from there! My overactive imagination is taking those two boys' comments too seriously. I'm just bored, but it is good for my book!

Longhorn speaks up behind me and nearly makes me topple out of my chair, "So, what is wrong with that idea?"

"What idea?" I answer back to him.

"Building K Horse to do battle against the villainy of society!" His voice is almost demanding.

"Look, Marshal, I thought about many silly concepts during the last weeks and that's all they are... concepts of a bored, crippled man. I shouldn't be hiding my recovery from Jill or anyone else. It is ludicrous to think I will become some dark vigilante righting the wrongs of this world. This body is crippled, and even with my improvement, I will be far from an Olympic contender in the crime fighting arena. Facts are facts, even with my cracked brain and disability, my reality is real; I am a cripple with brain damage and delusions of a long dead marshal that needs a bath. I know you are not real, even though your company has been good... I know you aren't real," A strange sense of regret flashes before me. That was really cruel to say to my figment, "I'm sorry. You don't deserve that comment."

"Look, partner, I have ridden the dusty trail for too many miles to let anyone hurt my feelings. But when you go see that psychiatrist fellow, I just may have to tell him you are giving me a bad time. Be that as it may, you have some ideas that may be a good way to regroup and re-enter this world with purpose. As I look at a dilemma, the first thing that needs to be done is to step forward with the first imprint of what needs to be. You have to look at the whole picture, but to avoid being overwhelmed, Think of each stage as your immediate focus. Then move onto the next. At the end you will look back and see what I mean.

Or you will look back and say to yourself, *What a stupid idea*! Either way you need to get started on the K Horse."

"I am, just not tonight." I just need a break, and with Jill, it will be a good one.

Out we stroll and roll to get some sunshine. Image stays to my side and Longhorn blazes the path ahead. Lawmen like us are a dead breed; pardon the pun. We live and breathe our job only looking for the next challenge. There is an old saying; '*Live by the sword and die by the sword.*' What a dumb way to look at life, I'm not looking to get shot just because I chase bad guys. Well, that's all irrelevant now anyway, I have been *struck* by the sword.

The coolness of the barn is change to the bright heat outside. As the three of us are enjoying the vitamin D intake, Jill is out of the house and heading toward us.

I look up at Longhorn and pass on some important information, "Jill is staying the night, and even though we are not going to have any *activity*, it would be mighty nice of you to leave us to our privacy."

Longhorn pops out of our company.

"Time for supper," Image steps up to her, and Jill cradles Image's head in a big hug, "How's the bravest horse in the world?"

Jill puts Image back then comes to push me inside.

Jill's dinner is incredible, but like earlier, I need to take only small amounts to overcome the intensified taste. Now, her cooking is good, but I now know why. The seasoning and preparation is more than obvious.

***

Bedtime is a lengthy dramatic procedure of embarrassment to me; a time to wash out all memory of it, and give credit to Jill for the horrible requirements to prepare me for slumber.

"After all that, I know it isn't the most romantic prelude to us being together, but if you like you can sleep beside me on the bed. Your company will be the best warmth to me, even though I can only be company. There are those pyjamas of mine in the drawer for you to wear if you like." I wish Jill and I could really spend a more romantic time together but... after being married for fifteen years and then divorced, I feel shy and awkward.

Jill goes into the bathroom to get changed. She comes out looking rather... *pyjama-y*. She still looks good. I'm not in a position to dwell on her beauty and need to stay focused on what cannot be.

Chapter Four

The doctor's office vibrates sounds even through my plugged ears. The worst is that cursed phone ringing.

The receptionist pokes her head in the waiting room and calls, "Mr. Harden?"

Jill stands up to push me after the receptionist. Finally away from that phone!

The room has a couple of lounge chairs and an examination table. On the walls are *'happy'* pictures to express the beautiful things out there that make us have happy thoughts. I feel like smearing graffiti all over them!

Two people come into the room. One is my neural surgeon, and the other is a woman.

The doctor began by introducing the lady as Dr. Dunley, a psychiatrist.

I'm doomed now to wander the halls of some facility for crazy people. They are going to evaluate me and determine that for my own good, they are enrolling me in a program to help me look at the happy pictures and be able to smile. I will go kicking and screaming if they do that to me. Where is Longhorn and his guns when I need him?

The doctor did a physical evaluation and commented that my physical healing is doing very well. I didn't expose my real capability.

Jill speaks up, "Bill has been telling me that his hearing and taste have become hypersensitive."

"With the medication we have him on there are sometimes side effects of misaligned brain function. The chemicals from the medication reacts with the areas of the brain that they aren't targeted for. I could go into that technical and medical explanation but simply put, his side effects are only that; side effects. They will not cause any damage and will subside after we reduce the doses. Just try to keep the food to a more bland content, and what he is doing with the ear plugs is a good idea."

I'm sitting here, with the doctor talking passed me like I'm a crippled person with brain damage. I feel like telling him I can think and speak too. Anyway, I will just bite my tongue and pretend I am chilled.

After the doctor is through with me, they ask for me to get comfortable back in my wheelchair so the shrink can do her thing.

Jill can see my frustrated look and whispers in my ear, "Be cool, my dear, and I will take you for a great lunch."

The lady shrink starts, "Mr. Harden, you have been through a lot, so we understand that it is hard to manage with your injuries. I am here to help you through the emotional and psychological adjustment towards a normal life even with your restrictions. Brain trauma can bring forth emotions such as anger, frustration and depression, but all of these are normal and we can work with you to get control of them." Her body language amplifies what she is saying with gestures and facial expression.

Ok, now tell me something I don't already know. I am about to tell them about Longhorn, but decide that won't be such a good idea since I value my freedom. And as that crosses my mind *poof...* there he is, my alter ego.

Longhorn sits on the examination table and draws my eyes in that direction away from the doctor.

Longhorn knows I have zero patience for a lecture and smiles, "I should have been a doctor. I could have told you all that, and I wouldn't have charged you for it."

I smile.

"Mr. Harden. Mr. Harden. Do you understand what I am saying?" She tries to get my attention back.

Longhorn moves behind her so it will seem like I am taking all what she is saying into my databank.

Now, I know she is here to help me and what she is saying is pertinent to my condition, but my attention span is one second or less.

Longhorn starts up again, "We didn't have all these fancy doctors in my time. If we had a problem, we bellied up to the bar for a drink, or went out and shot a bad guy or two. It was the best therapy a lawman could have. All these words are fine and dandy, but getting out and busting loose is so much more fun. Want a beer, compadre?"

I almost answer him! Though I *could* use a beer.

It had been really great having Jill with me last night. I wonder how Brandon is making out with the chores. I wonder what I can have for lunch that doesn't send my buds into orbit. Yep, could use a beer right about now.

"So do you understand what I am saying, Mr. Harden?" My *'mind'* doctor is looking for more of my input.

I reply, "Hundred percent!" Can we get out of here now?

"Well Mrs. and Mr. Harden, I think we made great progress today and I should get together with you both in a week or so. Here's my card, just call my office to make an appointment."

Jill rolls me out to the truck and helps me in. After she gets positioned in the driver's seat she puts the key in the ignition and pauses, "Did you hear anything she said?"

"Yep! I heard we have to make an appointment with someone." Really, that's all I heard. It gave me time to think about the truck build and she was a good way to focus.

The truck engine comes to life with the wheels now in motion. I am having a rough time saying what I should, along with refraining from the not. There is no doubt Jill is having a difficult time dealing with my aliment. There is just no control on my part.

It is a good thing for my ear plugs because even with them the racket in this restaurant is deafening.

It seems my thoughts are more and more adrift. Considering a verbal interaction with anyone now is stretching my patience. I would assume being in my company right now wouldn't be a happy time either.

Thoughts of the day I was attacked are haunting this moment. Having such a cold-blooded creature like him get one over on me is like a curse on the soul. His sadistic face showed no remorse for his violent act of cowardice. Here I sit broken and tormented with no recourse. To make matters worse, he had to get killed with someone else's bullet. I feel robbed of my justified release. Shadowed for the rest of my life.

"Are you done feeling sorry for yourself, partner?" Longhorn takes up a third seat at Jill's and my table.

I look at him and slam my crippled hand down on the table and yell, "NO, I'm not!"

The table shutters, knocking over our water glasses. The restaurant shoots to silence as I became an unwilling center of attention.

I look up at Jill and apologize for my outburst.

She reaches over and takes my hand in hers, "I can't imagine what you are living through, but I know one thing to be true. You are not alone and *we* will get through this." Her eyes return to the menu, "Now I would suggest you don't have the spicy hot sauce burger. After that outburst, your sensitive taste will send you up against the ceiling!" she smiles.

"I'm sorry. I just can't control myself sometimes." I smile back, realizing the great gift that has been bestowed upon me.

"That's better, partner. Look to the sun where there is good." Longhorn is out of character with that mushy stuff.

Shifting to his direction, my mouth almost replies.

***

It is now nine o'clock in the evening with the only souls on the ranch being myself, Image and an intruder by the name of Longhorn.

The flash of my camera lights up the barn as I take pictures of the *before* Knight Horse. This is to keep a photo record of the build not only to give me a journal, it gives me a reference if I don't remember how things get re-constructed. Image is free in the area to explore what is going on, but a set of extra hands would be an asset: aside from Longhorn.

The '89 has been tough through the years. I remember looking at it brand new on the car lot. She has rolled over some rough terrain through the years with me and never complained. The dents and faded paint are testament to her experience.

Rising to my feet on unstable legs is a difficult operation. Trying to work with *my* rusted body parts is going to slow restoration down substantially. But I feel good. My mind is at rest for the first time in a while.

Bolt for bolt body panels are exposing the naked chassis. As I look to her stripped frame, the ideas for re-build and modification are swelling my thoughts. She has to sustain a heavy barrage of assault against her, so new technology will be integrated into her systems. A nasty 454 cubic inch motor with a five speed manual transmission will propel *Knight Horse* through her duties.

Throughout the disassembly Longhorn peeked over my shoulder in curiosity. This iron horse was constructed in an unknown world to him. Mechanical travel vehicles didn't exist during his time, other than the railroad locomotives. The technology fascinates him. His barrage of questions interferes with my work, but it is his profound appreciation to his teacher that makes it worthwhile. The only problem I have is that his new-found knowledge has no physical benefit towards assisting me.

***

The sun is peeking over the east range and it is past five in the morning. It is time to pack up and get to bed. I moved the old girl into a more hidden part of the barn so nosey visitors won't ask questions. Jill only comes to the front of the barn to see Image so I don't think she will notice the truck has been moved.

Through the night, my strength is building and my mobility is taking a giant step. The muscles all over my body are yelling back at me for tormenting them for the first time in months. I am going to be sore today but every tweak of pain is worth it.

The grit soap removes most of the dirt and grease from my hands, but the modest previous use of them has changed to a more rugged beaten look. I will wear some cotton gloves today to cover them up. If anyone asks I will tell them that they are sore and the gloves warm the pain away.

No sooner than I sneak to bed; the nurse arrives to come in to check on me.

"Mr. Harden. It is morning and I have your morning meds."

Well, that was the shortest sleep I ever had, "I had a rough sleepless night and I just want to stay in bed for now. I will call you if I need anything. Okay?"

"Of course. Your buzzer cord is right here." She positions it so I can readily reach it.

Ah, silence again. My eyelids feel like someone is tugging them down.

***

This time of year the sun sets around eight o'clock. It is dark outside. The toils of the previous night have overworked my inactive body. The pain in my shoulders and arms are intense. Even my restricted movement is harder to accomplish. All I remember of this day is the isolated vague procedure of taking meds and a short visit from Jill.

The last duties of the night nurse start with little cooperation from me. I am so stiff and in so much pain that even the meal she is stuffing down my throat takes my full attention.

I won't be working tonight; that is a definite.

Just as the nurse is finishing up with me, Jill walks in, "You have been sleeping all day. Are you alright?" Her soft hand covers my cheek.

"Ya, I'm okay. Guess things just caught up to me. Can you help me up and into my robe? Are you going to stay? Maybe we can watch a little TV or something." The rising out of bed is an experience. Feels like I have been run over by a truck.

Jill notices my cotton gloves, but before she can ask I tell her my excuse. I can't tell if I convinced her or not.

My schedule for building the K Horse is going to have to be reconsidered and then planned more precisely. To sleep during the day just isn't going to work.

As Jill and I are sitting out on the deck taking in the moonlight, my consciousness becomes overrun with overlapping brain activity. Thoughts and mental conclusions are being resolved, then packed away to make room for new ideas. Solutions to build concepts for the '89 processed data with lightning speed. Memories of almost everything my eyes have seen and read were flashing past my subconscious. I can remember what I ate for supper on any particular night going back to childhood. Everything in my memory is sitting, just waiting to be pulled forward for re-access. I have heard of a photographic memory, but this is ridiculous.

My head jerks mildly in different directions, enough for Jill to take notice.

"Are you alright?" She grabs my arm and shifts her line of sight to the front of me. I am going to call the doctor.

"No, I'm fine, just had some crazy day dream sparking my imagination. Not to worry; all is good." I smile at my enlightenment and take Jill's hand in mine.

I thought long and hard as to whether I should share my dilemma of what has really been happening. If she were aware, I could easily complete my project and move on with my now focused intent. On the other hand, she would worry that I might over step my capability and risk further damage to my condition. I so want to stop deceiving her. She is my greatest purpose on this earth. So far she has weathered my shenanigans in good faith. The decision is made, she will be told in the morning!

***

My sleep was interrupted throughout the night. I would wake, and see Jill next to me with thoughts of getting her to wake and listen to what I must tell her.

After breakfast we are again out on the deck having a coffee. There is no more waiting. What must be said needs to be told.

"Jill. I have been thinking long and hard about asking you to come back to our home. Because of what has happened to me and my condition, I didn't want you to stop your life just to come here to care for a cripple. If I ask you to come home with me, I want it to be because you love me and for no other reason. I want you to come back because you truly want to." My partial face paralysis makes my words deformed but the meaning is true.

Jill's eyes water as she responds, "I never at any time desired to be apart from you. I let the divorce go through because I understood your work was so demanding. You lived for every day out there seeking what is your destiny. There has never been a day go by that being next to you wasn't on my heart."

"There is no way to express how sorry I am for putting you through all this. I want and need you with me. If you say you can't, I will understand."

"Well Mr. Harden, this lady does want to come home." Her grip on my hand tightens.

"That's great, but there is just one thing I must tell you before we set that in stone. If you change your mind after what I need to divulge to you, I again will understand." My body is shaking from anxiety.

"Can you push me to the barn away from prying nurse's eyes please?"

As we roll toward the barn doors it seems like an eternity.

I can hear the heavy breaths Jill is taking and the pounding of her heart. I am having second thoughts about this decision. It could forever destroy our relationship because of some stupid idea.

The barn doors creak open. Now my heart is pounding out of my chest.

My head lowers to make my final gamble.

Jill pulls a stool out in front of me and patiently awaits my withheld information.

My lungs fill and empty several times, "If I tell you what is going on, I need you to promise to keep that information between you and me only, even if you disagree and tell me to take a flying leap. I need you to promise me this, Okay?"

"Just tell me! I will not say anything, I promise."

"Since the incident, I have struggled with a multitude of emotional problems. The medication has and continues to give me problems that I just can't explain as of yet. There were times that I wished I were dead instead of trying to adjust to my injuries. Fortunately those thoughts have dissolved. My hours were eaten up by finding a sane way to purge myself of the negative by creating a goal to work toward. I found that goal because of some unexpected developments. These developments also affect how our relationship can survive. You know that I cannot deceive you, and you deserve to know the facts."

My body starts to shake radically with all this nervous excitement. My nerves don't need more stress put on them at this time.

Jill comes to warm me with her embrace.

We keep silent for a moment, then I continue thinking again. I start to wheel myself to the back of the barn, at which time Jill takes hold of the wheelchair to take over.

As we arrive at the tarped truck, I ask her to pull the canvas back. Jill is puzzled by my request and even more so after revealing the hidden project. She refrains from asking; knowing I will explain further.

"I needed a project to focus my mind on something positive. I thought that the old truck would be a way to restore my head and my body by restoring it. My healing has had a surprising twist to it. I know the doctors said I have permanent damage to my nervous system, but there are things that they have mistaken with me. I can't explain how or even why, but all I can understand is that it is happening for a reason. That reason I must pursue to solution."

I rise to my feet, and in a posture up to my healing, I stand tall. My hands uncurl to where I could to this point straighten them. In my semi-healed state, I walk over to the love of my life and wrap my arms around her.

"My broken body is healing itself. There is a long road to go, but all that matters is I can hold you with a promise to you that I will love you for the rest of my life, if you will have me back." I go back and sit down in my chair again. The overworked muscles from the other night are reminding me of my overindulgence.

"Why didn't you tell me this sooner?" She appears angry and elated at the same time.

"There is more. I started rebuilding the '89 the other night. The plan is to restore it with modifications for a project I have concocted. My plan is to go back to work, but with a slight difference. No one is going to know it is me. It sounds crazy but even with my brain damage I am quite sane; with only one exception; that I will tell you at another time." My eyes steer clear of Jill's. I am hoping she understands so far, and will see through the confusion shrouding me, to be there after the dust settles.

Awaiting her final verdict is causing more pain than my stiff muscles, but finally her silence is broken, "So let me get this straight; you are getting better; you are building a super truck for an elusive unknown crime fighter that is pretending to be a badly crippled invalid. Oh, and he wants his wife to fully understand his quest *and* be more than patient with him; along with keeping his secret life from the doctors and psychiatrists that will be probing his mind and body… so aside from the incredible good news of your progressive healing I should try to understand… well this has been an evening stroll of strolls!"

Again she stands silent as I await all heck to break loose.

As Jill ponders her unorthodox bundle of information, she sits back down again.

"So if I agree and support you with this… idea, are you going to pull back if you find it too much to handle?

"Yes, I will. This all sounds crazy, but if things don't function the way proposed, then I will return to whatever state my mind and body permits. I promise."

As Jill surveys the dismantled truck she continues, "You did all this work the other night, by yourself?"

"Yes I did!" My chest protrudes with pride.

"Okay my darling, I will go along with your plan, but with one condition; you don't over extend yourself." She smiles and gives me a hug and kiss, "I am so happy you are getting better."

I sit back in my wheelchair and as Jill pushes me out of the barn, Longhorn smiles and winks an eye of approval.

To say the least, the ride back to the house is a bit unsettling. I have divulged all to Jill and from the look on her face along with the silence; she is still processing all the data. It is substantially load lifting to have her aware of my condition.

As we enter the house, the attending nurse is packing up to leave on errands for a few hours. This will give Jill some time to come to terms with the event of this day.

Jill pulls up a chair next to me as I chase for a safe place to look other than into her eyes. I feel like a young boy who just got caught with both hands in the cookie jar. The more I thought of my explanation and confession, the more ludicrous it sounded. There is an opportunity to recover to a certain degree, but I need to complicate things by throwing in a crazy idea about chasing bad guys.

Longhorn crowds in to sit on the edge of Jill's chair, "Well, partner, I must say, you have a good woman by your side. Never did settle down myself. Had a fixin' to corral a wife once, but the call of duty pulled me in another direction. Reckon I should have started a family, but with getting shot and all, that thought died with me. You don't need to worry about your lady. She has it in her heart to be with you no matter what you do."

Jill starts to talk at the same time Longhorn is giving his speech, so trying to keep track of both creates a problem. Fortunately the big guy gave way to Jill.

"Have you had any of those spikes you were getting after you stopped your meds?" Her line of questioning is leading.

"No. There hasn't been another one since."

She continues, "If you are going to attempt to build the truck and get back on your feet, you must listen to what the doctor has to say and maintain your meds. Oh, and next time we see the psychiatrist; make sure you listen to her."

"Ya, ya, ya. It's just; I'm managing on my own without all the *copping stuff.*" As much as I understand why the shrink is trying to help, the best counsel I could get is from another cop. Guess since Longhorn is here, I will classify him as my counsel.

Jill's face has a smile from one ear to the other. Her eyes glitter like the diamond in her wedding band she still wears, "I am so excited about you getting so much better! Your project may be a silly idea, but if it gets you mobile and rebuilds your muscles, then so be it. My work at the lab can be reduced to a part-time schedule to give me more time to make sure you are behaving yourself. We can reduce your home care nurses down to a daytime shift, which will ease the pressure of your barn activities. Now tell me what plans you have for the truck. Maybe I can develop some products for it at the lab."

My eyes widen at her enthusiasm and new enlightenment. She is getting into my plans far beyond what I anticipated. What a relief. My stress level bottoms out. The more I thought of the future, the more elated my focus is becoming. Even if my healing doesn't get fully functional, we have a life back.

Jill is a chemical engineer for a military-subsidized research facility in Houston. This could result in a working combination, accomplishing much more than I anticipated on the truck build. She would have another top secret assignment.

After lunch we are going to return to the K Horse project and develop a full build plan with a parts list.

The change today is pushing me to stretch my legs along with my brain to hurry my healing process. There are still major hurdles to overcome, but I now have another ally in my quest.

Chapter Five

Four weeks have sailed passed without looking back. What has been, only reinforces our tomorrow.

Jill's hands are as greasy and cut imbedded as mine from our building of the K Horse.

As we stand staring at the now completed chassis, our minds encompass our work of art. Every nut, bolt and inch of the rolling undercarriage is replaced, rebuilt or refinished. Even without the truck body, it glistens as though it is brand new.

The engine is a 454 cubic inch fuel injected monster with a heavily modified five-speed transmission. The transfer case is also built to withstand anything I can put it through. The transmission and transfer case have a bullet proof housing. The drive shafts are also encased in an armor shield to keep them from being taken out by rough terrain or an explosive device. The radiator is armored by a honeycomb stainless steel shield in front to resist gunfire. A series of skid plates underneath give added resistance to undercarriage assault by explosives. Jill developed a rubber compound for the tires that does not allow bullet penetration or puncture damage from any road hazard. All in all, the chassis is more or less indestructible.

Then comes the toys! The rear weapons defense system includes the usual super-agent assault equipment, like; oil slick, tire spikes, and smoke. But the neatest weapon is the *'Idiot seeking missiles'*. These are self-explanatory.

In front is a 30 caliber machine gun for times when road rage isn't enough.

We are proud of our accomplishment and head into the house for dinner. My wheelchair is only a necessity when my leg cramps get out of hand. My mobility is to a point where my ability to walk, and even run short distances, is without distress. The wheelchair is more of a prop at this point. The doctor is aware of my new leg and arm function, but my brain trauma is still affecting my speech and facial distortion.

The greatest embarrassing product is now vacant from my daily routine. It has been the worst part of my recovery; the infamous diaper. My manly demeanor is now restored.

The psychiatrist requested I write a short story about my recovery and I decided to include it in the book Jill and I are writing. It is as follows:

As one stands at the bottom of a canyon looking up the steep rock walls it is time to understand why you are where you are. To reach the top of the cliff walls takes dedication, reflection, and positive spirit.

Many times I have been on top looking down and found myself plummeting back to where I began in the canyon base. These rises and falls are part of life and the important thing is how we react, learn and mature. It isn't because of anyone else's error but our own. We have all been given the spiritual and physical strength to overcome calamities. The answer doesn't get resolved consuming alcohol or drugs. On the contrary, the problems remain and the problems are amplified by a hangover.

I have learned that a positive spirit makes the journey less corrugated and more of an adventure. Appreciate the gifts that are given to us in bounty and not the bounty in the gifts.

Even though my climbs up the cliff walls have scarred my physical being and my soul, these battle scars only remind me of, and amplify the good given.

We may not live in a mansion or drive a fancy car, but if we are happy on a bicycle and dwelling in a tent, take no criticism for you are you. Give the person beside you on the cliff wall a hand. The climb for them may be more difficult.

She has no idea what Jill and I have been up to, but along with my figment friend and Jill, my mind is on the mend. Or so I am told.

Longhorn hasn't interrupted us during the chassis build, but his company has created somewhat of a one sided communication. There is no way I want to enlighten Jill about my bygone marshal. She has been secure with my sanity thus far and that just might put a hole in the boat.

Part of my rehab includes getting back in the saddle and going for short horse rides. Jill has brought her horse 'Moon', a Leopard Appaloosa gelding, their relationship is that of Image and I.

In the saddle and about to head down toward the creek for a dip, we want to take advantage of the last hours of daylight.

The clap of hoof steps is multiplied by an additional set. Longhorn has mounted up and joined us. It is the first time he has been on horseback since he came into my life. He sits tall in the saddle and is everything an old west marshal should be.

With Jill in the lead, I reflect on how fortunate I am to be married to such a wonderful woman. She is a pretty lady with flowing long blonde hair and a slim build. They say everything happens for a reason, my injuries have brought us back together. This I am thankful for.

We have been on the trail for about ten minutes and a twinge in my foot takes a turn into a full blown spasm through my body like the earlier attacks. The jolting shot of pain throws me from my horse to the ground. The thud to the ground turns my world into darkness.

"Wake up, partner," Longhorn's voice slowly brings me to, "Wake up."

I am flat on my back with the jolt of hitting the ground echoing the pain through me. My eyes slowly focus on Longhorn kneeling over me. He pours some water out of his canteen into my dry mouth.

"You had quite the fall, partner. How do you feel?"

As my senses come back, I realize Jill isn't at my side, "Where's Jill?" I turn to see why she isn't helping me.

"It's just me, partner. There is no one else here." He shifts his gaze to the surrounding area to show what he said is true.

Longhorn takes me by the arm as I struggle to rise to my feet. My confused eyes scan the area trying to figure where Jill had gone. Ah, she has gone for help. That's it, she has gone for help.

My foothold on the ground is firming as I dust myself off. My hand catches on the holstered gun on my hip and hurts my finger. Still dazed, my eyes analyze the fact that on this ride, my hip didn't support a western holster or a gun. Looking up to Longhorn for answers, he just gives me the '*What?*' look.

"I don't understand. Where did this gun come from, and where is Jill?"

"Well partner, you got that gun and holster last year in Tombstone, Arizona, and who is this Jill you keep asking about?" Longhorn shrugs his shoulders and cocks his head to the side.

"Tombstone! What is going on? One minute Jill and I are riding down to the river and next thing I'm packing a holster with you being my first vision. Ah, I know, I must be still out cold and I'm dreaming... right?"

"Bill, you and I have been on the trail since early morning and should be in Yuma in about an hour, if you get back on your horse." Longhorn makes sure I am stable and he saddles back up, "Come on get back on your horse, we are losing sunlight!"

"Yuma! We are on my ranch in Texas!" Dream or not, I'm getting mad.

"Just get on your horse and let's go!"

"Longhorn... if this is a dream or another delusion; can you fill in the blanks so I can play along, and hurry up because Jill and I are going for a skinny dip in the river before it gets too late. Oh! That reminds me. You can't watch!"

Longhorn just shakes his head like I am a crazy person and ignores me from this point. At least Image is on my side.

The sun is sinking over the horizon without my skinny dip. Now I'm really upset. Our ride of the last three hours has been in relative silence except for my query of what is going on. I have been ignored.

Over the years, Jill and I have been to old Tucson, and this doesn't resemble it at all. The streets are crowded with cowboys and wagons, with the roar of the saloon overwhelming the street noise. The dusk light of the town gives it an atmosphere of the old west. My dreams are so realistic I could reach out and feel the experience. As a matter of fact I can smell the old dusty buildings along with the barn smell of horses.

"Come on, partner, my throat needs to have a drink to wash the dust out of it." He heads for a hitching post in front of a drinking establishment straight out of the 1800's.

My shirt weighs heavy, my glance to investigate exposes a shiny silver marshal's badge. Don't recall putting that on this morning.

Longhorn half turns his head to me, "Cover your badge, partner."

Longhorn storms through the saloon like a gust of wind followed by his bark for two glasses and a bottle of Kentucky brew. He swings around to see where I am, only for him to get a stark that my person is right beside him.

"Let's grab a table, partner."

As my first shot of whiskey flows down my throat, my senses pick up on a stench at the next table. It is a combination of manure mixed with body odor. Turning to see what the violation to my nostrils is, Longhorn advises me that my nose is right on. The cowboy is the poke that we came to this town to bring back to Texas.

At our *bad boy's table* sit an odd grouping of saddle sores that Longhorn is twisting his memory to see if there are any others that requires our *attention for detention.*

This is nothing like I ever experienced or trained for, but not knowing any reality at the moment means what *'is'*, is my objective.

Longhorn stares at me like he is telling me what information I need to be aware of. He raises three fingers and with the other hand, portrays the act of cuffing. This tells me that those three are wanted. There is a fourth in the group at the table, so he is an unknown.

Longhorn's eyes carefully travel around the saloon. He is making sure there aren't *further* unknowns lurking in our midst.

Even with my years of law enforcement, this gives new meaning for the term *'old school'* by following his actions. Whether this dream is true or not is irrelevant right now. My partner is depending on me to back him up on this arrest. My gun and my skills as a cop are here to do whatever needs to be done.

Longhorn and I down our third drink and prepare for duty. He stands and walks toward the bar, then turns to face their table about six feet away. I head to a more central location, but out of a crossfire.

"John Parton, Billy Thorpe, and you, Jim Pike; you all are wanted under federal warrant and will hereby surrender your weapons." Longhorn's hand is warming the handle of his 45, preparing to release it.

John Parton doesn't raise an eyebrow in response to Longhorn's demands. His fingers slowly twirl the shot glass as he speaks back, "I don't reckon that will happen Mr. Federal Marshal 'cause my boys and I aren't finished our drinks yet."

The others keep their movements frozen, waiting for the outcome of John's death speech. With the threat of gun play, my hand rests ready to draw my sidearm with any threatening movement that would change.

John flinches ever so slightly before attempting to draw his gun. The split second it slides from the leather, my hand grips tight to my 45, bringing to target the shot glass in front of him. The thunder of my bullet firing and blowing the glass to splinters stops John from finishing his draw.

Longhorn speaks up again, "Now where were we… oh yes, you all are going to slowly put your empty hands on the table while my partner collects those nasty guns of yours."

We secure them in the jail cells and are walking back to finish our bottle.

"Did you see that? I didn't ever see myself draw that fast ever before. I kinda scared myself!" I relive the moment with Longhorn. "I have never worn a western style holster either."

"What do you mean; I have seen you shoot like that lots of times. Your falling off the horse today really knocked your memory into the water trough. Get yourself together, partner, we have a long trip home with these bad boys."

Taking a better look at my holster shows that there are four marks on the belt. I haven't a clue what is going on again, but I do know Longhorn, and we have a history together. This history is eluding me, but we obviously are used to each other's actions.

A voice from behind calls out, "Hey, marshals!"

We both draw our guns and swing to see who is now testing us.

There stands a small man in a city suit and Boler hat. Our guns pointing at him make him jump back, knocking off his hat.

He regains his composure with dusting off, "Scared me there! I'm a writer from back East and I'm out here to write stories about the hardened law men that are trying to clean up the west. I would like to interview you both and get your stories to put in your own dime novel. Back east the people are reading anything they can get their hands on about the gunslingers taming the Wild West."

We holster our guns and agree to spin a yarn or two. Longhorn is getting a charge out of the attention from the little guy.

"I have a fellow that takes pictures for me. Can I get you both on your horses for a picture?"

"As long as you hurry because we need to finish that bottle we started before it warms in the heat." Longhorn is getting testy by this little man vibrating around us, attention or not

Off he went, returning shortly after with this man carrying a big box. I saw one of those box cameras in a museum some time back. Digital cameras are so much easier... and lighter.

We sit proud on our steeds as the flash from the camera forever immortalizes us in history. I Think.

Back in our bar seats I pour us a drink to settle my nerves, "Not what I would recollect as standard operating procedure. In my day we..."

Longhorn screws his face at me, "I'm going to fetch a doctor to have him check out that bump on your head. You have been acting real strange since you fell off your horse today."

"No, it's okay. I'm just adjusting to my new delusion. Another shot or two of this rot gut whiskey and all will be within normal focus." I give him a sideways smile.

Deep into our conversation, our writer friend comes purpose driven through the saloon doors scoping the seating area for us. Don't know where he gets his energy from but he buzzes around like a bee being chased by a bird. He pulls up a chair and drops his writing pad down on the table.

Tipping his hat, "I'm sorry, gentlemen, but in all the excitement I neglected to introduce myself. My name is Wilbur Bigsbee from New York City." He picks up the pen and dips it in the ink bottle and prepares to write. "Now… who may the two of you marshals be?"

There is no doubt that Longhorn is getting right into having us written into a dime novel.

Longhorn shifts back on the chair, "I have read one or two of these books about some of the *Shootists,* and I might say writers like you do have a knack for putting more bullets in the gun than it can handle. My name is Longhorn and this is my partner US Marshal William Harden."

The little guy's eyes spread open like he had a cattle prod shooting pain through his body, "You mean you are *The* William Harden; better known as the *Widow Maker!"*

I have no idea about what he is talking about, but obviously my reputation is rather nasty. The nickname placed on my soul isn't what I would call encouraging on the side of the law, but if Longhorn is partnered with me, I guess the bad guys are *afeared.*

Wilbur continues, "I heard you shot six men, is that true?"

Longhorn steps in for me, "Bill only shoots those that need to be shot. He only has four marks."

To me, if all is true, I should be *afeared* of myself! If only there was a memory of what I allegedly have a reputation for.

The immediate area around us goes silent when Wilbur mentions my name. One left the bar in a hurry.

Now, my presence here may be strange to me, but there is always a shooter looking to gain a notch on their belt for taking a character like me down. Rather unsettling considering my lapse of memory.

Longhorn sees what I am mulling around in my head and is keeping watch on the door.

Wilbur makes notes of the information Longhorn shared with him about our exploits through a couple of hours. My mouth fell silent out of ignorance of my past. He is doing just fine exploiting our experiences to our new acquaintance anyway.

From what is being passed on; the *Widow Maker* has put any being pursued by him jumping at their own shadows. Apparently he... or I, is within the law, but just barely.

The sun has set and the night crowd turns the saloon into a crowded menagerie of cowboys and saloon girls. The clouded view of all is making us both uneasy. It is time to call it a night. We promised Wilbur an opportunity to ride with us a ways on our return to Houston tomorrow.

A sudden silence waves from front to back of the saloon. Through the doors enters a sole figure of a man that I had no idea as to his identity. But from the utter silence and Longhorn's facial expression, it means trouble.

One day in this new dream and already the fire is stoking.

The cowboy is a lean, well-dressed man that emulates gunfighter. A broad path spreads in front of him as his cold, dark eyes center on us. His purpose driven walk leads him to within a half dozen feet of our table. His presence before us is obvious and will meet with confrontation.

Both Longhorn and I have gun hands ready with eyes fixed on his every twinge.

The stranger's stare meets with Longhorn. Their mutual visual battle excludes me from the moment of silence.

Longhorn shatters the unearthly atmosphere with what may be his last words, "So you are still alive. Heard you took a bullet in Tombstone a spell back."

A cold, growly voice spaces between the stranger's lips as he slowly shifts a stare at me, "It's been a while Longhorn. I see the two of you are still partnered up. I will deal with Bill right after I kill you."

My ignorance of the stranger didn't impede my judgement or understanding that this man has a serious beef against us; More so over Longhorn.

Wilbur backs away from the table writing frantically in his notebook. For him to witness a battle with his own eyes will bring his words of the incident to life in his novel.

The untold revenge this stranger holds for us is about to be resolved. He must have a talent with his sidearm to take on the two of us at once. Fortunately, after today's arrest, my gun hand is ready to repeat another draw.

The stranger utters his final words, "Take a bullet like you gave my brother Longhorn!" His gun hand skins his weapon from its leather faster than I can even get started.

As the lead heats through the short distance from both shooters, Longhorn swings to the side after having the stranger's shot hit him hard in the shoulder. Longhorn meets his draw as fast and places his shot mid torso, throwing the stranger down and against the bar.

My sidearm is drawn and centers on the stranger waiting for his next shot to be in my direction. He settles to the floor with his eyes closed. My attention spins over to my partner who is set back in his chair in pain.

Holstering my weapon to help Longhorn, I hear a salon girl scream. The stranger lifts his 45 to fire again and I can feel the searing heat pass through my chest. Reflex returns a shot that brings his life to an end.

One knows when death is pulling at the soul. Blood is pumping up into my mouth with every drawn breath.

Longhorn drops to his knees to raise my head, "You took a bullet that was meant for me, partner." His eyes pool with tears as I slip into eternal slumber.

***

In the darkness I can hear a soft, familiar voice. Its gentle encouragement brings light back to my darkened sight.

As I lay on my back, the sunlight shadowed a beautiful vision. Jill is beside me calling for me to wake. With my returned awareness, I will abide by her wishes.

Her beautiful face welcomes me back to the real world, "Are you hurting anywhere?"

Rising to my feet, I dust off and check for bullet holes. To my relief, my person is free of lead intrusions.

"I'm fine. What a silly thing for me to do. Haven't fallen off a horse for years." I wasn't about to tell her I had another pain attack.

As my full vision returns, my glance about the area reveals Longhorn's absence.

"How long was I out?"

Jill checks me for abrasions or injury and finds nothing other than my embarrassment, "Just a couple of minutes. Are you sure you don't hurt anywhere?"

"Ya, I'm sure. Let's get down to the river." For only a couple of minutes, I sure had a lengthy dream!

As our ride continues to the river, my recollection of the experience with Longhorn goes into replay. It struck me that this real 1800's marshal is in my world for a reason. Fact or delusion, his presence is for a purpose. It crosses my mind to get Jill to do some research as to whether Longhorn indeed had a partner. The more I ponder the possibility, the more I convince myself to keep it a mystery. The truth will remain shrouded in the clouded conscience world that is mine.

The river is a cooling refreshment against the afternoon sun. It also subdues the bruising from the fall. This time with Jill is good. She appears to be happy with us resuming our relationship. The discussion about the truck construction has also shown her as being bitten by my bug. Her enthusiasm extends into the crime fighting aspect of the project. If she can't stop me she might as well join in on the action.

The subject in our talk is taking an off track from the truck project to the book we are working on. The content of said book is growing with every radical event that shifts my days with irregularity. The dream would add some spice to the story line.

***

The last visit to the doctor was a positive prognosis. With the active progression of my healing, he was very much surprised that with the extensive nerve damage that I could have any return of physical function. The exercise, including getting back in the saddle, impressed the doctor as a good step for therapy. Medication for my head injury continues, unreduced. My senses have increased a little more. The use of earplugs is now a necessity or my head would blow off with the decibel levels. Aside from the taste, my eyesight is strangely modifying as well. Distance detail is gradually growing. Fortunately, my sense of smell is remaining normal. With all the auto body materials and their strong odors, it would be nasty. The doctor still stands by his statement that the changes are side effects from the meds. Jill has done some research relating to such sense modification with surprising results. It seems the brain has a tendency to rewire itself sometimes. These alterations of self-repair can activate brain function unused normally. It is called *Neural Plasticity*.

Although my time with the psychiatrist has been reduced to a once in a blue moon, she feels my healing time with Jill, along with getting relatively mobile again has done wonders.

A month has passed since the trail ride incident and thus far I have been free from that cursed pain strike.

The progress on the K Horse build is slow but sure.

With the added light in the shop, working on the truck body is much easier. The cab is complete with paint and is ready to be mounted back on the chassis. We rigged a lift rail system on the ceiling of the shop for the bigger more awkward lifting.

"Okay, let's slide the cab over the chassis and we will lower it slow to get it lined up with the body mounts." I motion for Jill to push from the opposite side of the cab, "Slowly."

The body and paint on the cab is incredible. The shimmer of midnight blue gives the shape a look of toughness. Jill developed a primer and paint that will resist temperatures of up to five hundred degrees Celsius, and is bulletproof up to a high velocity rifle round. She is such a genius!

The groan of the straps supporting the airborne cab is hurrying its travel over top to frame location.

Almost in position, the front strap snaps and drops down on Jill's side. The heavy cab was only inches from the frame, but the thud down caught us by surprise.

I call out to Jill who is hidden on the other side, "Are you okay?"

"Bill, I need you over here quick, I'm pinned between the cab and the frame."

The shock of horror that she is hurt flies me to the passenger side to find her upper torso caught under the full weight of the cab. Without thinking, I grab the sill of the lower door opening and lift it up to allow Jill to pull herself free.

"Are you okay?" I check her over to see if there is any obvious injury.

Jill sits on the floor in a daze but appears fine, "Nothing is hurting. I shouldn't have been so far under. There was a void that I was caught in so there wasn't much pressure on me. I just couldn't move. I'm okay."

"I'll take you to the hospital to get you checked out!"

"No, I'm fine." Jill gives me an odd look, "This cab weighs about six or seven hundred pounds! You lifted it like it was nothing! Did you hurt *yourself*?"

"It was just the adrenaline pump of the moment. Let's call it a night. You go sit and I'll drop the other side into place. I'm sorry Hun. I don't want this project to hurt you. We need to be more careful from now on. K?"

***

Lying in bed this night, our ordeal with the cab brought the sudden lift of mine back to mind for scrutiny. Jill was right, I shouldn't have been able to lift that weight. To me, the lift was like picking up a cup of coffee. I am aware of the stories of people doing remarkable things when in a stress situation, but this is different.

***

All of my healing progression is now in the open with my commander and doctors. The deception still exists with the extent of my amplification of senses and strength. These items along with the truck build are mine and Jill's little secret. Unfortunately, my facial deformity and speech have had little improvement.

Chapter Six

This bright sunny morning is Jill's day. Today we are remarrying. The caterers are busy with final arrangements along with our friends helping with the setup on the ranch.

It is a good day for me as well, but the absence of Longhorn over the last while is disturbing. Whether he is a delusion or not, Longhorn is a special friend. If I had my way, he would be my best man today.

A vehicle coming into the drive has Jill's and my parents. They flew in from Florida to be with us for our day of celebration. Mom and dad came to see me when I was in my coma long ago, but their ages don't allow for much travel, so it is great to have them out again.

Superstition keeps most brides from being seen on her wedding day, but we aren't superstitious. Jill darts out to greet the four parents with open arms.

I'm glad my physical condition allows them to see me in an upright position. As they enter the house emotions take over and the mothers become motherly, scurrying around me like I am a kid again.

Jill saves me from a fate of motherly smothering by suggesting the dads and I go out to check on the horses; since our four-legged partners are part of the wedding party.

The walk out to the corral is an incredible feat. Just months ago the act of mobility was only as memory would allow. Image and Moon give their approval of our visit. My father helped bring both horses into this world. His bond with them is an unspoken world of eye contact. My dad has always told me that your horse is as much of you as your own legs. This was proven when my buddy saved my life.

Dad's name is William Harden senior; AKA 'Will'. As a retired US Marshal, he and I share a common quest. Jill has quoted that *'Cops never retire, they just tire!'*

Jill's dad's name is Jacob, and like her, he is in the engineering field. If only the two fathers could see project *'Knight Horse'*.

For the wedding, the project is secured well away from any misdirected eyes.

As Jacob and Dad reacquaint themselves with the horses, Longhorn makes his presence known. He stands beside me in silence for a moment, then speaks to me, "I remember my father. He lost his arm in a shootout, but he pressed on to become a lawman not to be reckoned with. He procured his form of justice with his mind and gun hand. My father may have balanced a fine line between the difference of justice and revenge, but never out stepped his moral duty. I look at what has become of law enforcement and have come to the conclusion what was, is now not a day of the gun, but a year of the paper." He tightens his jaw while slightly swaying his head, "No matter what you have planned, Bill, make sure all you do is in the name of justice and not to get even."

I responded, "Over these months I have been given many gifts, and thankfully in the wake of my recovery, I see the world devoid of my need to feel judicial anger. There is only a place to fill with a soldier against those that offend. It is not clear to me exactly what my quest is but I'm sure when the time comes and I saddle up *Knight Horse,* my journey will be justified."

Our group is joined by my commander Robert Dunham. In his hand is a six pack of brew, "Now don't get the impression that I am contributing to the delinquency of all of you, but it seems we need to bust open a cold one on this hot special day and have a toast to the groom." Hands go up and he continues, "To this day."

Longhorn is noticeably feeling left out, so although his consumption of a beer may not be practical, I put a word in for him, "To the Marshal Service, past and present."

My partner smiles and gives me his response, "Thanks, partner. Could use a taste of that beer right about now, though."

***

After riding up to the altar, our horse handler takes Image to stand slightly back from the ceremony. A true cowboy wedding doesn't include a tuxedo, but denim and boots. As the bridesmaids come down the aisle to join us, the sound of Moon's hooves approaching brings everyone's attention to the bride. Jill is as beautiful as the first time we met.

She joins me off of her horse.

Longhorn stands over by the horses and, unless my eyes deceived me, the big guy has a tear or two shadowing his eyes.

With our vows complete, we didn't get remarried as much in a spiritual sense, but reaffirmed the love that has always been with us.

We saddle up and ride off to a special place for the two of us. Our short ride is to our spot where many years ago I first proposed to Jill. It is our time to become one before returning to the reception. It is this time that one appreciates the bounty in the gifts given.

As we ride back to the reception the aroma of a Texas barbeque flows passed us.

In all the excitement I never saw the large group we had invited. Between Jill's and my work along with family, we could start a new community. Maybe I should have put another steer on the spit.

Tomorrow morning we head off on our honeymoon to Jamaica. Beaches, sunshine, with more beaches and sunshine, that's all we want. Don't remember the last holiday we had together.

***

The airport is a mass of organized chaos. Boarding the plane is our time to realize our vacation is over and heading back to the real world. Our time together over the last two weeks in Jamaica has been incredible. It was the best honeymoon we could have ever imagined.

Shuffling down the seat isle, a strong smell of gunpowder with the distinct aroma of the weapons oil hits my nose. The sensitivity still surprises me. It is common knowledge that firearms are extremely restricted on board an aircraft so I assume the gun belongs to an Air Marshal.

Jill is so excited about our holiday and is not keeping it a secret. She is hyper and glowing.

The flight isn't all that long, but with the loading and pre board, we thought we would never get underway.

Air Marshals are highly trained flight cops that fit in with the passengers. As I peer back to the person that was closest to the powder smell, he certainly blends in. His carry-on bag is clutched tight in his hands as though he is a frightened passenger not approving of the leaving the ground. Mind you, his behavior does draw my attention. The sense of discernment awarded me over the healing process gives me an uneasy feeling.

Jill is busy snapping pictures out of the window of the tropical landscape below as we ascend into the clear blue sky. She is having such a great time I don't want to disturb her fun with my mental observation of our fellow traveler.

The empty seat next to us across the aisle, suddenly has Longhorn filling it. For me to carry on a conversation with him would certainly have me committed, so I sit and just listen to what he has to say.

"Bill, you may not fully comprehend what I am about to say, but you must do as I ask of you. When we are in a more suitable situation, the facts will be clearer. The man you have been observing is not an Air Marshal; he is a courier. The bag in his hands has something in it that cannot be delivered to its proposed recipient. You must get that bag at all costs! He has a shoulder holster with a large caliber handgun. If he is found with that gun on him, he will be charged with a Federal offense and jailed. The gun is a way to put him out of the picture and give you a means to walk off with that bag he has. The next time he goes to the back restroom, you need to subdue and get him somewhere he can't be found until you are off the plane. The main thing is to get that bag and disappear after landing back home! If you understand, just nod."

I give him a confused nod and Longhorn disappears again.

The target is watching for the attendants to be busy before he makes his way to the restroom; bag in hand.

Impatiently I tell Jill I am heading to wash my face, intending to follow him back. Outside the restroom door my eyes make sure there will be no one witnessing my next move.

The stranger's eyes meet mine as he opens the door, meeting with my fist to the side of his face. His body falls limp toward me giving his weight to me to drag to the express elevator. The fit presses us to the limit, but I did manage to get him to a lower storage area.

The element of surprise rushes my blood through my body like a pressure pump. The actions of getting him here happened quick enough to avoid a mile high event with the crew.

A cord on the shelf allows me the courtesy of binding the subject's hands and his neck kerchief a muzzle. A dark corner of the storage galley will keep him tucked away until we were safely distant after landing. I place the illegal weapon he is carrying unloaded and on his lap. He will have a hard time explaining why he is tied and smuggling a gun on board.

The bag he carried is now mine and all I must do is get back to my seat in secrecy. The ride up the elevator gives my heart a rapid pace; almost to a point of me passing out. This secret agent stuff is hard on my healing body.

The way is clear as I peer out of the elevator window, so out to the passenger seating my shaky legs transport the rest of me.

As I sit back, Jill looks at my sweaty exterior and asks if I'm okay. "I'm fine, just getting a little airsick. I'll be fine in a moment. Guess the thought of getting home is catching up to me!"

Her stare at me tells volumes of disbelief, but fortunately she knows to await an explanation until later. Her eyes move to my new bag.

My anxious mission cools after landing. Clearing customs is easy when I present my Federal Marshal badge. At least I got one 'get out of jail free' card! Getting seated back in our car and seeing the airport in the rear view mirror lets me give my nerves the opportunity to play catch-up with my adrenaline. I'm a wreck.

The burning question flooding Jill's patience is finally blurted out, "What is going on? What is with the bag?"

My attention to the road and answering Jill's query is in disarray. Good thing for the traffic is light, "There was a passenger on the plane that was concealing a gun, and whatever is in this bag is of great importance for us to do something about it. The guy that had this bag is okay, but will be answering some nasty questions from authorities. I know this all sounds really strange but…"

"How did you know he had a gun and that this bag is so important?… IS IT A BOMB?" Jill is now freaking out.

"No, it isn't… or at least I don't think so. When we get home, we can check it out. I'm sure it isn't a bomb… my source of information wouldn't put us in that kind of danger. Trust me! Just believe that I haven't lost my mind… okay, maybe just a bit."

Both our curiosities don't last the whole ride home. We pull into a rest stop to check out the bag.

Looking at the bag between us, then into Jill's frantic eyes, I make a suggestion, "Maybe you should wait outside of the car."

"What I do know is that this guy is a courier. My source said I had to intercept this bag." Jill decides to stay with me as we explore its contents. My hands are shaking bad enough to interfere with the opening of the zipper.

Jill's uneasiness grows into impatience to see what all the hubbub is all about.

We are two kids opening a present.

As the sound of the zipper clicks its way down the length of the bag, we bang our heads together to peer into the growing access.

Now to describe disappointment would be to the extreme. Our eyes search for some rare, priceless object or a document of astronomical importance, but all we find is a small weathered notebook. It must have some inkling of value to be couriered by an armed guard.

Within my grasp, I examine the exterior to find some clue as to what is so desperate for me to beat someone up, steal his package as well as smuggle it through our border security. I feel so guilty now!

The notebook is without title on the outside and shows extensive aging.

Jill and I exchange eye contact showing our confusion.

The binding is old… maybe a hundred or a hundred and fifty years old. As I open to the pages, we gaze upon what we assume is a short journal, maybe thirty pages long. The writing is in fountain pen and very neat. Although the paper is old and tattered, the words are clear and unencumbered. There is a date at the top left of the first page. February 14, 1875.

Scanning further, my body shudders as the letters label its author. My vision goes in and out of focus to assimilate what I am seeing. My overactive nerves just received an overdose of stimulation.

I look up at Jill, "It is Longhorn!"

"You mean the old marshal from the cemetery?!" Jill is as shocked as I. She pauses to assess, then her eyes widen, "Who is the source of this mystery... and what are you not telling me?"

"My source has to remain a secret. I know this is really unusual, but you need to trust me that what has happened opened my eyes to what I need to do... as soon as I figure out what this is I need to do! This marshal must have been involved with something pretty radical to... whatever is happening." My quest is now coming to light. To all that we are is what path we must follow. I feel exuberance replacing fractured nerves. There is energy filling my body for there is purpose to my new step.

Taking Jill's hand in mine, my words try to give her peace, "The book we are working on is being told before us, my Love. What a great resource for our story!"

Jill smiles, "I'm going to have to build you a suit of armor! Let's get home now and settle in. We can read more later."

When a cop can't do his job anymore it is like losing a part of life. Being injured and forced to retire took my soul away. Longhorn's quest is now mine; bringing me back home again. The pages we will read in this journal will open a new world for us.

Chapter Seven

To tell of my visionary friend Longhorn would give Jill more understanding as to what I believe. Considering my brain injury and medication, hidden information may not seem relevant to my real sanity.

Our holiday was great but to be home on our first day of a new start feels awesome.

It would be so easy to just sit back and ignore the new acquisition of the mysterious journal, letting the world outside rotate without us. But there is a vacuum of duty pulling me into this adventure. Considering Longhorn is a part and parcel of my mind, the journal of his is real to both Jill and I. That can't be discarded as mental fiction.

We both are comfortable in our chairs on the veranda having a cold beer. Jill has the journal and is hesitating to open its story.

Her hands clasp the bound pages, "If you are ready, we can continue through this." Her fingers open to page one, and she reads aloud.

"February 14, 1875: The pursuit of a man by the name of Theodore Franklin has come to a violent end. During an altercation with said fugitive one of my bullets struck him dead. During the examination of his personal possessions I found a weathered paper map leading to a cave in Arizona. It apparently is not a hidden treasure

map, but pointed to a cache of information that was held in utmost secrecy by our Federal government. The package was stolen from a secured location in 1798 out of Washington, D.C. and hidden in its present location as described.

The fugitive I shot had a Federal warrant for treason. He was a former Confederate soldier in league with a branch of the Confederacy that maintained their hidden battle against the Union.

The map in his charge was vital to their cause and as such made him a wanted man.

My oath to the government means I will not conspire against it, but until my thorough understanding of what this all means is going to curtail my knowledge of this document to my office.

August 21, 1875: I have located the cave in Arizona, but cannot find any related information or cache. This may be an over manipulated bootless errand.

March 13, 1876: My office has assigned a new partner to help in my overworked duties as a marshal in the vast jurisdiction. His real name is hidden like mine and goes by the nickname of the 'Widow Maker'. My first thought is that my bosses are suspect of me harboring knowledge of what I am now calling the 'Undertaking Cache', and assigned a spy.

May 01, 1877: Any suspicions that my partner is a spy are deemed wrong. He has covered my back many times and I trust him. He has confided in me stories at home office that I do know of a national secret and may be under the gun.

May 30, 1877: Today I must go into hiding. The secret I hold has killed my partner. A shooter was sent to bury me and my secret. My partner took a kill shot and saved my life.

June 10: 1877: The map is hidden. There is only one person that will know where it is. With the map seek out the cave and find what is in the cache.

'What is done with that information after is of grave importance. It will be stained with the sweat when I am sheltered by its shadow.'

Jill lowers the journal, "That's all he wrote, or all I can make out. The rest of the pages are too water stained to make out. What a sad life."

She gets the *'Look'!* Her eyes widen and face tightens, "Oh no we aren't. We are not looking for this… This cache! No way!"

A broad smile crosses my face, "We need to get K Horse finished!"

***

Jill has kept quiet about the journal. I assume it is in the belief that I will forget about it and go merrily on my way about other things.

Knight Horse is nearing completion. We have worked diligently for the past weeks to get her rolling out in the night to fight crime.

As I prepare to start the engine for the first time, Jill gives me a kiss on the cheek for good luck. My head is bowed, saying a prayer for guidance and understanding. Although we will be fighting for justice; the means are going to kick up some legal infractions. Like the old saying; the end will justify the means… more or less!

My fingers press the ignition button bringing the thunder to life. The hammerings of the pistons are yelling out that they are ready to project this steel horse into the stratosphere.

Jill jumps in the co-pilot seat and orders me to take us out for a breakin' in run. She is as excited as I. The subtle blue lights in the dash and gauges illuminate all the vital functions of K Horse. Jill turns the police scanner on to hear if there is some fun stuff to get into.

Jill pulls a couple of neck kerchiefs out of her pocket, "If we do need to interact with the public, we need to cover our faces with these: just like the old days. Tie them so they cover our nose and mouth."

Considering the truck is not legally licensed and has more armament than a battleship… along with some new implements of super spy equipment, we had better not get caught.

In the windshield is an integrated night vision mode. If we need to be elusive in the dark, the system is switched to stealth thus seeing in the dark. A radar unit gives a topographic profile along with any mobile vehicles within a half of a mile.

The list goes on, but the scanner comes to life with a 1033 distress call from a Highway Patrol Officer. Units are responding, but are at least fifteen minutes away in his rural location.

Jill ties her face cover over her nose and mouth, and places mine on while I press the gas pedal to head and assist the officer.

We head off road cross country to get to his location in only a few minutes. With lights out and the heat sensing screen activated, we can see the downed officer only a hundred yards ahead. As we approach, Jill jumps out to assist the shot patrolman, and I kick the Knight Horse into low to chase the escaping vehicle.

My over exuberance with the throttle pert near run the bad guys over! I hit the red switch on the shifter and release a heat tracer to towards the car. The non-explosive projectile took out the rear differential rendering the vehicle lifeless on the ground. A man and woman bail out each side of the car and launch into a full run.

My familiarization of all Knight Horse's toys isn't complete yet, but the pretty button with a picture of a net on it looks like fun to play with. A ball of netting shoots out and covers the female. The K Horse comes to a halt and out I jump to tackle the male. He doesn't stand a chance against my amplified chase speed. I cuff them both, pack up the net and throw them in the truck box. Jill would need some help I assume.

As I approach, Jill had the officer's wound bound to stop the bleeding. He would have bled to death if she hadn't been there.

A set of headlights is approaching off in the distance. There are no red and blues flashing, but we have to vacate. The two escapees are against the cruiser waiting for the good guys to arrive.

We are away in time to evade identification.

I am so proud of Jill. She kept that officer alive.

The excitement shakes her to the bone, "I now understand why you miss your work. The adrenaline pump I got is incredible, and we helped someone." Her hand covers mine on the shifter.

The next morning:

Jill turns the TV on just in time for the morning news. The reporter is talking about the incident last night. *He* was the one approaching as we left. He beat the emergency units to the scene. He, like us, was monitoring the scanner.

As he gives his report, he tells of a dark truck leaving the scene and the packaged criminals. His latest report is that the wounded police officer is in stable condition in the hospital.

He also states, "Whoever these people are, they saved the officer's life. The handcuffed man and woman are facing attempted murder charges and are being held without bail." The reporter pauses, "As I came to the scene, there was a name painted on the tailgate of the truck. It said '*Knight Horse*'. If these people are listening; the family of the injured officer thank you."

Jill is now in tears.

***

We sit together out on the veranda having our evening cold beer. Jill is taken back by the overwhelming emotion of our previous night's adventure.

"Jill, you worked wonders with all the gizmos on K Horse, but you are going to have to instruct me on all of them. I don't want to push a button and blow up something that doesn't need blowing up! She did good last night... just like you. I love you, my crime fighting... what do I call you now. You aren't a side kick or tech geek. I need to give you a name. How about... what's a good name for you? I guess I'll have to give it some thought."

In all the action last night, something remarkable happened. My face isn't paralyzed anymore and my speech is straight again. My prayer was answered in an incredible way.

Dad and mom have made a return trip to visit us and their car is pulling up the driveway.

Their visit will give us grounding again.

Mom sits with Jill while dad goes to grab a beer out of the fridge.

As he sits back into his chair with us, the swish of the can tab made me jump.

Unbeknownst to Jill, I want to talk with dad about the family history, "I know that you were a marshal, and granddad was also, but you haven't said anything about any further back."

Dad hesitates to say anything but starts his recollection of our ancestors, "In the mid 1800's your great-grandfather was born. His name was as yours. After the war he joined the US Marshal Service. He was young and battle scarred from the Civil War. I don't know why they called it that because there was nothing civil about it. Anyway, he had a hard start to his life and as he grew into his twenties, he became as hard as the criminals he chased down. He never married but he did have one son by a dance hall woman. That woman took our last name and that boy became your grandfather. Apparently your great-grandfather didn't know about his son. His reputation for a harsh justice became his only life. At the age of twenty eight, he was shot and killed in a shootout in a saloon. He is buried in an old cemetery in old Tucson. Not much is known about his life other than his enemies called him '*The Widow Maker*'. My father, or your grandfather, didn't get much in the way of his story."

Longhorn stands silent listening to dad spin the tale. He and I know what really happened.

There are no medications that alter what I see as the truth. As brutal as it may be, Longhorn owed him his life. The truth was buried with him about so much.

For the first time, I notice two initials on Longhorn's gun belt. They are '*GA*'.

My first question to dad, "Did he have a partner with the initials '*G.A.*'?"

"Not as far as I know," Dad falls silent to think.

Longhorn returns my gaze, and then vanishes.

The conversation moves to more homely discussion before going inside for dinner.

Dad notices the scanner and comments on my addiction to my former work, "And don't think because you feel better that you can even consider returning to your job!"

"Naw, just keeping in tune with the excitement. My boss and the doctors keep telling me to just relax and enjoy my retirement, and that is exactly what I'm doing, right, Jill? I have considered a new hobby that will make me feel more than occupied in a constructive way."

As dad and I wait for supper, he clicks on the local news. The story about our incident happens to be airing again. His attention to the report is unbroken until the reporter finishes the story.

Dad shakes his head, "Never in my day did anything like this happen. This *'midnight avenger'* had better be careful or the cops are going to think he is a vigilante. It is probably some young kid that couldn't make it into becoming a cop and is getting his head too far into something he knows nothing about. Mind you, saving that cop's life is a good thing."

I choke on my beer, "Ya, probably some kid! But at least he is trying to do good."

"There are trained people out there to do that job. Someone could get hurt." Dad is too old-fashioned.

The rest of the evening nestled into a card game and early to sleep.

A month later

Knight Horse has made quite the impression after making the news through the past month. The scanner responses have turned our night escapades into front page coverage. We do have concerns about copycats, but our spur of the moment action cannot be duplicated.

Since my visits to the Houston Marshal's Office are rather frequent, I get any Intel about what the law enforcement agencies are up to. According to my research, the Knight Horse is not at risk of being hunted down. The street officers know that whoever it is will not jeopardize the safety of the public. The only victims are the bagged bad guys. They are also aware that we are a man and woman.

My focus is now back on the pursuit of the hidden map Longhorn spoke of in his journal. He refuses to relinquish any information regarding it to me, for what reason I don't know. He is either the most stubborn delusion I have ever met or he suffered a loss of memory from too many mind-hauntings.

His clue at the end of his journal never even occurred to me as a map location until I had too many beers. In my stupor it hit me: the sweat is, his head in his cowboy hat, and his hat is with him in his grave. What better of a secured location than in a hundred year old cemetery! Now my concern is how to tell Jill we are going to break into a graveyard in the middle of the night, and dig up some old dude to get a map out of his hat. To me it sounds like a job for the two... we really need to come up with a name for us. All the comic book characters have super duper names. We aren't in the comics but if we get caught we will be in the funny pages.

***

As a break from our errands in town, we stop for lunch at that café where the two young boys inspired me. Now it may be coincidence, but while we are eating our lunch, the father and mother come in with their son and his friend. The two boys don't have their super hero action figures this time, but re-enact the reported events of the Knight Horse and what they call '*The Knights'*.

Now, as '*The Knights'* make our way home, we discuss the alleged location of the map. Since my deductive reasoning is called into question, I change the subject to the dilemma we face about using K horse during daylight hours for purpose driven activities. The truck is going to have to take on a different appearance to fit in without suspicion.

Just like the genius woman I married; Jill has a solution. What a woman! She integrated an overabundance of pearl into the paint. Pearl will change the shade of the paint in different lighting, but she has rigged the body to an electrical impulse that shifts the added pearl into a directed shade. She can turn the truck from dark blue to whatever color she wants. Totally awesome! Now we can utilize K Horse during daylight hours. It will make things easier when we head to Arizona, instead of skulking around only at night.

Jill has also devised a face cover that is flesh toned to give us a blank look. Not very radical of a character appearance, but they are functional.

Our plan for this day is to head to Tucson to visit great-granddad's grave. Not much to learn, but the interaction may inspire me to understand him more.

With the K Horse secured and arrangements made to cover our absence over the next week or so, we hit the road. The anticipation of our plans in Tucson is mixed.

Three days later.

Jill searches the web and determined great-grandpa's burial location. She is noticeably distressed by what she has discovered.

In his time, Tucson was substantially smaller and the Court Street Cemetery was on the outskirts of the northern part of town. As time passed and the town expanded, the cemetery got swallowed up by the population boom.

The cemetery was first established in 1875 and was last used in 1909. Its history has been shrouded in debate. As the town grew and the cemetery was so under maintained, the sites were left to the elements. It was classified as an eyesore. Many gravesites were moved to another cemetery, but several remained and records are in as much disarray. Jill was fortunate to find information on great-grandfather's site number.

The entrance and landscape resemble that of a scattered, abandoned old cemetery. The ground is natural dirt with little to no vegetation. The markers are heavily weathered and neglected. This is not a respectable resting place for any dead soul.

As we search the area for my family member, my body moans in disgust that these years were vacant from our hearts for our lost father. This man gave his life for another and this is how his memory is honored.

Deep into the vast barrenness, I see Longhorn standing atop a small rise. His hat is off showing he stands close to where we need to be.

I motion to Jill to follow me to the gravesite.

Approaching the granite head stone, the name *Harden* shows what lay beneath. Longhorn holds back his emotions as my heart is torn from my chest. Jill gives me physical support to keep me from collapsing to the ground. It is my time to weep. This, my great-grandfather, shall not be forgotten anymore.

Being here shoulders the thought of desecrating Longhorns gravesite, but ends any thought of it. The mystery can lay buried with him.

Longhorn looks up at me as his words echo through me, "William Harden is my friend in death as he was in life. The bullet that took his life still burns my soul. He needs to be taken from this place to where I am laid to rest. When you lift him from here, keep his hat for what you seek is within. He was killed because of it." He fades away.

***

We remained in Tucson until we were granted permission to have his body exhumed for transport home to Houston. The Marshal Service is going to have him buried with honors.

Chapter Eight

As was told, there was a tattered map in grandpa's hat.

It is good to be home again with having the Tucson horror behind us.

Spread out on the kitchen table, the old document resembles a small section of a broader sheet. The old ink and weathering make it almost illegible, but we determine the location of the cave that Longhorn spoke to me about.

Longhorn stands beside me as Jill makes final notes from the map. I want to turn to him and let blast with my impatience, but since Jill is present I refrain, but aloud, make a comment regarding the map. It is more directed to him than a query for Jill to answer, "I wish we could just have someone simply tell us the information of where and what this is all about so we can put this matter to rest." My eyes meet with Longhorn's.

He speaks to me, "I am truly sorry, but I can only guide and make suggestions to you. There will be no answers from my mouth."

This only compounds my frustration.

"Jill, let's head out tomorrow morning to locate this alleged cave. Since we can camouflage Knight Horse we will take her, along with the horses."

The smell of death not only permeates my nostrils from the old document; there is a far deadlier history behind what we investigate.

The next morning.

Jill packs a small lunch in the truck cab as I finish loading Image accompanied by Moon into the horse trailer. The journey through the heat for the horses will mean frequent stops. The truck is nicely air conditioned, but the horse trailer is not.

As much as I want to open up on the throttle of K Horse, towing the trailer subdues my desire. Jill fills me in on all the toy functions on the truck as we make our way toward the Texas border. I fully understand why the company she works for has her on staff. I had no idea she was so talented at making these defensive, along with offensive apparatus. Jill is using K Horse as a test subject for a few new ideas she hasn't told them about. The best addition to the truck is the bumper sticker, '*Equipped with Idiot seeking missiles!*'

Over all the years we were married before I hadn't taken the time to get to know Jill. She is a wonderful woman. Having her as my partner in this crazy project really opened a new door for us. Most couples go on holidays to romantic sightseeing locations. We, on the other hand, are chasing bad guys in disguise, as well as the quest Longhorn has saddled us with.

The smell of the desert flowers vents up through the air conditioning to give a natural scent.

The sun is setting for the night as we enter a lone motel along the highway in New Mexico. A local rancher is caring for the horses overnight. Before leaving, Jill made arrangements along the route for them.

It has been a long day so a lengthy shower will feel good. Just as I get my shirt off, preparing to peel the rest for the shower, Jill's cell phone buzzes an alert.

She tells me to keep my pants on and grab a gun; someone is tampering with the truck. For some reason she is smiling.

The dull lighting in the parking area affords us no immediate awareness of the perpetrator, but as I circle to the passenger side a young man is calling for help. His partner is hoofing his escape in the distance.

We stand a few feet away from our victim who is still feeling the Taser shock from the passenger side door handle.

I look at Jill after I handcuff him to the front tow hook under the bumper, "He should be good here until morning when we will call the Sheriff. Just remind me, so I don't drive off with him still hooked up."

Jill responds, "Don't depend on me to remind you. I have a worse memory than you!"

Our sad excuse for a thief is now crying that we can't leave him locked up like this! He has rights.

Jill smiles again, "Hun. Let's go have a beer while we discuss what rights he has. But remember, we can't do what we did to the last sod that tried breaking into the truck. I feel so bad that guy will never be able to have kids. Oh well, at least we learned to make sure we have the safety on, on our handguns."

It is so sad to see such a tough guy crying for his mom.

Just when we were maybe, possibly, considering calling the Sheriff, we hear the squawk of a siren. Apparently the motel manager beat us to the punch.

This is the first time I have seen a felon thanking a cop for taking him to jail. He must be repentant for his shortcomings.

***

Considering our long hours on this black ribbon, my body is seeking a sleep reprieve. Keeping my eyes open and focusing on the road is becoming a secondary reality.

With little restraint from eminent danger, I slip into dreamland. Care and control of the steering wheel are now replaced by a twilight encounter.

At the top of the canyon cliffs my eyes fan over the arid landscape below.

From my distant vantage point, there are two saddled cowboys slowly making their way through the lower valley. They may be far away, but their identities are clear. It is Longhorn and the Widow maker. My great-grandfather's pinto is a stark contrast to the barren land they travel through.

To what purpose am I here? Seems pointless to view them from afar. To what lesson can there be?

The sky fills with dark clouds and the crack of thunder hammers. My footing slips on the loose rock and down I slide, uncontrollably careening off the cliff side. My breath is forced from my lungs as my fall leads me to a helpless destiny. A protruding rock scrapes my shoulder, jolting me forward.

My shoulder is gripped hard and a voice screams in my ear. A bright light blinds me. The grip tightens and now I see clearly again. The screech of the tires on the truck pulls us away from the oncoming vehicle. We again are safe from harm.

Jill releases the grip on me and the steering wheel.

It is time to stop for the night.

Days later

Deep into a box canyon the truck is overwhelmed by our road dust catching up. It is hot and dry. The towering walls of reddish rock give us little shade as the burning sun channels through the canyon.

From here we must travel on horseback. The terrain to the cave entrance is too hard for even K Horse to reach.

The temperature is well over a hundred, forcing our bodies to soak our shirts with sweat. The click of the horse's hooves on the hard soil is a sound like music to my ears. I could sail back in time to be quite comfortable in the old west lifestyle, riding from one adventure to another like my great-granddad.

Even with the scarcity of vegetation, the hard rock cliffs we travel through are an incredible canvas of landscape.

The matter of us talking with each other is curtailed by the need to just survive the heat of the day. As we ascend up the canyon wall toward our target, our pace is slowed to almost a crawl. We dismount to allow the animals a reprieve from us weighing them down.

Out here there is no representation of the modern world, just the harsh environment along with the isolation. Each heated step drains us of the last fiber of energy, but we press forward.

A short rest gives me a few moments to confirm with Jill that we are on the right heading. Off in the distance is a large column of stone that gives us validation. We continue on.

Hard to believe that a few short months ago, my vision of even moving my legs was a challenge, and here we are scaling a desolate mountain in the middle of an earthly oven in search of a lost artifact. Goes to show one that what must happen directs our future. The adventure we partake in this day is substantially better than what I faced then.

My feet are cooking in the hot leather of my cowboy boots, slowing my step all the more. Image steps forward, nudging me with her nose to give me more push. If she is doing this well in the heat, then I don't feel so bad. Looking back at Jill, I see the heat searing her as well, but she gives no complaint.

It has been four or so hours on the trail with the sun falling deep in the western horizon.

"Let's set up camp here for the night. The cave should only be an hour or so from here. If we push the horses or ourselves in this heat, we will just defeat our mission. When the horses cool down I will water them. After the sun sets we will be thankful for the heat of the day compared to the cold of the desert at night."

Our bivouac for the night is a small chunk of alcove along the side of the trail. Small sage brush borders the area, giving us a little wood for the night's fire.

Jill ties the horses off in another sheltered spot down wind. As much as I love horses, the smell of their droppings is not conducive to a good night's sleep. The sound like course sandpaper rubbing against stone grabs my attention. My eyes frantically search the surrounding area for the source. Between Jill the horses and I, I spot the slithering menace. A rattler has been disturbed from its daytime perch. Normally, the nasty reptile would seek refuge away from confrontation, but this one is heading toward them.

The horses pick up on the snake giving a defensive dance. Jill is no greenhorn out here and prepares for its attack. She draws her side arm and shoots a warning shot hitting near the now rattling snake. The pounding of the 45 slug slamming into the ground is enough of a deterrent, forcing it down and away. The horses settle down along with Jill.

I have a distinct repulsion to snakes, "I think I'm going to sleep in the saddle on Image tonight!"

"Oh don't be silly! That snake is probably half way to Phoenix by now. I tell you what; I will encircle the sleeping area with a hemp rope so you can feel secure with sleeping on the ground." Jill is so unsympathetic.

"That's just an old wives tale. I'm sure them snakes cross over a rope with no problem! I want the top bunk!" I'm still traumatized.

Jill doesn't let up, "That snake is more afraid of you than you are of it."

"Okay, tell that to the snake! I would rather face a man with a gun than those legless creatures. Even Adam and Eve had a problem with a snake, so I rest my case!"

I will put two rows of rope down, maybe three.

Next Morning

The cold air of the night is warming in the morning sun. Jill is already up perking a fresh pot of coffee on the fire along with bacon biscuits. I just love the smell of morning coffee with bacon for breakfast.

After my first coffee the world will be a safer place.

I carefully lift to my feet to check if my body heat has been harboring any unwanted renters.

Jill just smirks at my actions and passes me a coffee, "Not to worry my dear; I chased all the critters away first thing this morning."

Sitting near the fire with the one I love is now free of all that is a scourge on my being. I find peace in this moment of personal company, reminding me that the scent of the fresh desert air is sharing my place with all that is good.

Thoughts of the reason for this trek, escape my time with Jill, until the sound of a group of buzzards send signals of their presence down in the canyon below. Some animal has been taken into the jaws of another's for survival.

This day I feel no anxiousness. There is no deadline to meet or impending threat to alter my schedule. When we reach the cave it will be at that time and not with haste.

The forward trail is steep with slippery loose rock under foot. We lead the horses rather than ride. It will give them a break along with a bigger element of safety.

The time is only about six am, with the sun's heat quickly warming the day.

According to Longhorn, he found this cave, but couldn't find what he was led to find. He stepped this path well over a hundred years ago, forcing him into what changed many lives. Longhorn said that the secret killed my great-granddad. Resolution for this mystery is on my doorstep now. This map has been hidden for over a century, so any pursuers will have been long buried. The fact that the courier had Longhorn's journal though, must mean it is a concern again.

The only lead toward us is the airline passenger list. If the item is important enough to have it couriered by an armed guard, the interested party may be on our trail as I think. There has been no indication of surveillance or a tail since our flight so we may be clear for now.

Once we find this cache of history, we can evaluate what we will do with it at that point.

Nearing what is labeled the entrance to the cave, we see markers carved into the stone face of the rock wall along the trail. It appears to be very old from the many seasons upon its past. There is a symbol of a star, two wavy lines and a sun. Below the symbols are a series of Roman numeral numbers.

Jill brushes the area to get a better look, "According to this it says '*one thousand, one hundred and thirty*'. That's odd. Why would someone put numbers on a stone way up here?"

The electrical impulses between the neurons in my brain are hammering messages back and forth until the current hits my frontal lobe, "They are not just numbers, but a date. It is 1131 *AD*. But how can that be? Other than the Vikings landing in the northeast around 1000 AD, there was no settlement by Europeans until the1500's. Or so history has been told to us."

Jill moves lower on the rock where there is one more symbol; that of a triangle.

"Jill. We need to find this cave. Let's move on."

A faint wave of sound hits my ears. It has a continual rhythmic thump to it, "Do you hear that? Jill, do you hear that?"

Jill shifts her head to zone in on my question, "No, I can't hear anything but the wind."

The sound fades into oblivion, "It's gone. Let's move."

In a deep crevice in the hard rock mountain is another symbol. We tie the horses off and venture into the dark cavern.

"This is it!" We light our flashlights. The line of light moves all over the cave sides as the beam explores.

I can understand how Longhorn would be unable to locate the cache in this massive hiding place. There is no distinct location marked on the map because of the damaged areas. It is a guessing game from here.

There are large spots covering the walls with what seems to be ancient depictions of sea craft and cultural history from a land unfamiliar to what this area's history could relate to.

The dyes and pigments have lost most of their color, but the symbolism is quite clear.

The humid smell of the cave is strong with a breath of something else. I can't quite make out what it is, but directs me into a crack in the right side of the cave, As I grow closer the smell grows as well. Jill sees me following the scent like a hound dog and keeps pace with me.

"It's here; somewhere around here. I can smell it! It smells like old leather." I reach into a small hole, feeling for any man-made object. My fingers probe until they touch something soft. A shiver shimmies through me as I thought I maybe tickling another snake, but I continue. Grabbing hold, my hand extradites the cache of which Longhorn spoke.

The package obviously has seen many centuries of seclusion within its life. The leather wrap is dark with weathering. It appears to have a small bulk of documents within but we need to get this home before it is opened. With its unknown contents we have to take extreme care in the opening.

A reverberating re-enactment of the earlier sound is bouncing through the cave, and as before, it disappears, "Are you sure you don't hear that?"

"Hear what?" Jill just wants out of the cave.

"Never mind."

We are blinded by the brilliance of the sun as we exit the cave, "Let's mount up and get out of here. We can easily make it back to the truck before dark if we hustle."

Jill shows her concern for my rushed attitude, "Is there something wrong?"

"I don't think so." It isn't the answer she is looking for.

Four hours later

The horses are pushed too far, but approaching the truck at the end of the decline would let them catch their wind back.

Packing away the saddles gives Image and Moon a cooling time from the desert breeze.

That infernal sound returns, which this time seems closer. My eyes try to shift with my hearing to pinpoint the illusive irritation.

All is packed as I fire up K Horse for our journey back. The sun settles over the mountain top putting the narrow canyon into dusk. We are on our way.

The truck vibrates from an external thunder, other than her own. A beam of light from above lights the road ahead, giving me the answer to the sound I heard earlier. It is the thump of helicopter rotors.

Jill tries getting some identification as to who is following our movement, but can't get a consistent visual.

It is strange having a chopper in this area at this time of day. It could be a search for a missing hiker or law enforcement. The canyon is too narrow, with wind gusts that make flying low dangerous.

Streams of light shoot down ahead of us striking the ground.

Jill yells out, "They are shooting at us! Those are trace rounds! They are chasing us!"

"Yes, I would say they are either giving us a warning to stop or we are going to be dodging an attack. Kill the lights and let's go dark!"

Jill hits some switches, bringing the imaging of the road ahead onto the windshield.

"I can't drive any faster or try to lose them in the gorge. Stopping isn't an option either."

Live rounds of 50 calibers spark across the front of us just out of lethal contact.

"They must have night vision. These boys are on a mission to get us. If these are the boys we got the journal from, they may be a little perturbed at us." Managing the road ahead is hard enough without having bullets being shot at us.

The rap of the rotors slowly dissipates again to nothing. The canyon is giving us a small reprieve from the attack.

Our pace continues as Jill checks the topography ahead for a strategy of offense. They may not be able to chase us now, but once we are in the open, we will be fair game for them.

"Jill, if these are the people we took the journal from they obviously assume we have custody of the cache in our possession. This gives us a small advantage. They will not want to destroy the artifact. It obviously has great value to be hidden for so many years. Longhorn must have an agenda to risk all for it as well as get us involved.

"If we make it through this gauntlet, we won't be able go back to the ranch, or at least not right away. They must have been watching the ranch and followed us here."

Pursuing this matter is important enough to have the resources placed against us so the first priority is to get to a safe place and evaluate what is so critical about this old bundle.

"Jill. This may sound really strange, but I know what happened the day great-grandpa got shot. Please don't ask how I know. Just trust what I do know as fact. There was a shooter hired to kill Longhorn because of the map he was thought to possess. Great-grandpa was shot protecting Longhorn from the shooter, or assassin. The story started a century before Longhorn got involved, so it must be a big enough matter to kill people over."

Jill responds, "Whatever it is will have to wait. We need to make our way out of here first."

The heat sensors are a gift from heaven. They give us sight in the darkness, giving us the chance of to avoid an ambush.

We are leaving the security of the canyon for open ground. The surrounding area is free of ground movement, but a blip on the radar shows our airborne enemy is approaching again.

Our speed is curtailed again because of the horses. Our only defense is to go on the offensive.

The chopper is approaching fast from in front of us. It swoops low and crowns overhead. The varying pitch of the rotors tells me it is circling back for another assault.

Jill prepares me, "Keep a constant speed without altering course. As the chopper comes at us I will lock onto its heat signature and let blister with my new deterrent. Got that?"

The chopper heads straight at us again, only this time its 50 caliber cannons spark each ignited round at us.

"Hold on, they are about to feel the wrath of a woman on the edge!" With her hand on a dash-mounted joystick, she shifts it to center on the target. Her finger squeezes hard on the trigger and a blue pulse light shoots out of the front bumper.

I expected an explosion of some sort, but the chopper just lights up blue, veering off to the right of us. Within a few seconds it hits the ground in a ball of fire.

"That will teach them for shooting at us." Jill relaxes her grip on the joystick and sits back.

"What is that?" I am impressed along with relieved they are out of the picture.

"I call it the *'PMS', Don't mess with a woman at that time of the month gun.* It is an electronic pulse weapon that fires at the electrical circuits on any targeted vehicle. It also pops great popcorn."

I will have to remember that.

"Keep it primed because I'm sure they have buddies around on the ground. We need to get the horses to a safe hideout. This trailer is holding me back. Oh, by the way, can the K Horse withstand a strike from a 50 caliber round?" I am still reading the forward terrain off the inside of the windshield. It is like playing a video game only the vehicle is real and moving at high speeds

"Never had time to test it. The paint and glass can take a close range shot up to a 308 rifle round, but if a 50 hit at an angle it would probably glance off. What the paint can't deflect, the internal armor plating will take over anyway."

The area ahead of us is relatively level. If we can make it to the highway we can blend in a little more.

Surprisingly, operating the truck in total darkness is rather simple. With all the gizmos and navigation devices, we could manage without an open *windscreen*. The aggression against us seemed to have little effect on Jill. My opinion on downing the chopper was a matter of self-defense. They were trying to take us out so they got what was a risk of their job.

The radar still doesn't indicate any other activity other than the odd rabbit or coyote. I guess they figured the chopper would convince us to surrender our precious cargo. Their overconfidence works just fine for us.

Jill isn't saying too much other than navigation obstacles. I'm sure she is worried about the horses, but we can't take the risk of checking them just yet. I never would have imagined in my wildest dreams the hidden talents of the women I shared a good number of years with. I'm just glad she is on the recoil side of the gun with me.

Couldn't help give her the odd stare to make sure she is who I married and not another delusion. She seems real to me for which I am truly thankful.

"I am really sorry for getting you into this." My eyes focus forward to avoid contact with Jill's.

Jill never alters her attention but quietly replies, "We need to do what is set before us in this world, to the best of our ability. To me all that has been, along with all that will be, is for us to use our minds to work out. And don't be sorry for anything... except the secrets you are still keeping from me." The blue shimmer of light in the truck cab accentuates her great smile.

The rumble of K Horse quiets our conversation.

"The highway is coming up in about three hundred yards. We will go north and circle back. There's a ranch about fifty miles from here that we can drop the horses off until we can figure out our next step.

Just before the highway, we stop to check on the horses.

The trailer shuffles side to side as we release the door handles to get into the rear of the carrier. Jill combs Moon's body for any signs of injury as I did the same to Image. They are slightly agitated by the rough ride and fireworks, but are in good shape.

Jill finishes with the animals as I inspect the trailer and truck for damage. The trailer is free from abrasion but Knight Horse suffered a few strikes.

I call Jill over after hearing her close the trailer latch, "Your paint stood up well my chemist partner. These strikes by the 50 caliber shots didn't penetrate. From the look of the damage, the hits glanced off. It seems K Horse got the worst of the encounter."

Chapter Nine

Now that the horses are safe with a friend rancher, Jill and I are free to interpret our next execution of survival so the mystery can be evaluated properly.

We rent a cabin far from civilization in the north end of the state. I would assume they anticipate our return to the ranch, so staying out and away remains the plan.

In the dim lantern light, I spread the documents out on the old wooden table. The items are fragile, with the folded confinement in the leather binding causing a golden tarnish to the paper. Some of the numerous documents stick together, giving Jill a problem, but are finally open for our curiosity.

The papers are a mixture of ships' logs, journal papers along with what we would classify as crude maps. There are several dates written in an old script that is easily determined for timeline. The question of when and where is more than evident on many of the papers as well. The earliest date is what appeared to be 1022 AD.

If these were just great artifacts for a museum collection, or a collector, their re-discovery would be newsworthy. My question remains as to why Longhorn was targeted for assassination over a hundred years ago, as well as the recent activity.

The maps are an extremely ancient version of a survey of a small portion of what are now Texas, New Mexico and Arizona. They include portions of the tip of

Florida. They are a broken layout of the interior of Arizona up to the Nevada border.

Further maps give a distinct navigation map of the Mediterranean Sea with explicit detail to the northern coast of Africa.

In many locations are symbols of a pyramid, and a version of an ancient sailing ship, much like the Greeks or other traders in the Mediterranean Sea would have used in that time period.

Just the maps alone are mind boggling for the history they possess.

Amongst the mountain of graphic exploration, is a distinctly different land survey of a journey to the west coast near San Francisco, along the northern states and back over to Lake Superior. The journey is continued on a subsequent map giving a survey to the east coast near North Carolina.

As we dig further, a map dated 1034AD, documents areas around Alabama and Georgia. On these, are markers of a triangle or pyramid with, oddly enough, what appears to be a Christian cross.

Nothing in all these maps would represent anything known to us as history.

Both Jill and I stiffen at the exact same moment at the realization of the gravity of the implications these documents present.

If these are authentic, they would present a significant alteration in history as well as the explosive claim these people would have on their early discovery, including the exploration of what is now the United States. If these papers became public there would panic. Groups would come out of the woodwork claiming ownership to the land, even though the natives to the country were the first here. As history has been told; the United States was born very differently. Before the English, French, and Spanish, the then 'North America' was unclaimed by invading overseas countries.

The present population would feel threatened that their property could be challenged by others. There would be economic havoc along with what could develop into an all-out revolution.

The scary thing is, we haven't got to the written papers as of yet and we are already crippled by what could in terms be, the end of our country as we have known it for two hundred years.

It is no flippin' wonder people are dying over these papers. Whoever hid them years ago knew what they meant or figured when the time was right, they would be presented as their claim to the lands covered. Whoever was involved those centuries ago were lost in history until now.

Here we stand in possession of a critical world-changing event without any place to go to find support or relinquish our responsibility. This is one time, I wish a delusional dream is what I wake up from.

My first thought is to destroy this cache of destruction and let what is, be. No matter what we do at this point, is going to have us pursued by the forces faced.

How can Longhorn place us in this crisis? We have dealt with enough through the recent months and now this. I understand that these papers have been hidden in a secure hiding place until Longhorn wrote his journal. How it surfaced is beyond me, but he should not have documented such a catastrophic artifact. Mind you, he may not have understood what these documents incriminated.

Longhorn stands behind me following my reaction, "I didn't."

I respond in anger at him, "You didn't what?"

"At the time, I only thought that the map led to a treasure hidden by the Confederates as a way to resurge their lost cause. I had no idea that this is what it is. But as Jill said, all is for a reason."

"There is no reason to place Jill in the middle of this!" my anger burst.

Jill changes from examining our mystery laid out on the table, to her curiosity with me talking to myself, "Are you talking to someone?" She straightens up to give me her full attention.

"Yes, as a matter of fact, I am! I have been haunted by a version of Longhorn and he is now trying to justify why he has led us into this hell."

She just stands staring at me as she crooks her head to maybe get a different angle on my psychotic event, "You are talking to Longhorn?! He is here with us?"

"Never mind! Maybe I am losing my mind!" If I could crawl out of my skin right now I would be happy. If it weren't for the reality of Jill confirming what is at this moment, I would commit myself to the psych ward.

"Hun, considering how you knew to get the journal from that guy on the plane and other strange things that you… share with me, I have no doubt that some sort of apparition is a part of your consciousness… did you take your meds today? Just kidding! About the meds, I mean! I believe you." She encompasses me with a bear hug, giving me some stability.

My eyes gaze upon Longhorn with empty thought, which is grounding me to the hollow space I sit in this moment. How are we to know what to do with this information in our care? The extraordinary power to destroy in the wrong hands would hold the world ransom. Jill and I are simple people in an explosive, complicated situation far beyond our understanding. It is not our decision to make.

Jill makes me jump as she speaks again, "When you questioned what quest lay before you, I would imagine this was not what you could have expected. But you know what; we are here so let's kick butt. I'm confident we will make the right decisions." She peers about the room looking for Longhorn's location.

"He's standing beside you," my tone is almost a whisper.

"Right." She shifts sideways.

"I'm tired and need to get some sleep," maybe this will all just fade away.

"Okay. I want to examine these more. Just go rest. We'll figure this out." Jill has a way of relaxing me with her voice.

I mumble to myself, "At least we aren't fighting aliens!"

My eyes slip into a stare at Jill processing the papers. I am still spellbound by her hidden abilities.

She realizes my stare, "Is there something wrong Hun?"

"No, just thinking. We were married for so many years. How could I have been so blind, and why didn't I know more about you. Your job never crossed my mind as being so complex. You amaze me."

Jill smiles, "I wouldn't have been able to tell you classified information anyway, so let's chalk it up to us getting to know each other all over again... K?

"Okey dokey."

My last sight was the flickering of the lantern.

***

Now this morning the room is filled with the radiance of a new day. Jill is slumped over the table in very much the same place she was last night. She is going to be stiff this morning.

It is my turn to get the coffee on and make breakfast. Opening each of the cabinet doors is putting a damper on my determination to surprise Jill with my breakfast cuisine. All I find is condiments with a few boxes of breakfast cereal. Fortunately for the world, I found the coffee.

Longhorn stops in for a visit. I'm still perturbed at him, "No, I'm not making coffee for you!" The 'GA' initials keep drawing my attention, "Again! What do those initials stand for?"

"That isn't important right now. Just have your coffee and look at the bright side… okay, there isn't a bright side, but just look at something. Thinking back now , your great-grandfather was just like you are now. You are a spitting image of him, even with your attitude. He was a gentle soul, but get his fire started, any bad guy that made the mistake of crossing him got powder burns. Rather ironic though, his nickname being the '*Widow Maker*'. In his entire career as a marshal he only killed five men; the last being the one that shot him. When he had a shootout, he would often only wound his opponent. It was told he killed many, but you know how stories grow."

Longhorn sits at the table as though waiting for a coffee, "I remember a time he faced a low down snake that I would have shot without throwing my drinking hand out of sync with my mouth. He had every right to shoot him after skinning his gun from leather to shoot your granddad in the back. The stories in the dime novels tell of lightning fast shootists, but there were very few. He did let blister faster than I ever saw though. By the way… thank you for having him moved to Houston. At the time he was buried in Tucson things were different. Not befitting a man like him to be buried in such a place like he was."

Longhorn draws his weapon to give the cylinder a spin. The sound of the clicking as it rotates stirred the gun fighter in me, "Yep. Those were the days when men were men and bullets were cheap. Days when those stupid enough to be lawmen felt they were doing something that might change things for the better. Mind you, nowadays marshalling is more paper work than target practice on a no account law breaker. Couldn't survive today without having to shoot something. Especially those buttercups with their britches halfway down their butt. In my day, a man stood proud with fire in his spirit and lead in his pistol."

His company is so real I pour him a coffee and sit with him.

"I appreciate the coffee my good man, but my ability to consume said refreshment is rather difficult in my state of being. Now where was I? Oh ya, pansies. I've been watching the news on your TV. This world is a state of real stupidity. If I were God, I would look down, shake my head, then go see a counselor to find out how I could raise such an idiotic world."

As strange as this morning coffee is, I feel rather calmed by his attendance.

He continues, "I'm rather pleased to be reassigned to help you out. It was rather mentally laborious on my last posting. Got to catch up on all the newfangled contraptions and gadgets though, so I'm not so behind the times with you. My down time can really be dead. I'm really glad you didn't decide to dig me up before you went to Tucson. The maid has been unavailable, so my domicile is a little dusty."

He goes to grab the coffee cup but slipping his hand through it ended that attempt, "Been a long time since I tasted a good coffee, or downed a cold beer." His eyes show malcontent, "But at least I have a hobby."

"Your wife sure can pack a wallop with those shootin' irons she built. She's a good woman, Bill. I never got the chance to settle down. That mangy varmint that shot me in the back ended any potential romance I could ever have."

It is my turn to speak, "You don't get out much, do you?"

He gives me a crooked grin, "Nope."

Jill stirs so I offer her Longhorn's coffee, "Gave this to Longhorn, but he had a rough night so he gave it to you."

"Well, that is mighty neighborly of him." She comes over to the table and sits down.

"Not there! Over in this chair instead." That is awkward.

Jill stops and shifts to another chair, "Sorry, I'm still half asleep and not fully aware of ghosts yet! Who should I thank for the coffee?"

Obviously Longhorn is amused. He is going to stay for the meal along with the show!

Jill yawns, then lowers her head with her eyes lifted to mine, "Are we alone?"

"Nope."

"You do realize that if I told your psychiatrist about your friend they may sedate you." Jill's head remains, but her eyes scan around the table area.

"Yep."

"If I discuss what I found in the papers last night, can our invisible friend know?"

"Yep."

"Just let me know if I am going to bump into him or... anything... k?"

"Yep."

"This is really odd, even for you."

"Yep."

"Is that all you can say?"

"Nope. Do you want some sugar for your coffee?"

"Yep." Jill is such a good sport.

She gets up again to grab her notes, but hesitates to sit again.

I shake my head to give her clearance to sit.

"Okay, now that we have all the... stuff out of the way, I found many interesting things in the journals. First, like you, the thought of a land claim seemed reasonable. In a way it could still be a threat, but that in my humble opinion is not the main agenda. As these wayfaring explorers made their way around the country, they did deposit items of strategic, as well as historic value. In the matter of land claim they could establish each area as theirs by proof of the placed items. On the other hand, these items could be used to establish themselves at a later date. Use them as trade goods or whatever. Their limited understanding of where they were would be based on wealth on hand. It would be like in later years when the Spanish invaded Mexico and South America to secure gold for the home country. But this is like salting the new world to get ready for their claim. Confusing, I know, but bear with me. Somehow the explorers lost communication with their country of origin and would have been thought lost in the *'big sea'*, as we know as the Atlantic. Remember, these souls did not know much about any land outside the Mediterranean. Now there is much more of the story, but at the time of the Civil War, someone, somehow found out about these hidden '*treasures*' and felt as originally assumed, that the Confederacy could rebuild even after the war."

She takes a breath, "Now there are many possibilities' as to who is on our trail. It could be treasure hunters, southern fanatics still bent on resurgence, or our own government concerned for their national security. Anyway we look at it, we need to determine what we should do with what we have and establish an end to the pursuit. Any of these people will not want us to leak information, so consider us on the *'Hit List'* no matter what we do. That is my simplified version." Jill slumps back in her seat and takes a good gulp of coffee.

Longhorn's jaw drops as low as mine with Jill's presentation, "Wow! Bill, if you decide to divorce her again… I want to marry her!"

"Sorry, big guy, but she is going to stay with me."

Jill regains attention, "What?"

"It's nothing. You just have a hundred and fifty year old admirer."

"Good, so if you don't listen to me, you have competition! I'm hungry; Guess I should make breakfast for all of us. Do ghosts worry about fat in their diets?" She rises to go to the counter.

Longhorn deems it necessary to disappear.

Over breakfast we discuss options.

"With K Horse we can get around in relative freedom. They couldn't have bugged the truck without me knowing."

Jill did let me know that the locations are marked well enough to be found on the maps regarding the several '*treasures*'. I personally don't care about whatever is there. To me, all I want is to put an end to all this.

The previously discussed option of destroying everything comes to mind again, but they would still hunt us down. Now, we could use what we have to keep us safe too.

I wanted a quest, but not quite this substantial.

We could start a new institution and call it the '*Treasure Hunters Protection Program.*'

I need a beer!

***

First thing we have to determine is who is on our tail and why. The disposable cell phone we bought will serve its purpose. It will be hard to trace to us. My big concern is that the investigation with the airplane incident will pinpoint us as the perpetrator, getting the government on our backs.

"I'm going to phone John Striker. I have worked together with him for years on Federal cases and as he said at our wedding to give him a call at any time to keep in touch. Since he is with the FBI, I will pick up quickly if they suspect us or not."

I'm a little nervous as the FBI operator in Houston answers the phone, "This is the Federal Bureau of Investigation Houston; how may I direct your call?"

"My name is Bill Harden with the Marshal's Office. Can I speak to Special Agent John Striker please?"

"One moment please, I will connect you."

A million thoughts of how to explain myself jockey for position in my head.

"Hello. This is Agent Striker."

"Hi, John. It's Bill Harden."

"Oh, hi, Bill, how is retirement?"

"Not bad. Trying to keep busy. Jill and I are on a road trip right now with the horses to see some new country." I am looking for any indication that all is not well with the big boys. I really don't want to be chased by the people on my side for implications that would hammer us into the ground and a vacation in a federal jail cell.

"Oh that's great! I guess you didn't hear, but you and Jill happened to be on a plane with some action on it when you were coming home from your honeymoon. When we checked the passenger list, you guys were on that flight."

My nerves are vibrating, "Really? What happened, because I didn't see anything out of the ordinary."

"The flight crew found a man bound and gagged down in the storage area. He had a gun in his possession so he is going away for a long time. It was strange, but when we interviewed the Air Marshal he admitted that he bagged the guy and didn't want to alert anyone to the problem. His actions weren't according to protocol, but worked out for the better. The armed man had a list of previous federal charges and how he made it through security is being investigated.

"Wow! All that, and I missed the action! Could have turned a quiet trip into something else for me if I would have known." Odd that the Air Marshal took the credit, but as I analyzed it, I could see that the marshal was just covering his butt. If what happened went unnoticed by him, he would have a lot to answer for. He had to assume responsibility. What an enormous break for us. So whoever is after us must have just figured things out from the passenger list. That I can deal with.

"When you both get back home, let's get together for drinks. By the way, how are you feeling? Bob says you are improving."

"Getting better day by day. I have a great nurse. I guess we should get mobile. So take care and I will call when the trip is over. Bye for now."

My attention is now on Jill, "I had no indication of a problem."

Jill spreads the maps out on the table so we could devise a plan to find out exactly who is hiding in the shadows.

"So… where do we go from here? Do we look for the noted map areas and see what they have placed there or do we go after the bad guys directly. You're the cop. You tell me." She wasn't being facetious, just solemnly asking.

"I don't think we need to look for them because when we show ourselves again, they will find us." I pause to think about her other questions, "It would have made things really horrid if our government thought we were felons on the run. It is hard enough dodging bad guy bullets. I think we should not set a pattern to our search, is my first thought."

Taking a long drink from of my coffee refreshes my brain connections.

I really love the smell of the old wood as well as that calming aroma of the wood stove. They simplify everything for the moment.

My eyes gaze around the room with blank retention. My head is in a space of deep concentration.

Jill's voice invades my stupor, "Are you ok?"

"Ya. I'm just thinking… and it hurts."

Sounds from outside draw me into a different dimension. There is the faint rattle of roadway gravel being driven on, with the pump of vehicle engines, "I hear something!"

The odds of anyone up here to visit isn't expected, "There are two vehicles together. Let's pack up and get mobile. I don't want to take the chance of being corralled."

Jill starts K Horse remotely to get her warmed up for our exit. She bundles the papers into their leather envelope and searches the area for anything she may have missed.

I grab another coffee to go. Sometimes there are more important things than treasure.

"What color would you like K Horse in today?" Jill adjusts the switch and poof, the truck takes on a camouflage look, "We aren't a tree, but it gives it that mean look. Don't you think?"

I'm really glad Jill isn't taking this adventure in a negative way! She is having too much fun with all her gizmos. Her confidence in survival is refreshing.

"We only have one and a half ways out of here Jill. Which route would you like? We can meet them head on heading out or take the cross country trail."

"Well, my love, K Horse is a four by four. Let's see how she performs building her own road." She straps me into my four-point harness, then she secures into her's for the ride, "Don't scratch the paint, Hun."

"These vehicles may not be the bad guys, but let's not take any chances." We head deep into the bush.

Jill turns on other switches, bringing up a radar screen along with a topographical placement of the forested area ahead of us. She hammers out directions to me, guiding the route through to a lower connector road.

A loud scraping sound accompanies a branch travelling down the truck side.

"Don't worry, Hun. It will polish out!" Jill is presenting a side of her she kept hidden for so long.

The truck bumps and rolls over the hard terrain with only the odd moan of revolt, but never gives way to the mountainous challenge.

According to the screen, the forest opens to a small clearing just before a main power trunk line cut a trail.

The power line gives us a good service road to travel on, but we are exposed for any aerial pursuit. So far, what may have been our enemy, has not shown any signs of a threat, but I don't think they would have expected us making our way the way we did. No matter what, the ride was worth it.

"According to this, there is a paved road that runs parallel to the power line about two miles from here. We will have to find an access to it off of here. Once we get onto the highway, head northwest. There is one of the sites about eighty or so miles away. I will let you know how and when to exit the highway. When we get to the turn off of the power line, I would like to check the truck." Jill gives me as glance to get a response.

All I can do is smile. She is so hot!

As we stop for the inspection at the highway, it is a time to crank down the heart rate to something close to normal.

We both examine the lower chassis for leaks or damage, but found nothing. Jill gives her a hug, "Good girl! I'll give you premium gas later for doing so well."

Now it is my time to worry about *her* sanity!

I am hungry. The ration of cereal over the last couple of days is not conducive to maintaining a couple of kids like us, "The first restaurant you see, let me know. I'll let you buy me breakfast."

"Good idea. In all the excitement I forgot how hungry I am too." Jill checks another screen and advises of an eating establishment just ahead.

It would have been interesting to find out who those visitors coming up to the cabin were but, oh well.

The truck stop is crowded with an abundance of patrons allowing us to blend in more. After ordering Jill is fidgeting with a controller similar to a TV remote. "What's that?" I ask.

"It is a remote radar device connected to the truck. Before we left the cabin I affixed a signature to those vehicles we were avoiding. If they come within ten miles of us the radar will alert us of them."

And I thought my hyper senses are intriguing! "Is there anything you haven't put into Knight Horse?"

"Yep. I didn't have room for a beer dispenser!"

Jill continues with our now new assignment. She draws a rough map on the napkin, "There is an old road trail right about here. We can almost drive right to the location but will have to hike for a half mile or so. If we can see exactly what these people placed there, we can get a better picture as to their ultimate goal."

The hefty portion of breakfast gives us a second awakening. The coffee isn't as good as mine, but the caffeine boost turbo-charges our already charged state.

Walking back to the truck, we see a highway patrol car parked across the back of K Horse. The officer seems enthralled by the radical appearance.

"Your truck?" The officer pokes his head up from under the back bumper, "I like your bumper sticker about the idiot seeking missiles. Could use those myself sometimes. Texas, hey? Long way from home."

Jill fills in the blanks for me, "We are on our second honeymoon. Thought we would explore the back country around here."

The officer presses around the truck and notices the bullet skid marks, "Are those bullet damage?"

"Naw, we were four wheeling in a canyon and had some rocks come down on us. New paint job too! Never fails when you wash a vehicle it rains… paint it and rocks chip the paint."

"So where you heading?"

"Just driving to wherever we end up." Jill is getting impatient with all of his questions.

I step up and flash my badge, "We are up here after a dangerous felon and you are bringing a lot of attention to us at this moment. It's great you are checking out things, but you really need to smile, wave and say goodbye."

"Oh, I'm sorry, Marshal. If there is anything I can help with just feel free to ask."

"Thanks, but we really have to get back on the road." I sound rude, but he is bringing too much attention to us.

Jill jumps in. She raises the remote, mentioning we have company.

It isn't fair on the patrolman, but... "There are two vehicles heading this way. You need to call for backup and check them out. Our Intel is that they are transporting drugs. But be careful, they are really dangerous. Above all, DO NOT say anything about us! Just be really careful with these criminals! Make sure you have backup."

The officer shakes his head, jumps into his cruiser and he is off.

We did the same.

A few miles down the road, I have a sudden nagging urge to check out our pursuers. I also want to make sure the cop is okay, "Jill..."

She is already changing the exterior colors, "I was thinking the same thing. Let's go make sure he is okay."

Just after turning around, another police cruiser passes us with lights and siren. There must be some action.

Slowly we approach what appears to be Christmas. A half dozen police cars surround the two SUV's with enough red and blue lights flashing to light up a tree.

The four men from the two vehicles are spread eagle against the police cars. A number of automatic weapons of theirs are laid out on the hood of their rides. They are going to have a lot of questions to answer. This will give us a little time to elude them. Their plates are Louisiana.

Jill suggests we continue in the direction we changed to, and travel on to a different target.

Doubling back is a great idea. The more confused we keep these characters, the better.

Our next closest eastern target is a little over a hundred miles. This gives a short time to think about how we are going to live through this project.

"Good thing for that radar toy you have. You have given us a great advantage over our enemy. I hope they figure we are still heading west. My question is, how are they locating us? Are you sure we don't have a bug on us or the truck?"

"They could be following us by satellite. But if that is the case they will have blind spots. I'm sure we aren't bugged." Jill's types away on her laptop, "We aren't using our own cell phones, so they can't triangulate our location that way… we must be doing something to catch their attention."

I'm not the electronic whiz that Jill is. All I know is the methods we use in the Marshal Service for tracking. None work in this application, "Well, the only way to beat them is to keep one step ahead."

No matter what, we are putting a distance between us and them,

"These boys are obviously well organized and probably ex-military from the looks of their weapons. Since our boys aren't on our trail, I would assume that since these fellows are from the south, our theory about a possible resurgence by a Confederate extremist group is very likely. This theory I base on what Longhorn dealt with and also killed my great-grandfather. This aggression would have been literally buried for all these years until Longhorn's journal popped up again."

I pause to think and continue, "If these ancient deposits are a hidden treasure, the cause would be well within a possibility. But why try to start another civil war? All that would accomplish is throwing the country into a deeper economic struggle. Just doesn't make sense to me."

Jill is off in her own world while I babble my theory. She speaks up, "I'm rigging a cloaking on us by jamming any electronics that they may be following us with."

***

We still have a number of hours before sunset so as we approach our target area, the closer we get, the mental exhilaration intensifies.

An old forestry road leads us within a few hundred yards from the site. The isolation in the middle of nowhere provides the target a secure hiding place.

The ancient explorers must have had a strong understanding of navigation using the stars, because their precise documentation is extraordinary.

Jill and I bury the truck deep into a bush area and continue to locate the unknown. The landscape must have taken on a different profile those thousand years ago, but the rock outcropping would remain the same.

Jill presses forward following her understanding of the location. Our steps echo with the cracking dead branches along with the thump of our boots compacting the ground. Following the lead of the GPS we are getting close. Jill's walk quickens, turning into the front of a small rock face.

The overgrowth encompasses most of the hard wall. She begins pulling away the overburden, "There is something within a few yards of this location. What it is I don't know, but should present itself. There is a thousand years of vegetation since they have been here so it won't be a neon sign."

After an hour of de-landscaping half the countryside, we come up as a blank.

Jill flops down on a dead log in exhaustion, "It has to be here somewhere!" She pulls her notebook from her pocket to review her notes, "It has to be here!"

Having adrenaline hammering through one's body can spend all your energy, then forces the mind to continue. Jill covers the whole immediate area with her eyes, trying to locate some inkling of a clue.

When nature calls, I usually respond, "I need to go release all that coffee from earlier." My feet kick away the underbrush as I move to relative privacy. A forward step kicks an overgrown stone in my way, forcing me to the ground.

Either we are overtired or I am getting clumsy in my old age. Picking up off the ground and dusting off, my eyes zeros in on an anomaly unbefitting this location. It is a well-constructed mass of stones. Unless the animals have taken courses in stone masonry, I would say this is what we are looking for.

"Jill, come here! I think I found something!" So much for my restroom break!

Limping back from the stones, "I got a boo boo!"

"Well, that's what you get when you have radar toes." She pulls the growth over the stones back to get a good look.

Obviously the rock creation is man-made. There are three larger base stones a couple feet across with a similar placed atop of them in the middle.

Jill sweeps her hands over the top one to clear away any debris filling the large chiselled markings, "This is it, but may only point to another site or be the crown over the *Treasure."*

Money or treasure is not the issue for us. We don't need either, but the mystery behind all, is the only issue to be resolved. Longhorn, along with my great-grandfather, deserve an answer for what they died for.

Chiselled deep into the rock surface are the same marks as on the map; an old single-masted ship with a pyramid or triangle below it.

Jill closely examines the art work then gives her first interpretation, "We can rule out these being made by the *'Knights Templar'*. These emblems predate them by at least two hundred years. The triangle more represents an Egyptian pyramid. The consistent replication of a small hulled ship strikes me as what is described in the journal papers and depicted on the maps. They are definitely Mediterranean from that time period. I will research that later when we return to the truck." She pauses, scanning the area with her eyes as though she is sighting in on a target. She mumbles under her breath in search of a light switch giving her an answer or two, "Let's take this crown stone off and see what it is hiding underneath. It has to weigh three or four hundred pounds though. We need a lever or something to pry it up and off."

"Let me give it a try," I move over to it and position myself to give it a trial lift. "I would say it is around four or five hundred pounds." My fingers grasp under it and I lift. Preparing to be defeated, I put all my strength to bear. My over exuberance set me on my butt as the stone lifts with ease and throw it to the side.

Jill's eyes widen, "Remind me not to get you mad at me. Where did you get that strength?"

"I don't know. I guess since all my other senses have developed to the maximum, my body is adjusting the same. All those hollow points in my brain have come to life. Pretty wild, hey?" In all my years as a cop, I have never punched anyone. Given this new strength I will have to refrain even more.

Our attention returns to the exposed rock cavern.

Like two children peering into a new surprise, we dug around to find some hint of an answer.

Nothing on its surface would tell us anything.

Jill requests a shovel.

Digging ever so softly to avoid damaging anything under the dirt, Jill probes.

The daylight is fading fast, so our efforts to discover the contents seems like slow motion. We had to remove the three border stones to accomplish a deeper excavation. The hole is now a couple of feet deep with nothing to show for our determined effort.

"The maps only show a location of these markers. They would have instructed more if the item, or items were in another location. Whatever we are looking for must be in this spot." Jill is getting tired.

Down to the full length of the shovel, our reach is waning.

As I drive the shovel deeper, there is a shuddering clink against something solid, "We need to widen the hole."

Darkness is closing the door on our exploration as the sun disappears. I spoke out of disappointment, "We will have to call it a night. We can sleep in the truck and continue in the morning."

The look of disappointment crosses Jill's face, "Ya, I guess you are right."

***

There is nothing fresher than the morning air along with the crispness of a new day. The confined quarters in the truck didn't provide the greatest environment for a restful sleep. My muscles are locked in a pain position requiring an extended stretch.

Jill prods my attention to get up to the excavation site. Trying to keep up to her in my stiffened state is torture.

As we stood next to the hole, it took on a different look in the daylight. To think that the last people to stand in this spot, are now over a thousand years old. We are peering into the past.

Jill spares no patience dropping into the excavation to clear away the surface area to expose whatever the shovel contacted. She brushes away the thin layer of soil showing a flat stone. It is about a foot across and serves as a shield for the booty hidden below it. She lifts it to me and returns to the container partially buried. The soil compacted tight, requiring slow, precise digging around the perimeter, but finally gave way to its removal.

The box is approximately a foot square with no markings on its surface. The artifact is constructed of copper cladding over what seems to be a wood base. Exploring a way to open the lid without damaging the old contents, which is sealed in a pitch like substance, I run my knife along its circumference freeing its cover.

We both breathe in deep to ready ourselves for our first discovery. Lifting the lid off, shows that the liner is indeed made of wood. On the inside of the lid is inscribed several lines of text. Again, there is the symbol of a boat with the triangle below it. There is a date, but only a one and zero are legible. The last two numbers have faded through age.

In the belly of the box is a solid item wrapped in an old cloth. The smell is that of a thousand years of history. I could only imagine the people who buried this treasure so many decades ago.

Jill removes the heavy contents and places it on the flat stone that marked the burial site. She folds back the wrap opening to full view what we have been questioning for so long. The object glistens in the morning sun as though there is a light within it. The golden surface and weight determines it is of solid gold. It is in the shape of a triangle with another triangle formed on its surface.

In itself, the gold is extremely valuable in today's market weighing about ten pounds. At eighteen hundred dollars an ounce, the treasure is indeed. To me this discovery speaks a language other than treasure. The lack of abundance in this site shows that the deposit of gold is only a representation of location. The translation of the text is the next clue to who and why.

We wrap the gold artifact in a towel and pack it with the box in a storage container. The lid remains out to determine more. Jill takes some pictures of the cover stone markings and we head back to the truck.

Both of our minds are washed with imagination as to what we have found. The mystery of the hidden treasure only intensifies with our confirmation that these sites are authentic with significant history. If each of the sites contain a similar find; the dollar value is substantial. It is understandable why the Confederate postwar movement had an interest in them. It could fund a resistance to the Union. The historical value seems to take a back closet to the need for the money.

The significance of these sites points out that real history has been hidden away for a thousand years.

Hearing the engine turn over on the K Horse is a calming sound. We need to get out of this area before we are located again.

Jill is excited by the find but without understanding what is said on the lid, we are no further ahead than the moment we start digging, "So what do we do from here?"

"I know a fellow in Minnesota who has a lab that analyzes old things like this. He did some work for us many times over the years. I'm sure if I ask him to do an unofficial *'investigation'* he would help us out. He searches for strange finds around the country that don't fit into known accounts of the past. He would be tickled to dig into this. He can date and give a location as to where the linen wrap came from as well as translate the text on the lid."

"Are you sure we can trust him?" Jill is thinking like I do.

"I know I can. Whatever he finds out for us will remain untold outside of his lab."

Chapter Ten

We travel several days to arrive here at his gate. We come unannounced so if in fact we are being followed, there wouldn't be a welcoming party waiting for us. Our buddies from Louisiana must still be explaining things because we have had no indication of hunters on our trail.

"His name is Jeremy Wright"

The country home is buried deep in the Minnesota countryside with heavy iron entrance gates. Stopped, I press the intercom button.

"Yes, can I help you?" A man's voice vibrates the old speakers.

"I don't know if you remember me, but my name is Bill Harden from the US Marshal's Service. My wife and I would like to speak to you regarding something you may find interesting."

"Harden. Harden… Oh yes, I remember. You had a garment from an old murder you had me analyze. I remember you, come on through."

The gates creak and groan as they open.

Pulling up to the front entrance of the house, Jeremy stands waiting.

"Good to see you again, Marshal, and this must be your wife."

"I'm Jill," She stretches her hand out to Jeremy's.

We proceed inside.

"So what brings you so far away from Texas?" Jeremy asks us to sit, "Can I get you a coffee or something?"

"No, thank you. We would appreciate your help with something. The *something* is our personal investigation and requires that whatever information you pass on to us must remain confidential."

I look over to Jill, "Jeremy has a reputation for digging in places the government would rather keep silent."

My attention goes back to Jeremy, "You must understand that what we have is wanted by persons unknown, so if you feel you would rather not help us then that is understandable. These people have made an attempt on our lives already so if they find out you are involved, they could come to visit."

Jeremy dips his head slightly, looking up through his eyebrows at me, "Are these boys Feds'?"

"No. As far as I know the Feds' are unaware of what is going on. But if they are, we have two wolves at our heels."

He shifts his weight, moves his mouth from side to side, then continues, "Well, Marshal Harden, I guess we'll have to just keep this to ourselves then. So what is it I can help you with?"

"We found an old journal of a marshal from the late eighteen hundreds describing a hidden cache from the 1790's. When we found these papers, they laid out sites around our country that were established around a thousand years ago. From the limited information, these sites are by someone that traveled from the Mediterranean area and failed to return home. We have excavated one of these sites as described in the cache. We confirmed what is in the journals. Jill has some pictures of the marker stones and the find we uncovered buried under them."

Jill passes the pictures to Jeremy.

He looks intently at each photo without looking up. His facial movement along with the odd 'Ah ha' is tormenting our curiosity.

"So I am right!" Jeremy opens with personal satisfaction, "I knew we had early explorers to the continent long before Columbus, or even the Vikings. There was word of a story similar to this, but seemed only to be that; a story. So what more can I do for you?"

"We have a sample of cloth that the artifact we found in Montana was wrapped in; if you could try to date it to determine from where and when it originated. The writing on the lid is obviously important, so if you could sample the wood liner and let us in on the literary log. We will pay for your time." I still feel at ease giving Jeremy our information. His reputation with me is ethical and solid.

He doesn't hesitate to answer, "Of course I can. Do you have these samples for me?"

Jill reaches into her pocket to retrieve the two evidence bags with the scraping's of wood along with a cloth sample, "Here you go." She passes them over to Jeremy.

"Why don't you park your truck in the garage to keep prying eyes off of it. I will be in the lab." Jill goes with Jeremy.

***

After several hours of Jeremy putting the samples through his testing, he approaches us with his findings.

"I'm sorry. I have been a bad host. I should have offered you both something to eat. Sometimes my interest in a mystery makes me forget about eating."

Jill jumps in, "No. That's fine, Jeremy." Her eyes are fixed on the results in his hands.

"Oh, okay. Let's see... first, the fibers from the wrap. They are a textile commonly used between 900AD and 1000AD. Their origin is from the north Syrian area. But remember, during this time, the trade between the known world back then was common. There are trade items that made their way all around the Mediterranean. The wood in the liner is from a tree in northern Italy from around the same time. So, in consideration of said trade, these items could've had any ethnic owners at that time.

"Now comes the inscription on the lid. It refers to a lost tribe of the Hittites out of Canaan.

"There is a lot of confusion as to the history of the Hittites. They were a driving force from 2000 BC to approximately 1500 BC. Their tribes were scattered in small groups and classified as Semitic. Apparently they were in conflict with the Israelites. This I find odd because the text is in ancient Hebrew.

"Now, if all their exploration across America a thousand years ago is true, then they could change history as we know it. These explorers could lay claim to the marker locations. Now, rationally speaking, this would meet with severe conflict, but would still shake the economy to the roots. If a descendant group still exists, they could wreak havoc. Land owners would feel threatened that they could lose their ownership, even if, as I mentioned, it would be practically impossible, but would be the ultimate terrorist plot on our country.

"Now you mentioned something about the Confederacy being interested in the cache back in the 1800's. Again, if they acquired this information, they could succeed in a hostile takeover, or at the least destroy what was taken from them after the Civil War. There are critical factions that could ultimately do substantial damage to our way of life." Jeremy sits back in his chair drained.

"What you have here is rather nasty. In terms of an archaeological find it is incredible. But in the sense of the implications; it is death in a box. Question is, what do you intend to do with this now that you have it?" Jeremy stares directly into my eyes.

Out of what he has described, we have Hell in a hand basket, "Jeremy, I didn't seek out this nightmare, it came to me. In a way I am glad it did so we can put an end to it somehow; I hope! Jill and I have been given a charge far beyond what we are capable of doing."

Jeremy interrupts, "Capable is not what is at stake here. You have been awarded an instrument of faith. It is up to you to fulfill what needs to be done."

"That's my problem. What can we do?" I am exhausted. I turn my eyes to Jill, "I am sorry for bringing you into this."

She speaks back, "Well, my dear, you did want a quest. Next time, specify how big you want it." She smiles.

"Jill, I really don't want to chase all over this country digging up all the sites so no one else can take up where we are now. The thought of us destroying documented history rattles my bones, but that seems to be the route we need to take. Now like I said before; the bad guys won't believe the artifacts have been destroyed;

which leaves us with another problem. How do we end the chase and get back to life as it was?"

I turn back to Jeremy, "What would you do in our predicament?"

"Given all the evidence that supports the information is now in the right hands, I would destroy the cache at your earliest convenience and go on the offensive against your pursuers. All we have shared is now undocumented conversation, but if there is any way I can help further; you know where to find me. Let lost history be lost forever. Oh, and I charge no fee."

Jill stands, "Thank you, Jeremy, for all your help. Not knowing why this… this quest is so challenged is dynamite with a short fuse. Your help today clarifies a lot. Can I use your washroom?"

Jill scoots off to do her thing.

Jeremy shifts back to me, "I look at the two of you being chosen to fulfill what needs to be done. You have a strong, wonderful lady with you. Can I offer you both supper before you go?"

"No thank you, the sooner we evaporate this paper the better." My tone expresses my mood; it's hard to hide. "I really appreciate all you have done for us. You have shed light in a dark cavern."

Jeremy lifts with a smile, "You have quite the truck outside. May I have a look?"

"Certainly!"

Jeremy walks around the truck, gazing at its proud being, "Who did the build? Gives her a hard crust with an attitude."

"Jill and I restored her. She is the *Knight Horse!*"

Jill returns, gives Jeremy a hug and we are off into the darkness of the night.

Some miles, into a back country spot, we stop and burn all the paper we possess. The gold artifact is wrapped and put into a bus locker in a secured location. Just having rid of everything makes me feel a little better. After all this, we can retrieve the gold and grind it into powder. The other sites can retain their treasure without my remorse.

***

It is dark as we head south toward Louisiana. Neither of us can sleep so we will press on until we are too tired.

The dash lights along with the gizmos create a glow on Jill's face. She moves next to me and holds my hand, "He's right, you know; about you being *given* the task of stopping this madness. Unfortunately, no one will ever know what has transpired except the bad guys. It's too bad... but I know." She kisses me on the cheek.

"Go figure! Saving a country in distress without anyone realizing how much trouble we are in. Oh well... I got my reward. How about another kiss?"

I miss seeing Longhorn. Too bad I can't thank him for the fine mess he got us into.

Jill calls to see how the horses are doing. Apparently Image is put out that we dumped her in a strange place. I will make it up to her when we return.

**

It's now four in the morning with Jill fast asleep against my shoulder. A bright light from a car approaching from behind is blinding me. He is in quite the hurry and closing the gap.

I shake Jill, "Wake up, we may have company!"

She moves over to activate some of the electronics.

"I may be wrong, but we can't be complacent." My eyes keep checking the rear view mirror.

There is a bright flash of yellow light followed by a ricocheting bullet off my driver's mirror.

"They have been triangulating off our phone! Toss it out the window! It's a disposable blasted phone. How could they know?"

Jill opens the window and gives it a toss.

More shots skin passed us.

Jill prepares to retaliate. She pushes a button releasing a drop of road spikes; followed shortly by the pursuing vehicle dancing back and forth on the highway.

Jill smiles, "That did the trick!"

Rolling over into the ditch the vehicle comes to a stop.

I lock up the brakes, twisting the truck back toward the crashed car, "Jill, when I get out, watch for anymore attackers."

The smoking mass of metal is on its roof by the time I get close to it. My gun is drawn as my step gets within range of the driver hanging by his seat belt. His passenger seems to not have weathered the storm as well as the driver, who is moaning from his injuries. I cut his belt dropping him free. By the shirt shoulders, my grip pulls him from the wreck back to a safe distance. The car bursts into flames.

My attention returns to the driver. He is semi-conscience as I shake his damaged body, "Who are you and who do you work for?!" I repeat myself a few times but only get a garbled response.

With his last breath, he mumbles a blood curdled last two words, "Mein Kampf!" He slumps in death's arms.

Feeling through his pockets I grab his wallet, a pack of smokes along with a book of matches.

Jumping back in the driver's seat I toss Jill my acquisitions and plant the gas pedal. The further from here we get, the better. I don't want some County Mountie asking questions about the two dead guys we left in our wake.

The crash from the jolt of adrenaline wipes my strength. We need to find a place to rest. I will head west for a bit then south again. That should lose them for a while.

It has been a couple hours since our confrontation with my eyelids heading south. Jill offers to drive, but she is as tired as I.

The flash of a motel sign is like a breath of freedom; heading off the main road to our temporary home.

Jill arms the beast against intruders for our slumber.

The pillow never gets a chance to warm before my eyes close.

***

It seems each new day, our adventure wakes with us. In the beginning, it was my understanding that this *treasure hunt* was just that, but the deeper into the secrets held for all these years, is turning what the ancient explorers did into a modern power struggle.

I twist my cooling coffee with my fingers trying to figure exactly what is going on.

In all the years in law enforcement, Jill turns out to be my best partner. She is totally untrained and yet handles each situation with a seasoned professionalism.

Jill has her laptop computer open and focuses on her research, "The words '*Mien Kampf* ' translated from German to English means; '*My Struggle*'. It is a book written by Adolf Hitler." She quietens to dig deeper.

"*My* Struggle! That lunatic murdered millions of people, and *HE* had a struggle!" I take a drink of my cold coffee to wash the words from my mouth.

Jill lifts up to give me more information, "Apparently there are groups of Neo-Nazi's still operating in most countries around the world. They don't have a strategic stronghold anywhere but they are based with the fundamental beliefs as was held during the Second World War of being a Master Race. It would seem rational that the people after us are, in part or as a whole, under this group. They have struggled over the years to maintain due to lack of financial support. So obtaining the gold from the sites would strengthen whatever agenda they have planned. The credible land claim that the ancients have surveyed out would also give them enough to disrupt the infrastructure of the United States government. Which, to me, would say they are partnered with Middle East allies, possibly descended from the explorers that set the survey?"

I respond, "Wow, is that all we have to worry about. And I thought we were in trouble! Too bad for them, all the maps and papers are now ashes. Those sites are now lost."

Jill continues, "My hypothesis may be wrong, but it does fit. The enemy after us is well organized with the ability to track us and have personnel in the area we are in, and with short notice. Get this; it is also referred to as *Neo-Confederate*."

"Jill. You should have been a cop." I know she is smart, but she is branching into another area of expertise, "You keep this up and I will be redundant."

"Not to worry. I'm sure I will find a use for you sooner or later." She tries to keep a straight face, but her smile gives her away.

"Jill, go through the wallet I got from our pursuer to see if there is anything that may give us a lead to their location in Louisiana."

She mouths further research on this group, "Neo-Nazism of post-World War II are social or political movements seeking to revive Nazism. Neo-Nazism can also refer to the ideology of this movement.

"They borrow elements from Nazi doctrine, including militant nationalism, racism, xenophobia, homophobia, anti-Semitism and initiating the Fourth Reich.

"There is organized representation in many countries, as well as international networks. Some European and Latin American countries have laws prohibiting the expression of pro-Nazi, racist, anti-Semitic or anti-homosexual views. Many Nazi-related symbols are banned in European countries in an effort to stop Neo-Nazism."

"So how can they bring this ideology to the States and get away with it?" I am glad I burned the cache of papers more and more.

"Well, because of the first amendment to the Constitution allows freedom of speech!" Jill chokes.

"Okay, freedom of speech is one thing, but what they are doing now against us is far from freedom of speech; it may well be an attempt to overthrow the government. That to me is a breach of national security. A far cry from parading down the street in a demonstration!

"Maybe we should contact the NSA." (National Security Agency)

Jill freezes, "We have nothing to prove what we believe: we burned the evidence!"

I feel stupid for a second, but, "They had to be destroyed. It wasn't worth the chance; the enemy could get a hold of them, or the gold. We made the right decision. Besides, as long as they were available, the threat existed against our country if in fact they were to slip into the wrong hands.

Longhorn may have prevented more than he could understand. This country could have been substantially different now."

***

I lay the contents of the wallet out on the table with the matches and smokes. Even though these boys may be professional, they always leave clues.

"Jill, I am going to lift the prints off of the package of smokes so you can run them through the database for an identity. I will give you the access codes." Haven't done a print for years, so I only hope with all the handling they haven't been smudged too badly. Using some crushed pencil graphite, I salt the package, raising a number of prints, "Can you pass me some of that clear tape from the drawer?" Rather crude forensics, but good enough for the bad guys I hang out with.

Carefully the tape provides a clear impression of a thumb print that I know isn't mine. Jill had the Justice program up, ready for the scan... "Blast! We need to scan it into the computer! Can you go into the motel office to scan it through? Then come back so we can re-link." We are taking a chance with exposure, but we will be mobile shortly anyway.

As Jill is dealing with the office, my scrutiny centers on the matches which had a bar name on the cover; *'The Barn'*. Again, it is in Jill's court to track this place down.

In the solitude of the small room, my mind chisels through the immense amount of information clarified to date, as well as the large pit of darkness we still need to understand. There is no doubt of a conspiracy amongst a rebel faction out of the south. My unsettled rationale with all this is why – when our country already struggles in a harsh economy – there must be some group to add more mud to the water.

Frustration is burning the fuse to my temper. I anger at the thought that there is always some psychotic idiot or group that just can't leave well enough alone, they have to disrupt. The old saying about the greener grass on the other side taunts the power seekers, but they fail to realize the grass they already stand on doesn't need a bigger lawn mower.

Jill returns prepared to start the search. Her fingers pound away on the keys then she sits back waiting for some sort of answer.

"It may take a while. The database has to analyze the print, then compare it to millions of recorded prints available in the system." My words are missing her ears. Jill just sits staring at the screen shaking her leg in impatience.

"Jill. Jill. I need to talk to you about something," I almost have to grab her by the shoulders to break her attention from the screen.

She gives in to my request, "Yes, my dear. What's on your mind?"

"I think this whole thing is much too big for just the two of us. I'm thinking of calling Bob to fill him in on what we are working on to get his point of view. We may need to call in the troops. The Marshal Service, I mean."

Jill's computer bings a hit on the print. She reviews the information, "Ramese, Franco Ramese. That's an odd combination for a name! Twenty six years old. He has an extensive arrest history going back into his teens. Mostly misdemeanor, assault and theft. He was connected to the Neo-Nazi organization out of New Orleans until about a year ago, but had a falling out with them because of his shared extremist activity with some other radicals. He, along with a small group, formed what they call the Arian Supremacy League." Jill speeds through the information to a more pertinent area, "This group is suspect in drug and gun smuggling, but has flown under the radar as far as getting caught red handed." She scans some more then lights up like a bulb, "Whoa! Get this! Ramese is from Lebanon; born and raised. Has links with Middle East extremists." Jill looks up at me, "How can he be a US citizen with a background like this?" She returns to the lengthy report.

"Ah! He is being chased by the Justice Department for warrants. He is here illegally now. Well, at least he was, until the other night anyway."

"Pack up, Jill, we are out of here. We need to get to the nearest Marshal Service Office. I want to call Bob to arrange a meet with him in New Orleans. We definitely need help with this."

***

Our drive to Kansas City is mostly in silence as Jill does her research in preparation for our meet with Bob.

Pulling into the Federal Building in Kansas City, the truck takes on a neutral appearance.

"I won't tell Bob anything over the phone, and when we do meet, the information we do give him will be restricted only to the cache of papers. The find of gold and our contact in Minnesota will remain between us." My sense of duty did not include getting us killed over a leak in the Department. My trust can only go so far with a prize like we found to tempt the weak.

The closing of the office door quietens the mass of ringing phones with the multiple conversations. My hand rests on the phone, giving myself a last moment to decide if my decision is the right one. The air expanding in my lungs and being released doesn't give me peace, but the look in Jill's eyes proves what we are about to do is right.

It takes a few minutes, but Bob answers his line, "Bill! How are you doing?"

"Well, Bob, it seems Jill and my trip has taken on a little surprise. I'm not going to go into it right now, but we need to meet with you in New Orleans. We are about a day or so out, but can we call you on your cell when we reach town?"

"Are you okay, my friend? You are supposed to be in a state of rest and retirement. I will leave this afternoon. Say hello to Jill for me. I don't know what you are into, but keep safe."

"We will. See you soon." The click of the phone hanging up ends the only connection to the real world at the moment.

***

Jill picked up on the radio signal these characters are using from the last time they chased us. It will give us advanced notice again when they are transmitting near us.

Stopping for gas about four hours out of New Orleans gives us a brief time to stretch our legs. With gas nozzle in hand, I peer over the battle hardened K Horse. Her paint has stood the trials of combat, but left it scarred. She has driven unrelenting.

A male voice startles my focus.

Longhorn stands next to me, "You remind me greatly of your great-grandfather. He never backed as a shadow. Your wife Jill impresses me as well. You both would make your family proud that the ground walked is justified and true. You are right about me not being aware of what was really going on back in my time. It was to me a simple undertaking. The path now is in the light." He bows his head, "There was a time that my partner and I fought for justice, with bullets as our reward. This day I see why. William Harden, this is not your quest, but your destiny."

He raises his eyes to the truck, "Never imagined a horseless carriage could do the things this girl can do. Maybe one day you can let me take the reins and take her for a gallop."

I see the loneliness in his eyes, "Longhorn, I don't mean to be disrespectful, but why don't you go *home* to rest. You have done your part. I appreciate our friendship like no other, but I don't understand why."

"Do you have any idea how slow time goes by when one is living as a mist? Besides, this assignment I took on willingly. There will come a time that you will have the full picture without doubt." He fades.

Jill was standing silent with her hands full of junk food for the last leg of our trip into New Orleans.

The rustle of her foot on the ground alerts me to her presence and makes me jump.

"How long have you been there?"

"Long enough." She doesn't move.

I finish with the fill up and get back into the cab. My hands caress the steering wheel while my words came forth, "I'm not crazy. I realize my brain is damaged, but I'm not crazy. Longhorn may only be in my head, but it is like he is real. I'm not crazy."

Jill finishes buckling into her seat belt. Her warm hand slips into mine and squeezes.

Just before I start the truck, "He likes Knight Horse... at least *he* isn't crazy!"

In most cases I would assume her silence is her attempt to humor me, but this is her way of expressing I am okay.

***

Darkness has set in along with an attempt to occupy my sense of adventure. Jill turns on the stealth mode. The windscreen pops with all that is now represented in a digital landscape.

Off to the right is parked a police cruiser. We must have created a dilemma for him as we scoot by without lights in excess of a hundred miles an hour.

His image pulls out into a pursuit, but ends after I kick in the afterburners. The bit of excitement gives me a few minutes of release. Feel sorry for the officer though, how could he call in a chase like he just encountered.

Okay, what else can stir up some trouble?

A buzzer flashes an alert on the dash scanner.

Jill stirs, "We have company and it isn't a County Mountie! It's the bad guys. We have two ahead about a mile and two coming up fast from behind. We will have contact in about ten seconds. They are boxing us in."

"I'm going back to headlights. Kill the screen. Arm the toys. This may get messy. When I say, flip on the forward spotlights. I need to blind the oncoming for a chance to bust through. Will that PMS gizmo work on a car?"

Jill answers, "If I can get a steady lock on the target, yes, it will, but we need to hold a steady course." She grips the joystick.

"How about we go right through the middle of them. Get ready with the spotlights, and let blister with the PMS when you get a lock!" Again, I need to be careful what I ask for. I go from boredom to nuts in two seconds.

The headlights of the oncoming assault, break the crest of the hill. They are side by side.

The gap is closing quickly and when they hit about a hundred yards, "Okay give them light!"

The sudden brightness hits them hard because their cars swerve slightly.

A blue pulse shot forward, giving the target a luminescence. The right car swerves erratically as we squeeze between them. Our target car slightly clips our back bumper, giving it its fatal nudge into the ditch.

We now had a clear road ahead, but three hunters are now on our scent from behind.

"Jill, let's go dark again! No point in giving them a lit target. Do we have another load of spikes for them?"

I'm getting quite used to this digital navigation. It provides more distance detail along with hazard alerts.

Whatever they have powering their vehicles, is a match for ours. They are closing the gap from behind without hesitation.

Jill is busy preparing for her welcome with our road presents.

The first car catches up and begins to come up on our broadside. It slams hard on my driver's side with the passenger sliding a long gun out the open window.

"Jill we have a gun on us left side!"

I pull hard left with the steering, giving them a second thought about shooting at us.

The rebounding assailant regains control and makes another bump toward us.

Jill presses a button releasing a couple of capsules out of the truck side. They smash against the windshield covering it with black oil. There is one last uncontrolled hit against us, but they slip into a skid that plants them into a telephone pole in the left ditch.

"Two down!" Jill is a force to be reckoned with, "Time for some spikes!"

The ground sparks as the tire eaters hit the pavement. Our tailing enemies swerve to avoid them, but one blew a tire. It came to a sudden halt in the middle of the road.

"Hope they have Auto Club!" Good thing she is on my side. Jill is starting to scare even me.

Automatic gunfire starts flashing out their passenger side, spraying the rear of the truck with searing lead. The heavy, thumping impacts are testing my patience. They are marking the new paint.

"Jill… they are knocking!"

She smiles at me.

Oh oh! Now they are in trouble!

Jill speaks through the noise of bullet impacts, "Obviously they didn't see our bumper sticker!" She presses the trigger and a swooshing sound shoots out from under the rear bumper.

The projectile struck in the radiator, but didn't explode.

"Jill, it's a dud."

She presses another trigger, "I hate tailgaters!"

The front of their car blew into fragments putting a halt to all that tangled with my wife.

There is only one thing more dangerous than my wife... nope, I guess there isn't! Forget having a beer right now. I need a keg!

Jill straps back into her seat belt, "I feel like Chinese tonight, unless you just want to have pizza?"

I just said, "Anything you would like, Hun!"

Chapter Eleven

After our short rest this morning, we pull into a restaurant for breakfast.

Across from me sits what appears to be, and for what I knew for years as a quiet loving person. Those traits still exist, but the warrior in her exploded last night. Now, I know the resulting carnage is not her desire, but they were trying to kill us. Any red blooded woman would have done the same...

"From what I read about the Nazi's during the war would curl your nerve endings. And these guys are even more extreme!" Jill attacks her hash browns with a vengeance, "And they tried to kill us!" Her eyes pool.

"Hun, we did what we had to. They just had no idea that my wife carried a bigger stick than them." I get a little smile back, "How didn't I know this, adventure seeking, lethal weapon side of you all the years we were married?" Figure I better not stir the dragon too much, but I'm dying with curiosity.

"Well. No one tried killing us before." Her assault turns now to the scared fried egg.

Tightening my lips as I shake my head in agreement, I respond, "That's reasonable. Can you pass the salt, please?" My eggs never had a chance to get scared. I'm starved.

Jill quietly speaks, "The more we make this trip, the more I understand how difficult your job must have been… and how it impacts everything around you. I'm sorry for not understanding. To think that I helped engineer a lot of the weapons over the years without seeing the other side."

***

It feels much better now we had breakfast; with our time to relate more about the reality of the universe. I hope we don't have to have these conversations too often though.

K Horse took a beating last night keeping us safe. For this we are thankful.

Being on the outskirts of New Orleans, I call Bob to meet us downtown at the Federal Building. I just hope he sees that what we are doing as a benefit.

The dim lighting in the building garage doesn't do the K Horse justice with the damage covering its crust.

Bob is just arriving as we get out. Waiting next to our beast may give us a quick escape if need be.

Although his interest is to meet with us, he gives K Horse the once over.

Bob shakes his head, "Are you two okay?"

I feel like we just got caught with our fingers in the cookie jar, "Ya. Had a little vehicle trouble on the road last night, but other than that we are just fine."

"You both look like hell. Let's get away from here so we can talk more freely. Meet me at the park on Fourth Street. I will grab us a coffee. Try not to have *vehicle trouble* getting there either!" Bob heads back to his car.

Jill and I return looks of relief.

Bob has been my boss, as well as a trusted friend for many years. He knows my integrity would never be called into question.

It is a bright sunny day that should be spent on some beach relaxing.

We beat Bob to the park and secure a park bench for our meeting. Considering my age and experience, it still feels like I am waiting for dad to get home to give me *'the lecture'*.

Bob arrives carrying our coffees along with cop pep food…. donuts.

I understood what Bob meant about us looking like hell. We appear as though our night was doing battle with aliens or something. At least we matched K Horse.

"What have the two of you gotten into? Bill, you are supposed to be healing; and Jill, you should know better than this. The puzzle pieces started to fit together for me about this vigilante couple wreaking havoc on the bad guys around the Houston area. Then poof, you guys go on a road trip, and a trail of wrecks started piling up. The media has been following the *Knight Horse* escapades with due diligence. We got a report about a Texas marshal tipping off Highway Patrol about a group of drug runners that happened to be wanted felons and connected with an extremist group out of Louisiana. Then low and behold, as these elusive masked avengers made their way across country, they stockpiled more of these characters." His eyes burn his feelings through both of us. "Then out of the blue, you two show up here looking as though you have taken on the world of crime all by yourselves." He pauses to take a swallow of coffee. His eyes check out K Horse again, "Now, given my many years in law enforcement, I assume the characters that are with me now are the responsible parties for aforementioned actions?"

"Well… I wouldn't say responsible! We got caught up in a conspiracy that is rather dangerous, so we… ya, I guess we are." No matter what, I know we didn't do too many things wrong.

Bob takes a few breaths, "I did some follow up investigation about the plane incident."

Oh oh… Busted!

"It seems the Air Marshal didn't have a clue that his plane had become a war zone and rescinded his report. Now isn't it curious that who should be on that plane? What you two have done isn't breaking the law… somewhat, or hurting anyone with collateral damage. But there is the matter of leaving several crime scenes, several breaches of protocol of the Marshal Service, building and operating a road weapon far beyond legal parameters and the most serious of all… not staying retired!" His hand shakes wildly as he drinks the last of his coffee, "By the way, the boys are taking good care of your ranch."

I try explaining, "Don't ask me how, but it all started with a journal. Then a cache of ancient maps hidden in the mountains telling of a land claim with hidden treasure. Then the bad guys started chasing us for the cache of papers so they could find the treasure. Then there is the conspiracy."

"Stop! Stop!" Bob flew his arms in the air. He turns to Jill, "Jill, I know you aren't the type to exaggerate… is Bill pulling my leg?"

"Nope."

Bob continues, "So where are all these papers and maps?"

Jill bows her head, "We burned them so the bad guys couldn't get them. There is a conspiracy to terrorize the government because of the land claim financed by the hidden treasure. Or at least that's our evaluation. Those men tried to kill us. We just protected ourselves. They even sent a helicopter after us."

Bob slumps even lower, "That was you guys too!"

"Yep!"

"I could arrest the two of you right now to keep the world safe, or let you loose to rid the world of crime. If this continues, the outlaws are going to *want* us to put them in jail for their own protection."

Bob tries draining the last drop of coffee out of his paper cup, "Because these felons are under Federal warrant, our office is involved. But there will be other federal agencies jockeying for position. We need to be careful not to cross swords with our own people. If what you say is true, then this needs to be addressed in an orderly fashion, and according to Marshal Service's protocols. Do I make myself clear?"

"Yep!" Jill and I answer at the same time. I have cloned a monster.

"I'm not convinced! Jill can you give me whatever you have on the group along with a full report as to what has transpired?"

She shakes her head yes and goes for her laptop.

"Bill, I really am concerned for you and Jill. If I let you go, you need to promise me that what is done, is within the law without getting either of you hurt in the process. Since the *Knights* are being pursued by this group, they will expose themselves. This will work to our benefit to round them up."

I can see the concern for Jill and me in his eyes. We have come this far, so quitting now isn't an option.

Jill returns and begins downloading only the information that is safe to share.

"This meeting never happened. But if the *Knights* are caught, my powers may be limited. Do you understand?"

Our meeting ends after pertinent information is shared. It is now time to locate a motel room to get cleaned up.

***

The Barn is our only location clue at the moment, so that will be our first place to visit.

The GPS leads us through an old industrial area of abandoned warehouses and collapsing buildings. Gang markings cover walls like the scars of decay that have ravaged the area.

The closer to where this bar we search for is supposed to be, the gang markings turn to swastikas with a knife crown.

Considering the new vehicles and sophisticated firearms our pursuers possess, this area is below their grade. I would imagine this dark corridor provides them a safe haven from prying eyes like ours.

Like most organized gangs, there is an abundance of lowlifes available to do the grunt work. These grunts are the IQ-less scrubs providing the street level protection from intruders. This is more than evident by the vermin glaring as we move deeper into their territory. We see the poverty level residents that are forced to reside within this portion of hell, scurrying around in fear.

The filthy road brings us into a business hub of old structures barely maintaining a commercial appearance. There is no government here, but what anarchy that is laid before them to survive.

There is reason for the Arian Supremacy League to operate from this castle surrounded by a rotting moat. Travelers that breach their borders glow a presence, just like us.

Most, including the ruling faction of this armpit of the city, would think anyone stupid enough to come here from the outside must be crazy. But what better way to draw out who we look for than the direct approach?

A tattered old business front gives us our journey's end. A bold sign presenting *The Barn Bar* lay before us.

I must say, a tingle of adrenaline pumped through my system. Jill is more than ready to defend against any idiot that attempts to breach the sanctity of K Horse's protection. She will remain in the truck while I go have a quiet beer in the bar, and gently ask reasonable questions of the group that is trying to kill us and to scoop our acquisition. I don't see any leaks in my plan!

"Jill, keep the truck running. I shouldn't be that long. I'm sure they will be more than cooperative with me."

I check both my 9mm handgun magazines to make sure they are full. And shove a round in the slot of the M16 assault rifle that I carry for a bargaining tool. This is a practical time for me to have body armor on as well. It clashes with my wardrobe, but... oh well.

"Do not get out of the truck no matter what. If things go south, just get out of here. Do you understand?" I give her a kiss.

Jill shakes her head.

"Remember, don't leave the protection of the truck!"

Drawing in a deep breath, my legs drop me out of the K Horse. A small group of *Skin Heads* crowd the door, but move to the side when I kiss my M16.

To my surprise, the inner sanctum of the bar is quite nice. The outer facade doesn't do it justice. The bar is comparable to that of downtown New Orleans. My entrance by now is expected, so it is my hope that the leader of the League will present himself. This is one time my hearing gives me an advantage against assault. Every vibration will be assumed.

Nearing the bar, the sweep of boots on the floor tells me there is someone coming quick from behind. I shift sideways, letting the attacker slip into my grasp. I pick him up, slamming his body onto the bar. The impact knocks his lights out and he crumples to the floor.

"Anyone else that tries to blind side me will be turned into a chew toy! Now can I have a beer? In a bottle; I don't trust anything served in a glass."

The bartender graciously passes me a cold one. Taking a drink of it cools my throat.

"Now, I don't want to be too impolite, but I understand that the maggot that runs the Arian Supremacy League hangs out here. His buddies have been trying to get my attention over the last few days, so here I am. Oh, by the way, that Supremacy League name is pretty radical. You guys must be real tough. NOW WHERE IS YOUR LEADER?"

A door in the back of the bar opens, giving a tall man, dressed in a modified Nazi uniform, step through. Two well-armed men accompany him; obviously his body guards.

He presents himself stiff and defined as a leader. His blonde hair short on the sides with the top slicked back. The man's eyes are deep blue cut deep into his skull. Walking as though militarily choreographed, he closes the gap to stand before me.

His eyes examine my person then speaks, "So, you are the soldier eluding my men. I expected someone... a little more... bigger. My name is Kruger, Himelic Kruger. You have something I want. My partners are getting upset for the damage and... casualties. Do you have my documents, Mr. Harden?"

"Oh, yes... I have them somewhere on me... I think. It's so hard to keep track of that paperwork." I pat my pockets, "Nope! Looks like I lost them. Mind you, I could have them in a little safer place than on me."

"What would it take to convince you to give them to me? I could even give you a reward. Maybe even refrain from killing you." His voice is breaking.

"I'm here to ask politely to call off your boys and just go back to parading around like you mean something other than the low life maggots you are." I could feel my face muscles tightening.

The hammer of a chopper rotor sweeps over the building, forcing my enemy and his guards to flee toward the back of the bar.

This was not part of my plan. The previously stalemated patrons now pull weapons to take me out. The first series of bursts from my M16 dissolve the first attack. My retreat back to the truck is followed by more gunfire. A searing heat tore through my leg, pushing me down at the truck door. Jill jumps to my aid and slips to my side. By the grace of God, she got me into the passenger seat giving her driver command of K Horse.

I look to the sky to see whose chopper it is that disrupted the negotiations. It circles around and makes it clear that the culprit is a local TV station. Somehow they got wind of our presence.

Jill maneuvers us out of the area.

"I need to get you to a doctor!" Her quick glances away from the road show her fear.

"No! Let's just get out of the city. They are going to move their location so we have to regroup as well. The bullet went straight through. Let's just get out of here!" I use a towel to wrap the wound. "Now we have to re-locate them! Blasted reporters!" Now I'm really agitated.

****

We have driven a few hours out of New Orleans to a secluded motel to tend to my wound and have some rest after the days blow out.

Jill grabs the first aid kit from the truck to see what she can do about the gun shot to my leg. There wasn't any time until now to feel secure that we were out of the lime light. Considering we started out trying to be elusive crime fighters, that exploded out the window today.

Jill briefly goes out to get us food and twenty six ounces of pain killer for when she is operating on my boo boo. Without any topical freezing, she feels an internal freezing would serve its purpose instead.

She turns the TV on to see if there is anything mentioned on the tube about the incident.

To our shock, it is ablaze with headlining news about the shootout and even video footage the intruding helicopter took.

The reporter recaptures all that was witnessed:

"Over the weeks we have told the story of two masked crime fighters who began their epic journey in

Texas. They travel in a custom modified 4x4 truck called *'Knight Horse'*. It appears to be bullet proof.

"In their travels through the western states into the Midwest, we have reported their violent battles against a group called the *'Arian Supremacy League'*. This gang of extremists have been exposed because of our 'Knights for Justice'. The FBI is now also involved in gathering all associated members.

"It is reported that the once governing body membership of the political party of Neo-Nazi's has given a statement denying any affiliation with the renegade group in any way. As a result, their party has been protested against publicly without being able to clear their policy.

"Our interview with the media liaison for the FBI shed no light as to who the *'Knights'* are, and advise that they are vigilantes and nothing more. There is a warrant out for their arrest.

"Now for our breaking news footage of today's firefight at the *'League'* headquarters in New Orleans. Be warned, the footage is very graphic."

The TV screen shows camera video from the helicopter circling the building as gunfire rang out inside.

"As the camera focused on the truck parked in front of the building, a man burst out of the front entrance firing an automatic rifle back into the doorway. Even though the camera zoomed in, a clear shot of the man's face was interrupted by his downward look and sudden movements. He appeared to be wounded in the leg and was assisted into the truck. The truck sped off."

The reporter's voice came back on as the camera panned the truck labelled *'Knight Horse'*. "As you can see the truck is in plain view of our camera. The graphics of a knight's sword is on the hood. The dark blue paint shows many marks from what appears to be bullets. It is quite evident that their battle against the *'League'* has been a violent one.

"So who are these people that fight in the shadows against evil. Are they our saviors in justice, or are they fighting for territory against the *'League'*? Are they friend or foe?"

The view keeps being repeated dramatizing the event.

Jill turns it off.

During our operation in New Orleans, K Horse had her real colors showing.

Aside from the pain, I am on the edge with the media, "Never fails. These story hungry mongers not only screwed up my plans for today, they are insinuating we are the bad guys too! I have pain in my leg, and the media is being a pain in the butt!"

Longhorn sits in a chair near the bed, "Who is the enemy here; the bad guys or these... what you call reporters?"

I respond, "The reporters!"

Jill queries, "What was that, Hun?"

I forgot Longhorn is only *my* invisible buddy, "Oh nothing."

Jill passes me the bottle of high test whiskey, "I think you had better take a few swigs of this before I start sewing your wound."

"Don't mind if I do, my lady." I don't normally drink to forget, but this is a good time to forget the pain.

Longhorn obviously wants a portion of my pain killer but... "I remember taking a bullet in the leg. Never did get over the horrible nasty extreme pain when the doc cut it out. Pert near passed out."

My eyes glare through him.

Jill washes the wound and waits until half the bottle had rinsed my throat.

I widen my eyes to try and focus, but for some reason everything wants to swim around me. I do see Jill though, "Yus are so priddy! If ever I wanted anyone to sews me up, it twould be chu. Yuspriddy! Sissgointhurt?Yus so priddy!"

Longhorn shares his observation with me, "Partner… the last time I was partaking, was with my friend the Widow Maker. But I seem to recall he wasn't so *womanated*. Not criticizing you for your attention to Jill, but don't ever do this in a public establishment."

My lips are going numb, "If I want du says stuff tood me wife I shall dude it anywares I like… partner."

Jill is preparing to stick me with the needle, but backs off, "Hun. Are you talking to someone?" she sparks to her own question, "Ah, yes, our friendly marshal must be assisting in the surgery." She buries the needle for first stitch.

"Owww! Dat hurt… need more fain diller." The room disappears and the pain is gone.

Hours later

My eyes open to scan the room. Jill is nowhere to be seen, but good old Longhorn is still with me.

I quietly start a conversation with him, "Those reporters today really blew me away by what they did. They don't care what may be jeopardized with their actions. They just want the story. Reminds me of that reporter that interviewed us in the saloon after we arrested those three cowboys. He just wanted meat to put out on the public bone. I'd be curious to see what story the dime novel really told of us. Hum… shot in the leg I am. I thought that last shot that gunslinger got me with did me in."

Longhorn only sits, listening to what I have to say to him.

"He did kill me didn't he? I should have made sure he was dead by plugging another 45 into him. I slipped up, partner. He never got to gloat over killing the *Widow Maker* though."

My partner's face shows how dark his soul is shadowed from my words.

"But it is okay. I would do it all over again for you, partner. Yep, I would really like to see what that dime novel says about us."

I feel pressure on my shoulder and a voice.

"Hun. Wake up; you're dreaming."

The motel window had changed from bright sunshine to darkness. Jill sat on the edge of the bed with me.

"You were talking in your sleep. Are you okay?"

Along with the sore leg, I now suffer from a brutal hangover, "I'm fine. What time is it?"

"It's nine at night. You slept for a day, and were talking in your sleep. Do you remember what you were dreaming about?"

"No. Nothing I can remember." I hate hangovers.

Two days later

We can't stay stationary anymore. After getting packed up Jill fires up the K Horse to get underway.

There is no purpose going back to New Orleans again. The *League* will be on the move, centering on tracking us down again.

It still stifles me as to how they are locating us. We are not using cell phones anymore to be triangulated, and the K Horse is free of tracking devices.

I look at Jill, "How are they tracking us? What are we missing?" My eyes swing around the room to gather some inkling of an idea, but come up blank.

My leg is sore, but only slows my movement.

As I grab the last bag to go out to the truck, Longhorn's journal falls out and to the floor.

Jill keeps me from struggling down to pick it up and passes it to me.

Sometimes even a seasoned cop can miss clues that are right before them. In the expanse of the chase, the answers can hide in plain sight.

I stand with a blank look on my face as I receive some common sense being transferred from one part of my brain to the other, "They bugged the journal. It is such an important part of the puzzle; they would have bugged it for transport by the courier. That's how they knew who and where we were."

I pull my knife out and closely examine the journal. The tracking device would be a small chip hidden in the cover. That would be the only place to be unnoticed.

As my fingers feel the lining, I come across a small high spot, "Got it!" Carefully, I cut it free, "I don't want to damage it. We can use it to send them off chasing their tails."

Jill finishes loading as I crawl into the driver's seat. Fortunately, my sore leg is the gas pedal and not the clutch. It will work. I need Jill monitoring the gizmos.

Just after we get started, we pass over a bridge with a small river running under it.

I put the chip into a sealed plastic bag and strapped it to a chunk of wood. The river will sail it aimlessly toward the Mississippi River. They are going to get their feet wet.

Having the chip would provide them to us, but I would rather control their visits.

Jill put K Horse through a color change.

I look to Jill, "We should slow down on the paint changes or K Horse is going to have an identity crisis."

It is a good feeling to be more or less incognito again. No tracking devices or prying eyes. Gives us some calm time.

Jill speaks up, "So, where to now? They don't know where we are, and we don't have a clue where they are."

"We need to go west for now. Let the media advise *us* as to where the *League* is. Let's go get the horses. There is a cabin my dad used as a safe house in the north of Texas. It will give us a home base until we can resolve this mess, and it has a secure landline that is untraceable. We need to check in with Bob. I need time to re-bait my fishing hook. There is a satellite TV hookup there too."

***

It's great to be back in our home state again. The whirlwind of adventure has nearly drained us of energy and the cabin stay will give a chance to re-root.

The horses are excited to be back in our care. Image presented a problem for her keepers. She is my partner and in turn was uncomfortable about our separation.

During this *safe time* we will get some riding in, as well as rebuild our case against our foe.

K Horse's exterior has taken a beating over our savage pursuit, but even though she may not present herself as the shining steed she was when we finished rebuilding her, her armor has protected us from many assaults. She has done well.

Sitting here on the porch with my sight on the horses then over to K Horse sparks every nerve in my body. Without them, this time would not exist. Each has had an intricate role in our unusual experience.

Then there is Jill; my lady who has hidden so many unique qualities from me all these years. She exploded before my eyes into a *Lady of the Knight*.

It is rather ironic that the low life that attempted to end all for me months ago, created an all new world instead.

Taking the last drink from my coffee, Jill asks if I would like another. My eyes cannot hear as they read the distance between us, swimming my mind with thoughts of her.

The phone rings, shaking me from my momentary romantic freedom. Jill puts down my coffee cup and says it is Bob returning my call. The old style ring took me back forty years

"Hi, Bob," Thought I would keep it short and prepare for his blast at me for not listening to his orders in New Orleans.

"So, I see you followed my instructions and started World War Four. There wasn't much left for us to find after you managed to do what would take weeks for a demolition team. Next time we need to take a building down, we will call you. Good thing the camera never got a good visual of you or Jill." He pauses, "Do you have any information you can pass on to our office or do you want us to just sit back and eat popcorn?"

Wasn't as bad as I thought it would be, "The leader of the *League* is Himelic Kruger. We had a man to man talk, but a TV chopper interrupted and destroyed my chance of getting to the bottom of this conspiracy. I'm sure there are ties to a Middle East group. These bimbos wouldn't have the financial moxie to pull off a gig like this without big dollars backing them. The *League* is just a grunt organization to do the ground work. From my understanding of the alleged land claim, the offshore partners could create a virtual terror plot without setting foot on US soil. The unrest would undermine the government and public enough to create havoc. The land claim would only be a terrorist paper weapon. Now the treasures from the mapped sites would give the partners in the *League* a force paid for by the treasure. The *League* has their own agenda, I'm sure."

"Bill, I know you didn't ask for all this, but since you are the driving force, I'm going to designate you as a deep undercover operative. This doesn't mean you can continue to lessen the ranks of our enemies or shoot up bars. When this does surface as you and Jill being the hidden Knights, you both are my responsibility. Of course, all this information will remain within the restricted confines of the Marshal Service Office. Is Jill doing okay?" Bob's voice has concern.

"Let me put it this way. If I were the enemy, I would run for the hills, 'cause Jill has her gizmos loaded and is huntin' bear." I don't think I put Bob's mind to rest.

Bob chuckles, "I take that as an *'okay'*. This Kruger fellow is going to surface again soon, because half the NSA and FBI are chasing him. They are working with our office, since we have two operatives working on the case. I will let you know of any Intel'. Now both of you need to take care and get through this unscathed. The only person that knows of the *Knights* is me."

"Gotcha! Have to go, my coffee is getting cold."

I sit back out on the deck to continue my admiration of my wife and cup of java.

"So what did Bob have to say?" Jill is burning with curiosity.

"Well, I guess we are on the Marshal Service payroll again. How does it feel to be an active part of a major national security investigation; gizmo girl?"

Jill's face lights up, "Really!? Wow! Should I wear more makeup?"

Chapter Twelve

On the road back to the ranch, my nerves are vibrating like someone plugged a quarter into me. If I were a bed that would be just fine, but I'm not.

We decide to swing by the homestead to restock K Horse's defense mechanisms and do some minor servicing before going back for the horses. She has worked much harder than is fair, so an oil change along with a wash will be in order. I know how I would feel if I was running with dirty oil.

Seems like a lifetime since we left; or with that said, a matter of a different lifetime.

All the express miles we put on, there is one thing that has skipped past my notice. We haven't played any tunes on the stereo. For that fact: do we even have a stereo buried amongst all the apparatus in the cab?

Jill picks up on me searching for something and speaks up, "Are you looking for something?"

"Yep. I know this is a silly question but, do we have a music box in here somewhere? If not, you are going to have to listen to me yodel out a tune or two." If that isn't incentive to rattle the cab with a prerecord nothing is.

Jill shifts to the middle of the seat to access a panel where the ashtray used to be. The small door opens and Jill flicks an 'on' switch. In the glove box she retrieves a small remote, "So what would you like to listen to?"

Again, because of my absence from electronic understanding, my face twists in four different directions,

"Where's the tape or disc, or where is the music recorded? These remotes scare me now. Could push a button to listen to an old classic cowboy tune and take out a car in front of us with a missile."

"Not to worry. The remote is on a totally different frequency, besides that, all the music is via satellite. You can listen to whatever you want. How about we start with some old country?" She fiddles with the remote and presto, tunes to calm the savage beast.

Now with that situation fully reconciled with minimal damage to my pride, we can travel this ribbon of black in harmony with the satellite. Seems a lot more personable when I could just push a tape into the player and pick a track.

Jill stays beside me and sings along to the music.

She has been the best gift in my life. When I sat helpless in my chair, she was with me no matter what. If I could, I would send a message to every married cop to open their eyes to the person standing beside them and give them all they deserve.

I wonder what part of the Mississippi the bad guys are fishing right now.

We are a couple of hours away from home with the moonlit night casting an eerie glow upon the landscape. Driving with normal headlights is almost odd to me now that I'm so used to the stealth mode running dark. These gizmos can get habit forming.

Jill is showing signs of exhaustion. Her head nods down as she fights to stay awake. She succumbs.

There are no warning lights flashing or alarms blaring, so I will let her get some much deserved sleep.

The mellow thump of K Horse's exhaust is like she is talking to me; her voice in rhythm with the old tune.

The couple of hours of solitude gave me time to reflect on our ever expanding case. If the *League* knew of us destroying the only means of locating the hidden treasures, our reason for being here would take on new meaning. Their alliance with their offshore partner would be terminated, but in their ignorance, we have a chance of ending any further uprisings from them.

I was told many years ago not to make any more enemies than necessary. One needs all the intact bridges they can keep. These *League* characters have defied their base establishment, so I'm sure the Neo-Nazi Party would like to have this separatist wing disappear. They don't want to bring the heat of the Feds down on them.

Paying a visit to the ranch isn't the greatest idea, but I'm sure the limited resources of our enemy wouldn't expect us back home. They wouldn't have someone sitting out watching. Still, it is not a time for us to drop our guard though.

A distant view of the ranch tells me to wake Jill and get her to do a scan of the area for unwelcome visitors.

She reorients herself and begins doing her thing, "Looks clear, Hun."

The yard lights bring us home. It would be nice to be coming home with a finale to this case.

The crunch of the gravel under the truck tires echoes through the still night. The grounds seem abandoned, but we awoke it with a renewed presence.

Jill breaks out of the cab to open the barn doors for me to hide K Horse.

The ranch is so quiet. I pass one of my side arms to Jill to cover our flank as we enter the main house. The palm of my hand soaks the grip of my 9mm raised to react to any hidden intruder. Room by room we clear our space at home.

We are tired and need to sleep in the worst way.

Jill has armed the truck to our remote, so any vehicles coming up the road will be on our radar.

"It's time to change the dressing on your leg, so go have a shower while I fix us something to eat." Jill starts looking for a quick fix from the fridge.

The hot water streaming over my battered body relieves some of the pain, relaxing the stress from the day. My leg is strained from being back in action after the many miles we traveled today.

The terry towel robe insulated me from the chilled air of the early morning. The noise from Jill working in the kitchen quieted abruptly. It may be nothing but at this point I will not be complacent. I must be quite the sight in my robe and slippers brandishing a Colt 45. The thought of calling out to Jill crosses my mind, but in the silence it would be more realistic to be extra paranoid.

There are times when silence is not golden, and this particular time is rather disturbing. The closer I draw to the kitchen, the more my body prepares for confrontation. Even with my better hearing I only hear the mild breeze passing through the kitchen window.

To the edge of the wall I will get a glimpse of the kitchen area. My eyes peer ever so slowly to gain a view of the kitchen.

Plates are set ready for our dining but there is no Jill. My back travels the wall to get a further glimpse into the dining room. At this point all is not good. I await with uncertainty to what I now feel is going to be a deadly ordeal.

This visit back home, I believe now to be a mistake, but it is now a mistake with consequences.

In stark contrast to the stillness, my body shudders from a sudden disturbance in the lower level bathroom. It is the flush of the toilet.

Jill comes sauntering out unaware of the intense atmosphere. She comes to a sudden halt when she sees me standing with gun in hand. She whispers, "Is there something wrong?"

Considering her casual demeanor, I have been mistaken ,"No... I just... No nothing."

"Well, don't you look cute in your robe and big gun." She is crushing me with her smile, "Let's eat so I can have a shower and we get some sleep."

There are times that I wish would be forgotten; and this is one of them.

***

We woke with the midday sun streaming through the bedroom window. It is a late start, but the work on K Horse needs to get done.

With re-acquired energy and a roaring garden hose, the dirt is flowing down K Horse's body. Jill starts to sponge the surface with soapy water, exposing the bullet damage. Her facial expression shows her emotional re-enactment of the assaults against us. Our mighty steed protected her riders.

The hot sun quickly dries her surface, giving Jill the time to reload her armament without getting dripped on. I feel rather useless watching Jill do all the work, but I'm sure she understands.

We are keeping our stationary time restricted, so this late afternoon, we leave our home haven to go north to pick up the horses.

I'm sure by now our enemy has found our sailing GPS chip and will be regaining a dog to find out where we have disappeared to.

***

The dark highway travels across the state line into Colorado. I am maintaining the speed limit to avoid getting attention from the local Highway Patrol.

My vision shoots into a blur along with another debilitating pain through my body. My foot slips off the gas pedal giving us a chance to slow the vehicle. The sounds of squealing tires on the asphalt give an accent to the truck shifting from side to side out of control. Jill grabs the wheel to get the steering stabilized.

We come drifting slowly to a stop in the grassy ditch with the clutch-less transmission jolting to a stall.

The pain subsides. I look around to see if I am still within a modern time period and not zapped to another dimension.

Jill shoots out of the truck and around to my side, "Are you okay?!"

The pain disappeared as quickly as it attacked, "Ya... maybe you should drive for a bit." The pain is a problem, but I'm relieved we are alright and the year is still 2014.

Jill maintains a frown of concern, but knows better than to pursue the matter.

As the miles pass into history, my focus returns to the case at hand. There is no doubt our enemies are still seeking us. What we need is to draw them into a location on our terms this time. I would feel much better turning the tables on them and making them the prey rather than us.

I struggle with thought. The last attack drained me of a decent concentration. All *'cause and consequence'* are becoming a jumbled mess of puzzle pieces. My mind needs to realign so we can move forward.

The morning sun peeks over the eastern horizon. Jill is tired from driving all night and needs me to take over the beast.

A road sign posted our new intent to stop for breakfast. Nearing the restaurant, the parking area is full of bikes. Not that I have anything against bikers, but the *one per center's* crowd take the intelligence away from the *good* riders. From the appearance of the bikes, we have landed in a snake pit of stench, but we are both in need of food and a hot coffee.

Jill puts K Horse in a non-descript appearance then we stagger to the entrance. The interior again caught me by surprise with a rather inviting dining establishment. The restaurant split the bikers into their own section, leaving one side to have the sane clientele. Seated in the booth next to us is a family of four hurriedly finishing their meal. The racket from the rebel group keeps conversation to a minimum within the people trying to dine.

It always strikes me as odd that our entrance gathers attention from the *goon squad.* We avoided eye contact but nevertheless inadvertently attract two of the group. The waitress writes our orders with a shaking hand and is interrupted by our two visitors. Their smell preceded their arrival.

They stand by our table without saying anything, but eye both of us.

Jill looks across to me, breaking the silence, "Hun. You promised me not to shoot anyone before breakfast! Now, even though these two rejects from the psych ward are stinking up our time of peace, you can't shoot them."

I return her look, "But Sunshine, they are disturbing my *'Zen',* and you know what that does to me. Maybe I will just wound them."

They quietly go back to their buddies. A flurry of conversation amongst them ensues.

Our meals arrive and the bikers leave the building.

Jill is tired and needs rest. It is not a time to be jousting with these bikers. The open view through the windows allow us a visual of them outside. A dozen or so swarm around the truck.

There is great delight in my morning bacon and eggs. To rush through breakfast would unsettle my stomach. We took plenty of time and all is good with my digestive system.

The waitress approaches and says the meals are on the house as well as offering to phone the sheriff.

"No, that won't be necessary." I smile.

Heading toward the door, I tell Jill to have her gun in hand.

Our walk out to the truck is met with jeers and comments, then a big, long-haired member steps in front of us.

From his scuff worn boots to his patched leather vest, I assume he is their leader.

His words force us to stop, "My name is Pig. You will have to excuse my two friends for their behavior. They didn't have a proper upbringing like the rest of us."

He looks back at the truck and then re-scans us, "Word is out from our friends down south to watch for a man and woman who are driving a mean machine such as yours. From the bullet marks on your truck, and you both fitting the description, I would say you are them."

I tell Jill to get into the truck then start it, "And if anyone try's to stop you… shoot to kill!"

The group spreads slightly to let her through.

I unholster both my guns, aiming one at Pig, "You are going to be really nice and back away or I won't hesitate to do what needs to be done."

To my surprise they did, allowing us to leave without bloodshed. The unfortunate problem is we are now targeted again.

My eyes watch the rear view mirror expecting the bikers to mount up and pursue. They don't.

I take it that they are either afraid of us, or they were told not to do anything to us.

In my moments of contemplation my words come as a surprise to even me, "Turn the truck around and let's go back."

All I receive from Jill is a smile. My impression is she understands why.

As she stops to begin the turnabout, my eyes return to our biker boys. There is a scurry of activity. Needless to say they didn't expect us back. If they know what has happened to any that have threatened to kill us in the past; it is their time to worry.

Our re-entrance into the parking lot scatters most back onto their bikes, but the leader stays.

"Keep the truck running and don't get out." My tone is harsh but she knows my meaning.

There are times when being a cop has its rewards, and seeing this tough guy squirming like a worm gives me great pleasure.

Now back standing in front of him, I drag out my silence to exemplify my enjoyment of the moment.

He got my '*Harden*' look, "When you contact your Nazi buddies, tell them that they can reach me by radio. We have an FM two-way with a scanner. If they want to talk about what we have, that they want; they are now going to play cards on our table."

Pig just nods his head and backs away.

Sometimes I even scare myself.

Jill shifts back to the passenger seat while I take over as pilot.

***

Many miles have spaced since we chatted with the bikers, but we haven't received any communication from the opposing force.

The dusty driveway to our friend's ranch smothered us in a cloud. At the house we sit, to emerge free from our cloak of concealment. Jim and his wife emerge from the house to greet us. It is refreshing to be with friendly people for a change.

They know we are anxious to go see the horses, so our path goes straight to the corral. Moon scoots around the corral in excitement at the sound of Jill's voice. Image whinnies and turns her butt toward me in an act of defiance. Her head turns toward me so I can see her eye shimmering words of; '*Where have you been?*' She plays her game and comes for attention. It is good to be with them again.

Our stay had to remain short with our friends, so after a great country meal we load the horses in the trailer to continue on to our new location.

After a lengthy discussion with Jill, we decide that the operation will be on our turf; being the bush country of northern Texas. It will be a long journey back, but will put me in familiar territory again. The terrain for our proposed encounter will not allow our enemy the benefit of driving to the location. Knight Horse will be hidden and we will go in on horseback.

Chapter Thirteen

It has been said that one must love one's enemies. I understand the concept, but fail to find it in my heart to give greeting to someone who is trying to kill us. Jill is not out to take life, but when time calls for extreme prejudice, the reality of survival kicks in. The act is not without emotional consequence when seated in a moral aspect. As a cop, the daily encounter with violence is accepted as part of the job, but doesn't mean a residual internal conflict doesn't exist.

In my early years on the job there was an individual that was trying his best to make a get away from me. This violent offender was known to have no hesitation to attempt to kill another. Because he had escaped from a transport to his court appearance, we were in pursuit. When I cornered his escape, he attempted to take my life and I was forced to take his in my own defense. Contrary to what is seen in movies and TV shows, it isn't as cold in its reality as it is portrayed. The thought that one has taken the breath from another is unnerving to say the least.

When I was ambushed then left for dead, it was a stark reminder that it is a matter of staying alive at whatever means necessary. It is learned very quickly that hesitation gives opportunity to one's enemy. These conscienceless souls have no remorse, even if you do, and they prey on that fact. Your rules of engagement don't apply to them.

***

The Texas panhandle is a mixed landscape from beaten prairie to cavernous canyons, giving us a versatile battleground.

A rolling, treed area near the Trinity River is our target location. It is extremely isolated with the only means of ground access being on horseback or via the river. This gives us an advantage to a degree.

Deep in planning, the radio bursts alive. A haunting voice calls for the Knights. He repeats his call to us but we give hesitation to answer.

Gathering my thoughts, Jill lifts the microphone to respond, "Mrs. Knight here, who may I ask is calling?"

The answer is quick, "This is Kruger."

Jill again talks, "And how may I help you... Kruger?"

His voice crackles from our movement through the uneven country, "You wish to meet, I have been told. Do you have what I want?"

"When we meet you will get some of the answers you seek, but until then you have to wait." Jill clicks the microphone off for a second and grits her teeth, "You shot my husband. So you had better behave or I might forget who I am."

My main attention is on the narrow dirt road on the way to a hiding place for K Horse. Jill is handling Kruger quite well and describes a general area of our meet with a final spot just before the meeting. She also advised there will be no helicopters used by them with their only approach to be on foot or horseback. This would remove some of an ambush attempt by them. Jill hangs the mic back up and sits back quiet in her seat.

At our base, Jill camouflages the truck. It won't be visible by air or from the trail. From here we are on horseback. In our packs are two portable radios for communication with Kruger.

There are many rough roads into the general area, but where we are going, motorized vehicles would not make the trip. The river is an only alternative.

The air is fresh and a cool breeze is blowing from the northeast. Our day ride will be in relative coolness.

Getting back in the saddle after a stretch in time is playing havoc on my gunshot wound. My leg muscles are stretching, causing discomfort.

Image and I are back in our environment. She steps the trail knowing we are making our way to assignment. She can feel the vibration of my spirit.

Jill has a 30-08 long rifle with a scope packed in a hard scabbard and I have my trusty Winchester. In Jill's care is a portable array of heat sensors and other toys she felt would benefit in preparation for the meet.

The regular clop of Moon's and Image's hooves on the ground gain a sudden addition. With us, is now another set of hooves stepping the ground. I look back past Jill and see Longhorn has taken the path with us. He nods his head and says nothing.

It is now midday which warrants a stop to rest and eat.

Jill keeps looking at me realizing my distraction, as has happened many times before, "I assume that our invisible friend is present. You get the same look every time."

My gaze wavers from her query to watch Longhorn tie his horse up and start toward us. His walk represents a man who has spent many hours in the saddle. The weathered side-arm seems to be part of his anatomy. A swirl of reddish dust is stirred as his boots kick the soil. He comes from a rugged time in history, but our battles are still the same. I have a great respect for a man that has seen the harshness of his day; a man that stands for justice.

He takes a seat near Jill with his eyes breaking from under the lip of his hat, "There have been many times your grandfather and I were on such a trail. No matter what, we covered each other's back." He drops his head.

I can see he is still haunted by the day in the saloon, "Cheer up. partner. You are with us and I know you have our backs."

Jill's head searches for my friend.

"It is okay, Jill. I may be delusional sometimes, but I'm not crazy."

She looks to the side where Longhorn is seated and see's the dirt shift slightly where his foot is. She takes a slight jump back. Her eyes widen, then seek refuge in mine. There is pause while she gathers breath to speak.

Choking on her words, she attempts to say something, "Did I see what I thought I saw or are the events making me delusional too?"

"You saw that? Do you see him?" This may mean I'm not losing it after all.

She squeaks out an answer, "Well… all I saw was the dirt move like something moved it." She shifts over and away a bit.

I smile in acceptance of my new proclaimed sanity, "Awesome! You don't need to worry, unless of course you can smell him, then there might be a problem. He hasn't had a bath in over a hundred years. His horse is tied up over there."

My conversation moves back over to Longhorn, "By the way, partner. What is your horse's name?"

He lifts his head out of seclusion to answer, "Horse."

"I know she is a horse. What's her name?"

Longhorn's voice elevates, "It is *'Horse'*. Won her in a poker game... or did I find her on the side of the road? Anyway, I'm not a big one for naming my mounts. She seems to recognize it when I call her that so, so be it."

I look at Jill, "Her name is Horse... and don't ask me why!"

She shakes her head, "So, we are deep in an isolated rough country terrain. About to face some bad guys with guns and we are riding with a... dead guy that is our backup and he is sitting next to me. And he rides a horse *named* Horse."

Longhorn shakes up, "You mean I am dead?!" His broad smile feeds the strange conversation.

Cuddling up to Jill, my arm drapes over her shoulder. "Well if things go bad, at least we can claim insanity.

It is the first time I've seen her drink from a flask.

"What's in that?" I ask.

Jill draws back another and responds, "Gin! '*G*oing *I*nsane *N*aturally'. So would he want a sandwich I packed, or do spooks have a special diet?"

"Not to worry, he doesn't partake." I'm elated Jill saw something.

She sits quiet peering slightly to her side to avoid detection that she is curious.

I think Longhorn is getting a boost out of the way Jill is reacting. I know he doesn't want to hurt her, but is enjoying the free entertainment.

Actually I am too.

Longhorn restarts the conversation, "I am much obliged you all having me on this case. Been rather uneventful over the last hundred and thirty years. My throat is rather dry."

"We are honored you are with us to help." I was about to translate to Jill, but she just shoots her hands in the air tightens her lips and shakes her head no.

It is time to move on.

It is such a nice sunny day. If this were just a regular ride for us, the views of the countryside and the journey would be like a holiday. The thought of meeting this band of cutthroats is not pleasant, interfering with my visual.

Having Longhorn as part of the troop makes me feel as though we were in our pioneer past in hot pursuit of an outlaw. It must have been harsh. Jill and I have a home to go to and modern conveniences that make our time more comfortable. He had nothing to speak of other than a bedroll with a saddle pillow. And yet he is here helping us. Come to think of it, it is strange to have him here. I had no idea that dead people come back to help the living. It is understood his connection with the family, and he needs resolution, but none the less I can't put him on the marshal's payroll, or even put him in my report. He could be considered as unsolicited support.

As I started months ago, writing a story about an old marshal; I shall dedicate it to the great man it is written about. He is a hero in my book. Longhorn has been there for me, even though in questionable format, and has saved me from myself.

Getting to the designated spot in this late afternoon, we deploy an observation post several feet up a nearby cliff. It provides a critical view of the surrounding area. This would also serve as our base camp for the night.

The crackle of the paper map echoes through the still sanctuary of our camp. Plotting our location, and the lower location of our meet tomorrow, I advise Jill to radio the coordinates of the spot to Kruger.

Listening to her pass on the information to our enemies places us in harm's way. Knowing they will attempt some sort of counter plan is expected. Thus, our counter-counter plan. I can be so sneaky sometimes it even confuses me.

Anyway, we are prepared and the arrangements are made.

It will take them at least eight to ten hours for them to get to the site. For them to travel at night would be foolhardy on their part. Besides, if they did try, we would pick them up on the thermal imager. All bases are covered.

After our camp is set up, Jill stops as if she had brain freeze, "Hun. It just occurred to me. What really is the purpose of this meeting? We don't have anything to give them and once they find out it will mean a shootout."

I smile, "Honey darlin', don't you worry. We are just fishing and the artifacts are our bait. I never got to finish the last conversation with him the last time and I need some one on one with this monster of mayhem."

She reaches over to me, "Here's your meds. Take them!"

It is understood that no matter what happens tomorrow, there is purpose to my madness. Jill will take first watch and I will monitor the darkness later with the thermal imager.

Several hours later

Jill has succumbed to the long day's activities. Watching her sleep gives me peace of mind that finally she can rest.

It is close to 0300 hours as the slight crackle of crunching underbrush reaches my ears. The view through the imager shows several bodies moving through the underbrush surrounding the meeting spot. After seeing their final resting spots it is clear that we are not alone in this dark night.

We hold a trump card with the alleged possession of the artifacts, so our enemies won't take any chance of losing the opportunity of securing them. The Intel is invaluable to us knowing what we are walking into later this day.

The sky is clear with the full moon illuminating the ground like radiance from the heavens. Over my shoulder to the east is an ever so slight pre-sunrise glow that gives me orientation.

These solitary hours have given me much to think about. My memories resurge over all that has transpired, showing new life where the dark of evil shadowed. Our battle today is with a positive spirit.

Longhorn moves next to me and whispers confirmation of the hidden bodies below, "It is my job to be able to fire this sidearm with you. I feel so useless."

"Partner, you are more support that you think." I give him a smile.

***

Jill sits with me as the sun rises. She is obviously disturbed by the new day, "We don't have to do this. I can't understand why you are so persistent to put your life out there today. Why don't you just radio them and tell them the truth, that the artifacts and maps are destroyed."

I give her a hug before explaining, "Sometimes a person needs to do something that doesn't seem rational at the time but has to be done. These people will chase us unless we put a stop to it. Just trust that I know what I am doing."

"I do. It's just I don't want to lose you again." She cradles her face in her hands.

My terms are difficult for her, but are important, "I need you to pull yourself together and listen precisely to what I instruct. When the time comes, you will be up here with your long gun. You are going to be my back-up at a distance that you can see all in the area. You will be able to see up close with your scope. You will be absolutely sure of your target if it is necessary to shoot. Make sure of your target. Do not fire unless I signal you to do so. Remember what I say. It is very important to my plan in place."

Jill objects in no uncertain terms, "I'm not letting you go down there by yourself!"

"I promise you I will be okay. Just trust me. You are my most important post up here. We will be in constant contact when I am meeting with them. When they come into the meeting you need to watch, but don't do anything unless you clear it with me. Do you understand?" My demeanor is harsh but important.

She agrees.

***

The passing of time through the morning seems like slow motion but as the sound of several horses come into my earshot, I knew it was time. There were around a dozen men on horseback approaching from the northwest. The intermittent glimpses of our enemy pumps the blood harder through my veins. I saddle Image and prepare to ride down to the meeting.

Jill gives me a kiss along with a warning not to get hurt.

Although Longhorn is handicapped with his support, it feels good having him ride down with me.

Again, as we rode down the path to the site, it took me into the 1800's in thought. Back then they didn't have the capabilities law enforcement has now, but the ride is the same.

My heart is pumping hard, surging the blood through my body in hyper pressure. To be afraid is not an unknown consciousness with me. I fear to not see Jill ever again and miss my time with her. But fear is overridden with confidence that my plan works with the sun setting this day with peace in this valley.

As instructed, Jill went on the radio, addressing Kruger that I am on my way to the meeting, and she has a high powered rifle targeted on him. If any harm comes to her husband, he will be the first to go. Her tone meant every syllable.

Awaiting us in the clearing is Kruger, a native guide and about ten men. All heavily armed.

Their horses were tied to a dead fall so I had clear view of all against me.

I dismount and scoot Image off and away. In my right hand, my Winchester had one in the slot ready to fire and a Colt 45 in my left.

Kruger steps forward, "I am here to collect what is rightfully mine. There will be no more games." His eyes scan my person for any packages or pouches, "I don't see that you have anything on you." His body tenses with disappointment.

"Well Mr. Kruger, I love to disappoint you, so you won't be getting that package today or ever, and you are now under arrest."

The surrounding bushes come alive with camouflaged FBI and Marshal Services Officers.

Immediately I radio Jill, "They are friendlies! I repeat they are friendlies! Do not fire!"

She acknowledges.

The area breaks into organized chaos. The horses spook breaking free from their ties. The officers took the group totally by surprise and the men surrender their weapons without a fire fight.

Kruger used a stray horse as cover and mounted for an escape. Other horses followed in the confusion shielding him from being taken into custody. I had no opportunity to take immediate action to intercept him, but Image comes to me like she knows what needs to be done. At a run, my hands grab the saddle horn giving my legs bounce enough to mount. I can hear my commander yelling at me that a chopper is on the way.

With my legs rooted in the stirrups I radio Jill of what is happening, but dodging the branches knocks the radio from my hand before I could get her response.

The pain in my leg is numbed by the adrenaline pump.

Kruger had a slight head start, but the spread between us widens. We slow to a walk. If Kruger runs his horse too hard he will lose his advantage, and injure his mount. The only supplies he has is whatever is on his horse. He is in a harsh country with no guide. His chances of survival are slim.

From his track he has indeed slowed his pace. Making it through the thicker bush won't allow much anyway.

The approaching chopper washes out any possibility of hearing him ahead. I decide to stop at my location and wait for the team to catch up. To proceed further without supplies and a radio puts everyone else in the dark. I can pick up on his trail again.

Image did well. She is an incredible partner.

Dismounting again reminds me of my sore leg, so the tree stump would have to do as a lounge chair whilst I wait for the boys. I wasn't sure that my Winchester made it into the saddle scabbard, but I see that it did. In all the excitement I figured it had dropped to the ground.

The chopper buzzes above me, then takes off after Kruger. It shouldn't be too long before I have ground support.

My experience in bush hunting shares a commonality with my work. I learned that if hunting an animal, one needs to give it space to allow it to relax its escape. If I were to continue the pursuit it would only run harder and further. My hope is that Kruger will relax more. His track will be hard to hide from me. In my understanding; patience is the hunter with panic being the prey.

My commander Bob is the first to make contact with me. His first words to me, "Jill came down to us after she lost contact with you. She is ok and should be here shortly. She wanted to saddle up first." He shakes my hand saying how well the gig went. No one got hurt and the FBI are happy with the potential information they can get from the captured members of the group they have been after. Bob commended Jill on the excellent radio work. He was concerned that our target may figure the meet may be a trap, but he went for it in his desperation. All is good.

Transmissions from the chopper update us that there is no sign of the target. The ground cover provided too many hiding places. Kruger's horse is a dark brown which helps him blend into his surroundings.

The clop of hooves is a welcome sound announcing Jill's arrival.

She flew off Moon like she had wings to give me a hug.

Bob gathers the team together to assemble a plan of attack, "We are going to return to establish a base camp at ground zero. A perimeter is now being set up cordoning the area off for fifteen miles. Considering he is unfamiliar with the topography around here and has no supplies, it is only a matter of time to capture him. Bill will proceed on horseback to ground track Kruger. We need to get back and set up camp."

It goes without saying that Jill will be my partner on this track. She gives Bob a hug and straps the additional supplies to our horses.

We mount up.

Jill has a smile broader than the canyon we are in. It appears she is getting quite the boost from our adventure.

She catches my attention and expresses her feelings, "This is so awesome. I understand how you got so absorbed in your work! Let's get this guy!"

Hated to rain on her party, but… "Just remember, he is armed and dangerous my dear."

Her eyes widen, "Not as dangerous as I am right now!"

I definitely created a monster.

Kruger's trail heads to the southeast through the scattered dense bush. To our north is the cliff range that would either herd him more toward the river or he will seek high ground to try and gain an advantage. Kruger isn't an idiot, but I am not aware of his bush skills. The evidence of his escape will fully describe his abilities to me.

The stride of his horse's track has been reduced to a slow walk with him leading his horse on the ground. Not a good sign to us. He is saving his horse. Things are pointing that he knows what he is doing out here. The boot track is a heavy tread military boot that leaves a good impression on the ground.

The game trail provides an easier pursuit. Game paths provide wildlife easy routes to their water source or grazing areas. At night they seek the cover of the heavier bush for protection. This route splits to the south heading toward the river and more in a northerly direction toward the base of the cliffs.

Kruger is heading for high ground. His distance from us is a couple of hours, giving him a three or four mile lead. If he gets to the cliff trails, he will be harder to track as well as give him higher ground.

Jill has been updating Bob as to our GPS location on a regular basis. If we get into a bad situation he will send in the troops via chopper. Keeping the chopper out of the area is my request while we do the hunting.

Jill asks to make a pit stop which will give me a chance to review the topography map as a small creek waters the horses.

Seeing Jill come out of the privacy bush gives me boundless pride. Not because she is potty trained, but watching her step firm to the ground with her determination to work with me. She has realized what many cops wives don't ever. The job doesn't clock out at five pm, but moves its hands at random. She sees that the duty covers hard ground. On the other hand, I have been blessed with a woman of many talents that would compete with the likes of Calamity Jane or Annie Oakley. She makes me proud.

I spread the map out to see where we are heading.

Longhorn kneels next to me, "He's heading up and is no greenhorn. He knows what he is doing, my friend." His leather gloved finger points a trail to the southwest on the cliffs, "There is a goat path right here. It moves toward where he is now heading from the north trail. If you follow the goat path it crowns about a half mile south of where he would crown. It will be dark in about half an hour. His and the south trail is too dangerous to navigate in the dark."

I wanted to shake his hand, "Thanks, partner. We will get to the base of the trail and make camp."

Jill pipes up, "Thanks for what? I just went to the bathroom is all."

I call her over to the map, "Never mind. Let's get to this spot before dark."

Leaving Kruger's track is risky, but with my scout providing intel, I feel confident that Kruger and I will... pardon the pun, but... cross paths.

My belief now is that Kruger is no slouch when it comes to rural combat. The threat level has been taken to another stage. He has had military training.

We continue on to night camp.

The temperature this night is warm, fortunately, so a campfire isn't a necessity.

Longhorn kept reminding me in the past that he feels useless to help, but he now is leading us with proper direction.

We both need a good night's sleep. The possibility of Kruger attempting an ambush is little to none. He would not have our location. Jill stopped providing GPS sites to Bob when we varied our course to the goat path. He is aware that all is good. If Kruger does have a radio in his possession, it won't provide any information he can use.

We rest in sleep.

***

The morning smells of pine needles mixed with the sounds of birds, far surpassing waking to the sounds of car horns and sirens on the streets of the city.

Being familiar with tracking bad guys gives me peace of mind along with a calm that at this point there is no hurry to rise from the warm sleeping bag. On the other side of the coin is Jill, impatiently waiting with saddled horses and a handful of trail mix she is inhaling for breakfast.

She sees me stirring giving her opportunity to force my movement from 'I'm coming.' to 'Get your butt in this saddle!'. Rookie!

Even worse! I don't have my morning coffee. Kruger's life is now in jeopardy.

Jill is prancing impatiently like she has to find a washroom quick. So I drag it out even slower, "Don't worry, my dear. We will get him. A few more seconds won't make any difference. Where's my toothbrush?"

The stiff muscles in my leg slowed me down anyway, but I found no sympathy from the rookie.

A horrible thought just crossed my mind. It would be a bad thing for this mission to have leaked to the media. But I'm sure because of the nature of the mission that would have been quashed. We don't need a nosy media chopper interfering right now.

Jill is mounted so I take the time to give Image a quick brush along with some words of admiration.

She gets her wish and off we go.

The vegetation went from a thick canopy of green to pockets of bushes crowding the crevices of rock for soil and moisture. The rocky goat path is as Longhorn described, could barely fit our horses up its narrow ledge. The ascent up the side of the cliffs would be in direct sun so it will be a hot excursion.

It isn't long before it is clear to us to dismount and lead the horses. Looking down from the saddle over the steep edge is disturbing. I'm not a great one for heights as it is.

I take lead to make sure that if I found anything contrary to our safety, it would be recognized.

Several hours of gruelling heat and hard climb is taking toll. My leg is killing me and looking at Jill's sweat soaked clothing shows she is struggling as well. I would like to say we can take a break, but the path doesn't give way to a wide enough spot to safely stop. We are pressing on.

A quick look at my watch shows it is just past noon. My upwards glance gives relief with the summit within a half hour.

As Longhorn stated, our navigation will be within a half mile of a parallel trail of Kruger's at the summit. The upheavals of the terrain provide more than enough cover to be hidden from side view.

We find a shady spot to cool ourselves and the horses before giving them water. As hard as it is, it is difficult to drink, then hold it back from our mounts.

The map shows Kruger would have a much more difficult ascent so I am hoping we gained ground on him.

There are more trees on the summit, however sparsely grouped.

We are both exhausted from the climb, but must press over to intercept our fugitive.

Seeking the occasional shade to chill, we still lead the horses on foot. This would give them much needed recoup time as well as lowering our profile.

Some two hundred or so yards from our intercept point, we hear the pop of a handgun, then another and another. The shallow echo confirms it is a low caliber. Whatever is transpiring, is exposing only one gun. There are no indications of a rifle.

We secure the horses to a shady area then move toward the shots. Three more rounds pop through the rocks. Last echo again confirms direction.

My ears are now picking up the deep growl of a bear. The intermittent hard grunt means this creature is further warning that it is upset at whatever it has cornered.

There have been a couple of minutes of silence from the pistol shots then two more. We are now extremely close.

Jill readies her rifle in preparation for our mystery animal. I slowly charge the lever on my Winchester, sliding a 30/30 round into the slot.

The growling is now evident as we emerge to the back of a big brown bear. He is on his haunches trying to reach into a crevice at our man Kruger. He is bleeding from his left arm and shoulder, but is still doing battle with the furry giant.

The big brown swings his head when he realizes we were behind him. His movements are slow because of the multiple handgun shots into his torso. The low caliber handgun is injuring the animal, but unless a shot hit a vital area, would only aggravate.

He drops down to all fours to head in our direction. The injuries may or may not kill the bear in time, but it is sure he is suffering. I make the call to dispatch the animal. It is a sad decision, but it has to be done.

Jill stays prone behind a rock with her rifle aimed at Kruger. I go to peel him out of the rock.

He is bleeding badly, but will manage to live. The use of his one arm is restricted because of his wounds. I disarm him but feel handcuffs aren't necessary at this point.

I tell Jill to go get the horses and we need the first aid kit. I also told her to keep radio silence until I did some of my own interrogation of Kruger.

Kruger's clothing is in shreds from being clawed at. He is a hurting man. He collapses to the ground.

My head spins to see where his horse is but isn't in view.

On her way back, Jill had the opportunity to recapture Kruger's horse.

She takes over cleaning and tending to Kruger's wounds.

The bear did to him what I wanted to vent on him. He stands for all that is wrong in society, I will feel better the sooner we get him into a jail cell.

After an hour of getting him patched enough to get mobile, I sit across from him glaring into his eyes, "Your men tried to kill us. What is stopping us from thanking you for that right here and now? It would be justified self defense!" I know I couldn't do such a thing, but he doesn't know that.

Lifting his head, he stares at me with his half opened eyes, "I now know you, Bill Harden. When you came to the bar I thought you were someone we considered as our enemy." He cringes in pain then continues, "It wasn't my men that tried to kill you on the road, and what happened at the bar was a mistake on both our parts."

Jill gives him some water to help swallow some pain killers.

"I know your file, Bill Harden. You are a just and honorable man."

I interrupt, "Coming from you I wouldn't accept any compliment!" My teeth clench.

He continues, "I know that I can trust you. My name is not Kruger. It is Johnson, Brett Johnson. I am with the NSA. (National Security Agency) I have been deep cover for nearly five years, infiltrating the Neo-Nazi movement in New Orleans. What I am about to tell you is highly classified and you must not breech my words to even your commander. Do you understand?" His pain shoots through him and he passes out.

Having a bombshell drop on our parade is one thing, but this goes beyond anything I've ever encountered. This is much bigger than I could even imagine. This would also mean that we are still a priority target.

Jill helps get Brett in a more preferable position for him to rest.

Just when I feel we are out of the proverbial woods, a tree falls in front of us! I rest my butt on a rock to gain perspective of the situation.

Jill can see I am in mental torment.

"We need to get him, and us, the hell out of here. Get Bob on the radio, tell him that we are still in pursuit and will report tomorrow morning. Have him keep air interference away until we have secured our target. Did you get all that?" My body is shaking from what I can see is *'The cop shake'*, better known as Post Traumatic Stress Disorder. It is not the time for me to break down! "We need to get off this mountain!"

While Jill is on the radio, I search the usual places agents will hide real ID. Sure enough, his credentials are real. It is good and bad news at the same time. If he were lying we would be more or less in the clear, but he is one of ours and his story puts us back in the game.

Brett becomes semi-conscience enough to mount up on his horse. We do the same. As per the map, another trail descends down the mountain on the west end. We would be within a safe distance of getting back to the truck. If we traveled through the night we could be mobile by sunrise. I don't want to deceive Bob, but I will straighten that out when we are out of the danger zone.

We desperately need to get Brett to a doctor as well.

Our descent from the top drains all from our energy reserve, but we have no alternative other than to press on no matter what. I feel like one of those dreams one has when being chased and feeling the pursuer is dogging one's tracks. One can't get away fast enough.

We have three hours of daylight, so the more distance we gain the better.

Two hours later

Brett is awake but in severe pain. He needs to stop. Jill is maintaining well. I think the thought of being pinned on the mountain has adrenaline pushing us past exhaustion into survival mode.

We break for a bit.

Jill and I review the map. It doesn't seem that bad of a route down the rock. If I lead with a small light we should be okay. I don't know if I'm convincing myself or Jill.

Every step of the horses is another step to our freedom. Wild thoughts of internal conspiracies cloud my mind forcing me to trust no one. It is a brutal concept when, after more than two decades of service, we could be contaminated by the very things we fight against.

Six hours later

We have made excellent time, but it is still deep into the night when we reach the truck. Until we are out of this area Jill and Brett will have to ride in the back of K Horse. Moon and Image are back in the trailer. The sound of the truck starting is a symphony to my ears. Brett's horse was set free. Hopefully he will make it back to his home. Horses have that sense.

The K Horse is running in dark mode. Radar is up.

Just hit me! We need to get through the perimeter that has been set! I will figure that out before we get to that marker.

It is a slow back road, but we are making progress. On the radar is a couple of targets blocking our exit three hundred yards ahead.

My hand wraps around the radio. With pause, my finger triggers the transmit button, "Papa Bear, this is Baby Bear; do you copy?"

The crackle sounds for a few seconds, "This is Papa Bear. How are my lost cubs doing?" It is Bob.

"Well, Papa Bear, we want to come home. We found a stray. Can we keep him?"

Bob's voice had a tone of relief, "By all means! Are you coming back to the den?"

"Yes Papa Bear, by way of the garden path. You can drop the fence and we will growl when we get the stray secured. Do you copy, Papa Bear?"

"Understood! Take care, Baby Bear." Bob really understood. He knew something was up.

"Papa Bear, we will be in the dark for our last stroll to gain distance."

"Copy that."

Ten minutes pass and off went the fence. We had clear road at least until light. Bob is my friend. As my friend, I need to trust him as well as he trusts in me.

I help Jill move Brett into the cab. We make our miles.

***

We pull into a small town far from prying eyes. The K Horse took on her disguise outside a doctor's house. He sees our ragtag threesome and scurries to help bring Brett in. I show him my badge advising him that the injured agent, along with us, must remain anonymous. He has no trouble with my request.

Laying Brett down on the treatment table gives us much relief. He had lost a lot of blood requiring his wounds to be stitched. Jill had bound them well, but the last hours weren't the greatest of post-first-aid treatment.

The doctor's wife comes in to see the sad sight we are and gives us an opportunity to shower. We emerge clothed in robes provided us while she washes our clothes.

The doctor diligently works on Brett as we enjoy the great breakfast Mrs. Baker prepared.

It is hard to sit still in our position. Being half dressed does make an escape an unrespectable possibility. A sheriff's car pulls up to the front by the truck and I swallow my last nerve. He comes to the door asking who their patient is. She tells him it is a logger that cut himself needing stitches. He smiles, tips his hat and returns to his car.

Mrs. Baker tells us that they make regular checks. All is okay.

Jill goes into see if the doctor needs any help. He put her to work cleaning the patient up. Mrs. Baker brought in some clothes for him to wear.

Dr. Baker comes out after finishing, sitting at the table with me, "He was torn up pretty bad. A bear, I assume. He'll be okay, but you should get him to a hospital soon. He is very lucky."

"We will as soon as we are in a safe area." I take a sip of my coffee, "You have to keep quiet about this for our safety. I will get the Marshal Service to pay you when we get back."

He smiles, "Don't worry about that. Just get that lady back safe."

"She is my wife. She got caught up in this. She is a civilian." I feel guilty admitting I exposed her to this danger.

Mrs. Baker sits down with us, "Well, from the condition the three of you came in, you all need rest. You are welcome to stay here if you like."

"No, we need to get back on the road as soon as we get our clothes back. But it is much appreciated for your offer."

The doc can see I am struggling with myself, "I have been a doctor for going on forty years. I have seen many wounds, but I have seen many nonphysical wounds too. You are burdened, my son."

Pert near broke down in tears. To hear him offer help is like a gate opening in my head. I can now understand what my shrink was trying to do.

Jill returns to the table, "Brett is resting."

With the company of these incredible strangers, I feel warmth returning to a crushed spirit.

We sat and talked, giving Brett a couple of hours of recoup time. We could have used some sleep too, but our company of new friends gave us a revitalized breath. These people are why we do what we do.

Getting dressed again gave me a sense a power back. I felt rather exposed before!

Brett is in no shape to travel, but we must get back on the road. The most suitable hospital is over a hundred miles away. It will be out of prying observation.

The cab of the truck is crowded, but we don't have a choice. Jill gets Brett cushioned against the passenger door with pillows and then she tucks next to me.

When I have fully debriefed Brett, along with getting him into a hospital, I will contact Bob to fill him in. The Marshal Service can hide Brett until we can figure out what to do with him and his information.

***

Knowing that our new charge is in great need of medical care we stop just out of the city to get the information I have been patiently waiting for. We don't have much time, but Brett is more suited to the task now.

He begins his explanation.

"The NSA monitors any groups that may present themselves as a threat to national security. The Neo-Nazi's have been under the microscope of observation for decades, but have kept themselves within the parameters of the law.

"Information surfaced that they had come into an association with an extremely recondite group that has been simmering in the back rooms of politics since the Civil War. They are called the New Confederacy.

"After that war, information about a hidden treasure of gold drew their attention. It was said that an ancient group came to America hundreds of years prior to any recorded history. These people were escapees from a civilization destroyed by a giant volcanic eruption. They loaded several ships with their wealth and headed into unknown waters. Some managed to make it from the Mediterranean across to what is now the Americas. Once they reached the continent, they plotted their travels and hid their wealth. It is unknown where they vanished to or why, but documents were found by the Confederacy just after the war. They would have changed history if the old maps were located, but the courier was intercepted and the plan withered. Recently a journal of an old marshal was discovered that had information leading to the illusive maps and documents. The New Confederacy resurged their efforts to locate them. Then they were stolen from the courier; apparently by you!

"My infiltration into the Neo-Nazi group was because of a proposed alliance between them and the New Confederacy. It would be an unusual alliance, but greed and power always make strange bed partners.

"My five years has uncovered a conspiracy to bring down the Federal government. Politicians from the radical Confederacy have infiltrated all areas of state and federal politics. The funds from the *Ancients* and the information of early inhabitants from the Mideast would be used to undermine their opponents.

"My assignment is to gather a list of the politicians involved as well as monitor the search for the old documents and deposit locations. The Neo-Nazi's devised a plan to have me appear to separate from the main group as a renegade to take heat off them. Their plan was working until you put a wrench into it. By the way, where are the documents you recovered?"

Considering all, I answer, "They are in a very safe place."

Brett continues, "Anyway, the Neo-Nazi's are only being used by the New Confederacy as gofers'. The real power is in Washington.

"When you came to me in New Orleans, I thought you were a boy from Langley Black Ops to make sure we didn't abscond with anything we had recovered. Washington is inundated with Confederate spies and operatives. This matter could topple our democracy." Brett is beginning to give way to his pain.

Jill dials the cell phone to get Bob mobile to our coded next location; the hospital. We would admit Brett as a John Doe.

***

It is now after nine pm with a long, arduous day closing in around us. Bob has taken care and custody of our compadre, giving us a chance to get some much needed rest, for tomorrow we head north to Glacier National Park.

Chapter Fourteen

The mountain roads are layered with snow and ice making our journey's leg all the more interesting. From the information Brett gave us, the New Confederacy has concealed its main base of operations in the park for many decades: Wouldn't be hard to do, considering the numbers of theirs that populate politics. Obviously there will be branches of the military as our advisories as well. This cookie we bite into may leave many crumbs when all said and done.

Jill gives little indication of concern because of her constant monitoring of the equipment.

I break silence, "Far cry from the antics we were pulling in Texas, Mrs. Knight." My smile gives her precedence to relate.

"This isn't what the first plan was, for sure. But when you take a lady out on a date you get a little carried away." Jill squeezes my hand, "All this will be covered over so the public will never know what is truly going on. The cloak and dagger sub world around us is too complicated for me to assimilate all the data in one download, but in a way I understand why the public should never learn the truth. If they were aware of how close they are to being the inheritors of a country led by the losers of the Civil War as well as linked to a Nazi regime, the country would have a meltdown. Scary stuff!"

"Well, my little honey darlin', you have done rather well being *Mrs. Knight*. All said and done, we have played our part and hopefully we are still breathing at the end. Speaking of breathing... did you pack the winter gear I asked you to? It's going to be rather chilly where we are headed."

Jill hesitates a few seconds, "Yeppers. Probably more than we need, but better warm than a popsicle. There is a lodge about thirty clicks from here where we can set up our base location. It will put us within a stone's throw of the outer perimeter of the enemy encampment."

"Hun, you have been watching too many spy movies."

Jill is again projecting a hidden aspect of her personality.

The crunch of the hardened snow under our truck tires announces our arrival at the main entrance of the lodge. In keeping with the ambiance of the mountain park, the lodge is framed in large logs with massive arched windows. The entrance stair seemed to be melded out of a massive stone.

"I will park the truck and meet you inside."

The winter gear offloaded, including cross country skis, will make us as one with the area. Besides, we need the skis to explore the back trails to the hidden tunnels Brett told us about.

The parking area borders with mounds of pushed snow to clear for a lot full of expensive SUV's and high end limos. Our lowly truck is going to stick out like a beacon.

Trail signs carved information into their wooden logs to give direction to different areas of the lodge grounds and to the main entrance. Too bad we weren't here for fun with all the amenities posted.

The grand doors of the lobby have an Austrian Alps flavor with depicted mountain scenes. Not very American, but I guess it gives visitors a sense of being there.

Brett was right in saying the Confederacy has been an influence for decades. If the Nazis do post here, they are not very subtle in hiding it.

Jill meets me at the lobby desk where the hotel manager is giving her a problem because she wants to pay with cash.

The manager speaks with a strong Austrian accent, "I am truly sorry Mrs. Knight, but it is our policy to only accept credit card payment for accommodation."

His round spectacles are about to meet with Jill's knuckles, so I feel it is my duty to intercede for his protection. I pull a cover credit card that Bob issued me the last visit; been doing this too long to be hung on a technicality. With Bob's sense of humor, he put the name of William Knight on the card. Not a very secure cover, but what a way to break into the ranks of our enemy.

Jill gives me a dirty look because I denied her satisfaction. It seems I'm in a cross fire.

"Thank you, Mr. Knight," He returns my card with a code key, "Have a pleasant stay with us and if there is anything you need, just feel free to ask." His smile comes as a memorized facial muscle movement.

A porter scurries to assist with our bags.

Jill whispers in my ear, "He asked if there is anything he can do for us... he could let me smack him one good!"

I turn to the manager again to ask if the dining room is still open.

"Yes, it is, Mr. Knight. It's open until ten."

Being subtle is not one of my stronger traits so our visit to this amenity is my way of introducing ourselves directly to our adversaries. There is no doubt that they will assume we are with backup, so at least we are relatively safe. I hope.

***

The morning sunrise on a clear day gives me relief that we were spared a visit during the night. Our deep, almost comatose sleep was much needed for both of us.

The *'alpineian'* breakfast eating room overlooks a cross country trail packed with deep powder. My eyes analyze the proposed direction of our day trip, while the waitress attempts to get my attention for my order. I slightly respond, but Jill deals with the ordering anyway.

Before retiring last night, Jill did some research into the urban legend that the Nazis were in fact hiding large bunkers of equipment deep within the park. Now considering these legends, like many others, are based on fact, they can be debunked by the people that are the legends. Case and point is how the military hid Area 51 by blatantly denying its existence. They hide it with confusing gossip that becomes too unreal to believe. But since I am already suffering from chronic delusions anyway, my investigation can't be contaminated with diversion.

Apparently hikers have stumbled upon old railway tracks in places that would defy purpose. These and other reports of strange things go un-investigated. They are like Bigfoot reports; they don't want to be thought crazy.

Other than downloading her research to me Jill is very quiet this morning. As we dress for our cross country ski she stops abruptly.

Her eyes meet with mine, "Are we getting too far over our heads by coming here? We have ended any chance of them retrieving the treasure so they are wasting their time chasing us. Why don't we just end this and let the NSA deal with it?"

The sense of adventure for her has turned to fear; understandably so, "I'm sorry, my lady. I became so wrapped up in this that I didn't think of how much jeopardy I was putting you into. I will call Bob and have him come get you, but I must follow this through to the end, to 'end' this once and for all. We can't be shoulder checking for the rest of our lives." I draw back a deep breath to clear my brain.

I get the 'Jill' look, "Don't be silly. I can't leave you without me watching over you. Besides... I'm curious. What's the worst that can happen? We have been chased by armed men in SUVs, ambushed in a bar, pursued by the media and on and on. How can anything be more dangerous than that?" She faces a sarcastic grin, "I'm alright! Too bad they don't make snow shoes for horses. It would be nice to have ours here."

***

The mountain air gives us a chilled breath in, and is very sedative to the brain, but we are off. According to the research, the rail tracks are about four kilometers to the northwest, with a side trail of about two hundred yards; shouldn't be too hard to find in this brilliance of white.

As much as the scenery, coupled with the agonizing exercise, is a must for our investigation, the warmth of the south is much more appealing than the ice cube that is now my nose from the nasty bitter wind. The thought of a winter vacation here is now on my *'to-don't'* list. The downhill *slides* on the skis are a welcome refreshment, but then those blasted uphill's ruin my fun. Need to put a motor on these things.

Jill has been quiet as she focuses on the GPS readings. So complaining to her about my aching gunshot boo boo will meet with deaf ears. Oh, the trials and tribulations of adventure.

Longhorn hasn't paid me a visit for some time now. He must not like the cold either.

Dense pine trees border the trail like walls of wood giving us an ominous enclosure. At least The odd sight of deer reminds me that we aren't in the scary forest alone.

"Just about to the side trail. Watch for an opening off to the right. I tried getting a satellite picture of the area last night, but all that came through was a washed-out mass of blur. Either I screwed up the search or they have blotted out this section of the forest somehow." Her eyes stare further at her readings.

I only get part of what she said because of my ear plugs and the loud swoosh of snow under our skis, but she pushes forward so I don't want to break her concentration.

Never thought snow had a smell to it, but there it is. Smells like stiff fresh air mixed with the scent of pine needles. Another fragment of information for my memoirs.

"There it is. Just ahead." Jill seems relieved we aren't lost or ending up on the south side of the north end of the compass, "Should be just a couple of hundred yards further."

I'm glad she is happy with her navigational skills. Between breaths I respond, "Can we catch a cab back to the lodge after we get where we are getting to?"

I have a good deal of tracking along with back woods skills, but this is radical even for me. I give much credit to the old mountain men that forged their way through these mountains back in the day. They must have been part animal.

I hope my bullets aren't frozen!

A hundred or so yards ahead, I had to stop Jill from going any further until we gave way for a rest, "I need some antifreeze." The flask of amber rum in my jacket empties a few ounces down my throat, "Well at least my innards won't freeze. Aren't you cold?"

"A little, just anxious to see if these tracks really do exist or if we are chasing our 'tales'." A smile breaks on her face.

"Jill, I know this may sound strange… but I am picking up the slight aroma of axle grease and either tar… no creosote! Like what they coat railway ties with… and axle grease! We must be near something!"

The clear air gives me an easy trace to the target. Almost feel that I am part hound dog.

Nestled within an alcove of trees is a side track buried with snow and a couple of abandoned box cars. From the undisturbed blanket of snow and weathering, they have been here for a very long time. They are very much out of place in this isolated park. The cargo doors are ajar, but climbing out of the deep snow to the elevated deck proves to be more of an effort than anticipated. I give Jill a step up then she grabs my hand to assist me.

The box cars are empty with old chain shackles mounted on the walls.

Our eyes scan the interior in contempt, "It's a prisoner car. From the looks of its aging, I would place these at sixty or seventy years old." I am choking at my analysis.

The wind is pushing pass the outside of the rail car, making the interior a resonator of echoes. There is also a smell of death mixed with the rotting wood. This place is shrouded in a shadow of the past.

Jill raises her gloved hand to the wall, giving her texture to what she is looking at. "These are bullet holes!" She pauses and turns her head to me, "These are bullet holes! People died in here!"

I shake my head in agreement, "Let's get out of here and look for the main track line."

Our eyes investigate to see if there is anything we have missed as we make our way toward the door.

Jill leads me to the door, but comes to an abrupt stop, "Hun... we have company."

Outside the door stand several heavily armed men in white combat field gear. The park rangers are taking their job far too seriously!

The group leader speaks up, "Mr. and Mrs. Knight... or should I say, Harden. We have been looking forward to meeting you. My name is Brad Johansson of the 101st Division of the 4th Reich. Would you please step down here."

The clatter of long guns rises to make sure we behave.

Jill receives no gentlemanly assist to lower her from the box car, so I step down first to catch her landing. It gives me a chance to tell her I love her. This isn't a great midway of our winter wonderland holiday.

"Mr. Harden, it would make me feel much more relaxed if you and your wife would relinquish your weaponry."

Two men step forward to receive our means of defense.

The last I hand over is my Colt 45, "Be careful with that, I am still making payments on it."

"Please, if you will come with us. We have a warm domicile that you are sure to like." The sergeant speaks with a strong German commanding accent. His bright blue eyes give strong contrast to the pale, clean shaven face.

"We have transport not far from here so you will be free from your skis."

The trudge down the snow trail is made easy by the broken path of theirs.

Jill remains silent, nudging into me to confirm she loves me.

As we approach the snow machine, the sergeant speaks of Jill's widened eyes. The craft is nothing she or I have ever seen before. Her eyes bounce around its outer core in provoked amazement. It resembles a ground version of a stealth aircraft on belted tracks for propulsion.

The machine is downwind from the rail cars which explains why my hearing never picked it up. These boys aren't any greenhorn city slickers. They obviously have the skills.

The rear gate opens to a large passenger compartment and we are *encouraged* to enter. The slight sound of a whispering engine comes to life.

The sergeant smiles, "We have our toys too."

We shake into movement.

There are no windows allowing us the freedom to see where we are heading.

Jill soaks in the visual wonderment of the interior. The pilot guides our path via a joystick, using the screen as his exterior view.

Jill is beginning to drool.

After about ten minutes we come to a stop, but then continue on. The sound of a massive steel door groans open and closes after us. I assume this to be the entrance to the alleged hidden bunkers spoken of.

The quiet transport we are in must be electric.

All stop. The hatch reopens and the sergeant motions us to proceed out.

We are indeed within a mountain. The cavernous expanse is lit by bright lights giving the area no shadow. Off in a corner, Knight Horse sits with two guards keeping it company. Armed personnel encircle us as an escort out of the big room down a concrete encased hall.

"There is someone anxious to meet you both since you have intervened by the theft of our property. Right this way." Our captor seems to be gloating with his successful capture.

"Passing on our right is a large communication room with bullet-proof glass and titanium doors to keep unwanted people such as yourself from entry. We have an eye on every facet of communication. We monitor all the secure computers of all the branches of government and law enforcement. There is no shadowed venue that escapes our attention. They say that knowledge is gold, but to us it is platinum."

Obviously anything we learn or see here will never see the light of day again. Where is Longhorn? His help would be rather useful about now.

Our excursion through what seemed like the Villain's lair of a British spy movie brings us into another large room. It is paneled with old oiled wood with a stone fireplace near a sitting area. Off to the left is a solid antique wood desk. The walls were covered with what appears to be a collection of rare art from around the world. In stark contrast, is the three predominant painted pictures behind the desk. Two of the large portraits aren't familiar, but one is. It is of the scourge of humanity that destroyed so many millions during the Second World War. It is Hitler himself. The swastikas in gold borders the pictures.

This is no set from some spy movie. It is, in fact, a monument fortress of a sadistic force.

I'm not surprised at the Nazi soldiers or even the symbolism, but what I assumed to be gophers seem to be the leaders.

"Sit here." The sergeant commanded.

"No, thanks. We will just stand if you don't mind. We don't have much time because we need to go and put more money in the parking meter."

Jill smiles at my comment, but the sergeant isn't amused. His constant smile went to a tight jaw.

Before he could respond, a gravelly voice speaks from behind us, "Thank you, Sergeant, you may leave us now. Leave us alone. If I need anything, you will be called." The voice has a southern accent.

We were left to see the now empty room, shared only with this stranger.

He wears a tan corduroy suit with a white shirt and red tie. His tailor needs a good lecture. Half expected to see the head honcho wearing a decorated Nazi uniform. How disappointing.

His hand lifts a carved pipe to his mouth and strikes a match with the other to light it.

"The infamous *Knights*, I am honored by your presence. Would you like a drink of brandy... or something of your liking?"

Jill speaks before I can, "Well, you could give us our ride back and we will be merrily on our way. You can also take your swastika and shove it up your butt."

I am left speechless.

Our host just smiles and leans against his desk, "That could be possible... except for the butt part I mean. You see, you two have something that is mine. Of course, no matter whether I get my property back or not is not the end of the world, but the relics would make a great addition to my collection. You see, our... how do I put this... cause, is not teetering on success because of the things you have. It is merely something I wish to have in my presence. You see, I am a man of culture with a grand eye for art and history, just like my grandfather."

His eyes move from his sweep of the art work on the walls to us, "I am so truly sorry. I have been a very rude host. I've neglected to introduce myself, my name is Fredric Adolf Hitler; grandson of our great leader. My grandfather was far ahead of his time, but did make a slight miscalculation during the war. But as our family has proven to our followers, we will have command of our world again.

"It would be my wish that the two of you would cooperate with me. To have to shoot the only two people that have impressed me would be a shame. You could live if I knew I could trust you out there in our new territory… but shame… you are just too stubborn. Tsk Tsk."

Our problem is that we are in a heavy secured mountain, far from civilization, with no weapons. His option seems lucrative, but since his collection is lost I think it is time to say a prayer or two.

"We can go and collect your property, but we can't do anything from here," my voice is demanding.

"Now that would be reasonable, but that just won't happen. Oh, there is someone else you should meet. He has a great interest in our future." Fredric presses a button opening the office door. Out of the bordering room enters his new guest.

There are times in this life that a kick in the backside just isn't enough to teach oneself a lesson. Brett, seated in a wheelchair, is pushed in by the sergeant.

"You see, Mr. Harden, we have people everywhere, even double agents."

Brett has a sadistic smile on his face, "Thank you for keeping me on this earth. Since I am second in command of the New Confederacy, you two saved my post. The bear was a painful event, but it did provide us with an opportunity to corral you both before more information went public. In a way, I expected a more… shall we say, creative assault from you both. But, oh well."

To think we saved this maggot's life. I should have gone by my instincts and shot him in the beginning. There is nothing I can say to vent how I feel right now. I let us fall into a trap any amateur tracker would have flagged. Longhorn must be very disappointed.

Fredric is buzzing to continue his history lesson, "My grandfather came to the States in the thirties to build a stronghold here behind enemy lines that would hit them without warning. As you know, the attempts on his life and the collapsing third Reich forced him to seek refuge here just before the fall of Berlin. Our allies here with the New Confederacy made all this a testament to my grandfather's legacy. It has given us years of freedom to establish our next invasion of the world. Your Civil War showed us that we needed to be patient by using our Confederate friends to get us inside your government, so when the time comes it will be too late for you to fight back. It is funny how men of wealth in your country can switch sides when their fortunes are threatened."

I protest, "Hitler committed suicide! So don't give me that garbage."

Fredric stood fast with continuing his story, "Mr. Harden, would you have the courtesy of letting me finish. My grandfather saw that he was in imminent danger. He was no fool. He knew that no matter where he went that, if he was believed to be alive, he would have been hunted. His double was what the Russian scum found in the burn pit outside his Berlin bunker. That double had been painstakingly duplicated, even down to dental similarity. The Russians were idiots to believe the capture of the remains were real.

"My grandmother and grandfather slipped into this country very easily because you Americans were so busy gloating over your so called victory. Our brothers in the Confederacy shielded passage aboard one of your own submarines. Isn't that ironic?! Our great leader commanded our post until he died of old age in 1972. My father took leadership in accordance to his request, but succumb to cancer just two years ago.

"When my father died, I was told about the old legend of the Confederate search for an ancient treasure. Like them, I am intrigued with the old stories. My purchase of the journal of the old marshal's sparked a fun treasure hunt for me, but you ruined it."

Bret interrupts, "My friend Fredric sent me after his lost property. Isn't it strange how your chance encounter with our courier could create such a waylay. Our acquisition would have made a wonderful addition to our priceless collection. I'm sure you understand that we know you are aware of what the treasure consists of and our curiosity is overwhelming. If you tell us the information on it, it would keep you both from a long agonizing departure from this world. You see…"

Jill begins to speak, but with her interruption, I interject, "We most certainly know what and where the treasure is. There is no doubt either, that it is of great significance, but we will not tell you. Unless of course you let us go."

Brett responds, his deep breath shows he is losing patience, "Freedom? No, we have perfected means of getting the information out of you. So if you wish to go that route we have a man that takes his job very seriously and seems to get a thrill from it as well."

"Could you get him to give me a shot for the pain in my leg while he is at it." I couldn't resist, "I don't know what it is, but all you villains seem to have the same dark character with a needle and torture kit. You are going to have to stop watching all those bad spy movies. They are a bad influence. Might I suggest anger therapy?"

At least Jill is entertained by my remarks.

Fredric buzzes again allowing two guards in, "Take them to our holding cell." He doesn't portray a fulfilled villain anymore.

"I must apologize again, our holding cell doesn't keep visitors very long; they seem to expire in short order. Take them away."

Brett follows us to give an extended tour of the facility, "I must say, Mr. Harden, you and your wife are too stubborn for your own good. There is a room I must show you before our interrogation."

This complex is massive. Branches off the main tunnel lead to large rooms where the large numbers of soldiers can have living quarters and service areas. If this is only part of what I would assume is the main base of operations, our enemy is substantial, and a viable force as Frederic has bragged about. The information contained in the communications room is of vital importance. It would have contacts with the outside, giving us a list of who is in on this insanity.

The noise of Brett's wheelchair comes to a halt. A massive window exposes a room with war memorabilia. In the center are two glass coffins. The one closest the window has a resemblance to the painting in Fredric's office. He seems almost alive in his preserved state. He is Fredric's father. The other ornate glass enclosure contains the aged remnants of the scourge of human history. The dark, heavily adorned uniform, clothed a creature that was reported as burned outside of his Berlin bunker. The evident age puts him in his nineties. What Fredric said is true; Hitler lived amongst us.

"The room is climate controlled with intrusion alarms and deterrent weaponry." Brett gives us that look of *'don't even think about it'*. There is a plaque in front of the coffin shelves, *'Adolf Hitler. Leader of the World. Hero of the People'*.

They should supply vomit bags in the viewing areas! Brett stares as though Hitler is a god.

I just want to blow the place up.

Chapter Fifteen

The stark white confines of our prison cell is only broken by the warmth of Jill's presence. The only appreciation toward our capturers is that they didn't separate us.

I turn my eyes to Jill's, "Quite the pickle we are in, hey?"

She smiles, "Well, I guess my gizmos won't get us out of this."

"Ya, but we aren't out of the game just yet. We need to get to K Horse."

Jill crooks her head slightly, "That seems to be impossible. We are locked down in a mountain safe with no key and hundreds of bad guys armed to the teeth."

"Well then, we need to find a key and get some weapons."

I get the *'Jill'* look, "Hun, I love you."

"Good, then you need to trust me and follow my lead."

Her eyes widen, "Do you have a plan?"

"Nope… but I'm sure I'll think of something sooner or later."

"Well it better be now, 'cause there they are at the door!"

The key pad clicks as the soldier slides his security card through the key code allowing the door to release.

Two men stand in the doorway, "Come with us!"

As I walk forward, I reach out to grab the first by the scruff of his uniform swinging him passed me, he becomes air born hitting hard against the cell wall. He drops to the floor like a rag doll. Our second escort feels my back swing, making him twirl like a ballerina.

"Get their gear off, including their uniforms. We are going to become soldiers of the Fourth Reich! Hurry, we don't have much time before they figure we aren't showing for the debriefing."

Jill looks buried in her new oversized uniform, but will have to make due. "Do you realize you just threw a two hundred pound man through the air with no effort?"

"It's my new breakfast cereal. We will discuss it later!" My tone relays my rush to scoot, "Act like a soldier!" I am encouraged with the newly acquired items of protection. As I look at them closer, I see they are stamped with US Military markings.

Jill sees it too, "I may have had a hand in developing some of our enemies' armament. That transport we came in has electronics I have seen in our lab."

I smile, "Well then if that is so, you may be able to drive that rig we came in… right?

"Maybe so." Her tone doesn't relieve herself of her guilt that she contributed to the madness.

"Stand behind me… we have surveillance cameras! And pull up your pants!" I didn't show it, but my heart is pounding out of my chest. No matter what, I need to get Jill out of this place.

Jill whispers to me, "Do you have a plan yet?" A broad smile crosses her face.

"Just follow me, or I'll send you to your room."

All hell breaks loose. A reverberating siren channels through the halls. I assume they know we are wandering aimlessly through their complex.

My eyes search for direction, "We need a way out of this place!"

Jill pulls a folded paper out of her pocket and opens it, "Oh, you mean like this!" She scans for our present location. Her finger follows a line of direction with calm anxiousness. "We need to go back to a hall just back here. There is a passageway that goes directly past the communication room. But that would be like shaking a hornet's nest."

"They wouldn't expect us to take the direct route… so why not disappoint them. Besides, we need to get into that room. If we can breach that area, would you be able to get into that computer of theirs."

"Are we there yet?... I may. Depends." Jill continues to review the map, "Turn to the left," she almost pushes passed me.

A rush of boot noise comes up from behind. We swing around ready to fire our primed weapons only to see Longhorn standing there.

Aside from the shock of relief, I am overwhelmed by confusion. Jill stands frozen in place still aiming at our spiritual company. I expected her to turn back to me so we could continue, but she just stood there.

"Are you alright, Hun?"

She responds with a broken voice, "I don't know just yet. Do you see him, Bill?"

Jill doesn't usually call me Bill unless she is mad at me, "Do you mean you can see him too?"

"I see an old dirty cowboy!" Her gun arm starts to shake.

"Wow! I'm not crazy after all... or you have been taking my meds too?"

Longhorn crooks his head, "I'm lost!"

Jill sinks deeper into her uniform, "Ahh... just follow us." She turns back to me, "I don't want to discuss it right now! Let's go!" Beads of sweat pour down her forehead. She mumbles, "I don't want to discuss it... this way." She takes lead.

The absence of a fighting force against us concerns me. There should be troops swarming the halls. Then again, what do they have to worry about; they have cameras everywhere and the fact of the matter is, we are inside a mountain. We don't exactly have an option to just wander out.

The clump of Longhorn's boots behind us encourages Jill to quicken her pace.

"We should be getting close to the communications room very soon." Jill barely frees her eyes from the map to look where she is going. She must be radar tuned.

The hammer of heavy boots accompanied by soldier's voices races through the halls ahead of us.

Rounding the next corner we are met with a wall of men and the dirty end of their automatic weapons staring us down.

Longhorn pert near runs over me as I come to an abrupt halt, then expresses his voice as to our situation, "Isn't this where the calvary comes rushing into our rescue?"

To the head of the barricade, sitting in his wheelchair, our nemesis Brett. His smile projects how futile our escape really is, "Tsk tsk. Do you really think that getting away would be even a considered thought?"

The click of the safety on Jill's gun relays her intention to go out in a blaze of glory. The muzzle flares with flame spraying ahead of her with a blister of bullets. She drops to the floor continuing to pull the trigger.

Unlike in the movies, when the heroine does this sort of thing, people seem to be impervious to being struck; but considering the split second of a woman's anger, the floor lay littered with what used to be our captures.

She stands almost bewildered; lost in the moment of violence.

I stand lost in amazement that we never took a shot!

Longhorn backs to a wall, sliding down it to a seated position, "Wow! Bring me a beer! Guess they thought we would just hand over the guns. I now know that a woman with a weapon is more dangerous than anything I have ever seen before. The old saying that when a gunfighter hesitates, it is the day he dies: Case and point! Glad she's on our side."

Speaking of hesitating... "We need to get out of here." I put my hand on Jill's shoulder. "We need to go."

Brett is slumped forward in his wheelchair. Jill stops, looks at him, then back to me, "The bear shouldn't have hesitated either!"

Brett's key card fell to the floor, so considering the gift, I pick it up. "We will need this to get into the Comm room."

Jill stops abruptly, and turns around staring at Longhorn, "How did he get in here? I must be cracking under the stress."

"He just followed me home one day and has been *hovering* ever since," I smile.

We move forward again.

Looking at Jill in the lead, I couldn't resist commenting, "You know, if you took the seams in on your uniform by ten or twelve inches, you would look rather nasty… in a good way I mean!"

She calls back, "Look, big Hun, just keep your mind on the program and walk this way!"

"Oh darlin', that would be impossible with your hip movement!"

Longhorn chuckles, "You two keep this up and I'm going to need a keg. Chasin' bad guys sure has changed."

Finally, the sirens quit screeching in the halls.

At the hall corner, Jill peeks around whispering back to me, "There it is. There is only one guard at the door."

Breath in, chest out. It is my turn to shine. As I pull the knife from its sheath, the blade gave a metal on metal sound. Ominous in its character. The sound of death foretold.

With Brett's card in hand, my solo venture brought me face to face with the lone guard. My uniform raises no suspicion until my blade finds its target. He drops to the ground.

The card clicks the hardened door.

I whisper to Jill as she crowds next to me. "Ironic. The bullet proof vault hardened door, breached by a simple swipe of plastic. Don't you just love technology!? Jill, go do your thing. Download whatever you can, but hurry, we are on borrowed time."

She scoots over to the counter of computer screens. The white smocked nerds want no part of our intrusion and crowd against the wall with my weapon in my hands staring them down.

The buzz of computer relays and storage banks that line the walls amplify the location.

Jill's fingers dance over the keyboard with hyper speed. Working the system she turns to me. "I have a video link to security. I also have eyes on the motor pool where K Horse is. If I can link into K Horse's system, we may stand a chance of getting out of here." She plugs a memory stick into the slide, "I'm downloading a list of the military personnel involved. The list of politicians is too well encrypted for me to get into."

Jill stops abruptly again. She looks over at the Comm room keepers, "Hun… do you think I am a tech geek like them? I don't look like a nerd, do I?"

"My love… you are but a flower in a garden of thorns. You are *'Gizmo Girl'*, warrior against oppression… nope, you aren't. But we do need to get out of here." I think my prisoners didn't share my opinion though.

With a click of the last key on the computer, she stands waiting. Her body swaying slightly back and forth in anticipation of download on the memory stick, "Done! Let us go. K Horse is prepped for our arrival. The guards are about to get a real jolt out of their assignment."

Jill clears the door, and as I reach it, I toss three grenades at the computer bank. I yell over to the men I left behind, "You had better duck!"

Longhorn obviously is getting a boost from all the new things he is seeing, "What are those round things you threw in the room?"

"They are going to reprogram the computers to delete everything."

A massive explosion blows the room into fragments.

"See… deleted!" Jill smiles.

Our temporary prisoners unfortunately made it out of the room.

Jill yells back, "You guys are going to need an upgrade… your computers are now obsolete." She mumbles a few swear words under her breath.

Longhorn seems frustrated being unable to get in on the fight. But I'm glad he is with us none the less.

The opening of the cavern to the motor pool gives us sight of K Horse. If we could get to her, we would have a chance of breaking through the outer defenses. On the ground near the truck lay the two guards. Fifty thousand volts zapped them good.

Jill bursts into a run toward our steed.

I limp with purpose.

The blister of skidding bullets bursts passed us. At the entrance, another group of soldiers give fire at us. In the center of them is Fredric.

He yells out, "We were too complacent with your visit my friends. But we are now not so."

A slight burn scorches my arm as I reach K Horse. A bullet heated my arm, but didn't cause further injury.

Jill struggles with our door locks to get in.

I yell for her to get us in while I hold them off.

K Horse is again protecting us from gunfire, but we need to mount up and make a distant memory of here.

I empty clip after clip firing back, and am now at the end of my ammunition.

A soldier comes through to expose himself with an APG (Anti Personnel Grenade Launcher).

My yell seems to be in slow motion, giving Jill the command to clear the truck.

She throws herself low and away.

The trail of the missile shoots into the heart of our beast. K Horse explodes into a fireball of death. Knight Horse is no longer. The burning remains sears our nostrils of its final battle.

I crawl over to Jill calling to her, "Are you okay?"

Her shattered voice returns to me, "I think *I* have a boo boo now, my dear." Blood saturates her shoulder area.

The troops are coming closer.

The nearest transport is close. It is a vehicle similar to the unit we were picked up in. The rear hatch is open so at least we don't have to burn time to enter while our assailants moved ever closer.

We hear Fredric's voice over the speakers, "Sorry about your truck. I'm sure it will just polish out!"

The sound of laughter makes Jill grit her teeth.

I hammer the button near the entrance that closes the hatch. The pinging of ricocheting bullets off the hull comes to a halt. The weapon they developed is now turned on them.

Jill struggles in pain as I move her into the captain's chair, "Are you okay to drive?"

"I have to use my left hand so don't expect a smooth ride." She is hurting bad.

The motor sparks to life.

Jill swings her eyes all over the cockpit to find fire control *(weapons),* "We have missiles, fifty caliber machine guns and this other joystick with a red button." She grabs it and presses the button. The vehicle gives a slight shift, a swoosh of a pulse and… BOOM!

Jill shows me a broad smile, "We have a big gun. We call it a pulse generated missile or a PGM. It was in early stages of development, but I guess these guys perfected it. The weapon fires a projectile similar to artillery, but instead of a primer and gun powder, an electromagnetic pulse explodes a series of gases in the casing, pushing the projectile out at hyper velocity. Just the speed of the projectile creates a terminal impact in itself, then add a fluid that is twice as explosive as nitro, but stable until collision. On the destructive scale of one to ten… it's a twenty. You could line up three tanks side to side, and one shot would vaporize all three. I need to get an outside view to see the hole we just made."

Looking around near Jill, I find several screens marked 'Aft', 'Forward', and so on. I flick a switch turning them on, "We have visual!"

We both search for what our *Boomstick* just did.

"There it is!" Jill presses on the joystick to move us forward.

What used to be a heavy bunker door is now an opening to the secondary outer chamber.

I assume by the lack of assault on us now, Fredric's own machinery is our ticket out. They should have put some failsafe devices on board in the event of such a takeover. His own arrogance is now his enemy. For someone so smart, he is very stupid.

We track into the outer cavern to where the exterior bunker door awaits our remodelling.

Another blast from our new toy and sunshine blows through the opening.

***

Breaching the outer perimeter, we now understand why we were not chased by large numbers of enemy soldiers. Explosions clank against our exterior armor causing frequent shuddering. There is an assault force bombarding the large number of Nazi soldiers defending the mountain fortress. Vehicles similar to ours drew a defense line with light to heavy gun fire being exchanged.

"Jill. The attacking troops will obviously think we are the enemy, so we need to show somehow that we are not." The rock and jolts of attack on us knock me all over the cockpit.

"Bill, can you strap me into this seat please? This and the co-pilot seat have four point harnesses." She cringes in pain at every volley of impact on the hull. She swings the vehicle hard right, "Guess we need to take out one of our sister crafts to show we are friendly. Speaking of which... I could never understand why when our own side is firing at us, it is called 'friendly fire'. There is nothing friendly about it!"

She takes aim and presses the button, "Exit one enemy with a Boomstick."

The target disintegrates into oblivion.

"Well, my dear, our friendlies now know we are on their side, but now we are faced against two vehicles that have the same Boomstick."

Jill pushes the vehicle at top speed manoeuvring to keep from being an easy target.

"I'm going to tuck us in around that rock face and turn about. If they follow us, we will be poised to fire when they peek around to see where we have gone to. I'm sooo sneaky... I even scare myself! Hope it works."

While Jill plays hide and seek, I need to find more ammo for our long guns. There will come a time when we'll have to leave the safety of our temporary home to meet the outside world again. On the wall is a cabinet full of ammunition and loaded clips. I click free of my harness to scoop enough to ready our departure.

Jill quietly speaks, "Come on, peek your pretty armor around that rock. Be a victim of my rage. Let me give you what Knight Horse got."

No sooner do the words clear her lips than an armor unit shoots out around the rock. Jill presses the button and the front of the vehicle disappears, "That is for Knight Horse." She shifts the throttle forward to get back into the fight.

Ground troops and heavy equipment are scattered across the landscape making it hard to focus on the remaining threat. The chaos of battle ravages the beautiful park setting. The area seems similar to the battlefields of the cursed wars abroad. The residue of a distant war continued seventy years later on home ground.

It is my time to feel useless. My only function at the moment is to monitor the cameras.

A deafening explosion blows against us. The right rear corner is now missing, leaving us susceptible to intrusion from ground troops.

I yell to Jill, "We have been breached and need to get out of here!"

"We still need to take out that last threat. My guns are still functioning." She targets in on it, "Bye Bye!"

Even with the ringing in our ears, we hear the swoosh of the projectile along with the earth shaking from its impact.

"That's for just being a bad guy!" Jill snaps free from the harness and heads toward the now breezy opening, "Let's go link up with whoever is on our side.

The smell of gunpowder and death blanket the area in a shroud of combat.

The adrenaline pump from battle keeps Jill from feeling her shoulder pain, but soon she will be experiencing it. I need to get her medical care fast.

I scan the surroundings for one of *our* guys and yell for a medic.

Out of nowhere a soldier comes running. His Red Cross insignia on his helmet gives me solace in the moment.

Jill is cradled in my lap as he gets to us. Her injuries had collapsed her exhausted body to the ground.

The medic cuts away her uniform to triage her wound.

To see her like this tears my heart out. For me to take a bullet or even die is part of my job. To have her cradled in the arms of death is not what my mind can wrap around.

An MP approaches with rifle raised. He tells me to drop my weapon and step back with my arms raised, "Who are you?" His tone represents that of war.

"My name is William Harden, US Marshal Service. This is my wife Jill Harden." My attention wanes from his questioning to Jill, "My wife needs to get to a doctor, NOW!"

A familiar voice reaches my ears, "Well, Bill, you sure can make a mess." Bob is dawned in tactical gear pushing toward us.

He addresses the MP, "These are our people. Get a chopper for Mrs. Harden!"

The MP radios.

Bob kneels by Jill and grips her hand. "Hang in there, Mrs. Knight, we will get you to a hospital right away." His face could not hide his feelings. Tears form.

Minutes later the MP advises we need to get her to a landing zone clear of the action. He points to an area in a secured place. The four of us pick Jill up to carry her to the now waiting medi-vac.

The whir of the chopper rotors drowns out the war sounds. They are a welcome sound because I know she is on board and free from this hell.

Her hand is warm in mine. To lose her would be too much to be bare. She gave everything to make a stand.

Time stops, casing a vortex of silence in my head. There is no sound about me as the chopper makes its journey. All that matters in this world is this angel of mine. The soil that covers our bodies from our fight sears deep into our flesh. This is a horrible dream laced in reality.

I squeeze Jill's hand, bowing my head in agony. My eyes close to feel the words from my heart reach out in prayer to keep her with me.

"My friend… you are not alone." Longhorn takes his hat off out of respect for Jill. In all this time I have never seen him like this, "When your grandfather lay before me my guilt burned my soul. As I see you now, we share what cannot be changed, but faith will give you strength." He fades.

\

Chapter Sixteen

The familiarity with hospital emergency rooms is all too unacceptable to me, but knowing Jill is being cared for by the staff gives hope.

We weren't the only casualties. Military ambulances are offloading the more seriously injured soldiers. The temporary Mash Unit was overwhelmed spilling over to this hospital. Wounded from both sides fill the parking lot triage area. Military Police accompany the enemy wounded.

Amidst the hyperactivity of the ER, a nurse comes over to me to ask if I am okay. My tattered uniform and blood-covered body must be a sight. Never thought to check if I had any wounds I may not be aware of, "I'm fine, but could you check to see how my wife is?"

"You and your wife are the 'Knights', aren't you? Wow! I sure will check for you."

Bob comes into the waiting room, he sits down beside me without uttering a word. He could see in my face that I am struggling to keep from breaking down.

Moments later the nurse returns, "Mr. Harden, your wife is still in surgery. We will know more when they are done. She is holding her own at this time. Unfortunately, that is all I can tell you right now."

I can't smile or show my emotion, all I can do is peer deep into her eyes with my response.

There are tears in her eyes. An ER doctor calls her away.

Seven hours later

Each minute can stretch the soul to a breaking point. Ignorance of information tortures the mind.

A doctor comes out covered in blood, "Mr. Harden. Your wife suffered a severe trauma to her shoulder from a piece of metal shrapnel. No major arteries are damaged, though the injury may permanently restrict some use of her arm. Her blood loss was extensive, but she seems to be stable at this point. I'm sorry, I must go, I need to get back. You should be able to see her once she is transferred up to ICU."

I can't even thank him properly. I fall back in my seat.

In all the hours, Bob and I never shared words until this moment. My guilt finally overrides my silence, "I pulled Jill into something too crazy to imagine. She followed me out of blind love, and I took advantage of her. Why didn't I just stay a cripple and let well enough alone. My stupid actions did this to her." No matter what, my contempt of soul is swallowing me, "It is me that should be in the ICU... not her."

Bob turns to me, "No matter what today's outcome will be... you and Jill have opened a door that let our service, along with the FBI and NSA, an opportunity to access a damned part of our country that could have collapsed our government. Jill downloaded information that gave us a list of traitors against our democracy. An ensuing Civil War would have killed thousands, even millions. The two of you embarked on a journey few would have even considered. So the sacrifice is not in vain. There is nothing stupid about what you both did."

He cries like a baby, this man who is my friend.

"How did you know where we were?"

"I stuck a tracker on your truck. Did you think I was going to let you two chase bad guys without me knowing where you were? Oh by the way… we recovered what is left of it; sorry to say K Horse never survived the battle."

Bob tries to continue, but a nurse comes in and says I can see my wife now.

A swarm of reporters is now storming into the hospital. Bob speaks up, "Go to Jill, I will deal with them."

Jill's room smells of surgery, the chemicals bombard my sinuses. In contrast to my war-torn exterior, all is spotless. The nurse gives me a gown to cover my dirty body. She knows I am not ready to delay any time to be with my lady.

It is like I am seeing what happened to me months ago from Jill's eyes. She lay still. Her shoulder wrapped with thick bandages. The monitors sing a familiar song. The slight beep of her heartbeat on the equipment gives me assurance she is still with me.

Close to her bed, I sit with her hand formed into mine. All I want to do is be here. I lay my head on the edge of the bed and close my eyes.

***

The feel of a nurse gently shaking my shoulder brings me from a deep sleep, "Mr. Harden, a man dropped off some clean clothes for you. If you wish, there is a shower just down the hall for you to use."

"Thank you, I will. How long have I been asleep?"

She looks at the clock, "About an hour. Your wife is doing just fine." She saw my look at Jill.

Several marshals fill the ICU hallway. Bob figured we needed a shield around us for the time being. Our stay here is now on the news so our enemies may want to finish the job.

My body now clean and a little speed nap have given me a new sense of presence.

Coming back into Jill's room there is a nurse and two doctors. My nerves spike that while I was gone, she had a problem.

The nurse meets me and says all is well. They are just checking on her post surgery recovery.

From behind the wall of surgeons I can hear a drugged whisper, "Is my husband okay!"

"I am just fine." My smile emulates all that I feel in my heart, "How are you?" Dumb question, but I am at a loss for words.

Jill still is heavily sedated, but just to hear her voice gives me peace.

She smiles back at me, "Now I know how your boo boo's made *you* feel. I feel like I was run over by our own truck!"

***

The hours that pass, give us our time. Our time to believe we are still together.

Bob enters the room, "Glad to see you bright eyed, Jill."

I can see he is struggling to keep his composer, but he continues, "Bill… we have set up a press conference downstairs. The media is buzzing like a hornet's nest awaiting information about the military action in the park.

They are even more adamant about information on the *'The Knights'*. If you are up to it, we would like to have you present." He drops his head as though he asked far too much considering the last hours.

I look back over to Jill. Her smile gives me the go ahead, "Okay, Bill... go for it."

"Bob, can you give me a minute and I will join you in the hall? When is this news conference?"

"As soon as you are up to it; now would be a good time." Bob turns to leave the room.

I bend over to give Jill a kiss before my fifteen minutes of fame.

She whispers in my ear, "I love you."

A nurse scurries a TV into the room for Jill to catch the event.

The large conference room is full of overlapping conversations and secured by several armed military guards.

At the entrance door to the room we wait for our introduction.

The speaker announces Bob and I, so out into the nest we go.

Bob takes the mic first, "My name is Robert Dunham of the US Marshal Service. The fellow beside me is William Harden, also of the US Marshal Service."

Before he can continue there is a barrage of questions from the reporters.

"Are they *'The Knights?'*"

"Is the woman brought in okay?"

"Is she Mrs. Knight?"

The questions swamp in but Bob intervenes, "There will be an opportunity to ask questions later, so please hold off until then.

"Marshal Harden has been undercover conducting an investigation that involves a national security issue. Details into that investigation may be released to the media at an appropriate time due to the sensitivity of the investigation.

"The action of the combined federal agencies, including our office, the FBI and the NSA, involved several years of agents being in deep cover. Mr. Harden and Mrs. Harden were brought in during the final stages of the investigation. As a result of today's military assault on a mountain stronghold of the organization known as the 'New Confederacy,' one of our agents was killed in the action. His name will be released... as I mentioned, once we have completed the reports.

"Details of what we have found in the stronghold are at this time restricted information.

"US Marshal Harden infiltrated the stronghold with his technical assistant, Jill Harden. Their actions breached the enemy fortress providing us with Intel to commence our military action.

"Our present report of federal agency casualties is 32 dead and 53 injured. The enemy casualty numbers are unclear at this time.

"Now, the floor is open to questions."

The reporters struggle to get the attention of Bob.

"Mr. Harden. Can you tell us how your wife is? We heard that she is badly injured."

Silence overwhelms the room awaiting my response, "She suffered a severe shrapnel wound to her shoulder, but is in stable condition. The doctors have been excellent here and saved her life."

"We, in the media have been following the story of what has become 'The Knights' traveling around the countryside in a truck known as the 'Knight Horse'. Can you tell us about your investigation and your mean truck?"

"First of all, understand there are many people that have put their lives at risk in the course of this investigation. Today we have lost men that gave the ultimate sacrifice for their country. My wife and I are but a small part of the large picture."

In the back of the room stands Longhorn.

I continue, "There are times in our careers in law enforcement that we justify our job because of the actions of others. My great-grandfather was partnered with a US Marshal that inspired me to keep moving in pursuit of justice. When I was injured many months ago, this marshal's story lifted me out of my wheelchair to regain my place where I needed to be. When things seemed hopeless, his story and my wife taught me that nothing is impossible." I bow my head to hide my tears.

"Mr. Harden, as reporters, we often chase a story to the end of the world. We know how hard today has been on many families of those lost, but you and your wife led all the heroes, keeping our country safe from what your commander has said to be a threat to our democracy."

The room opens up in cheers.

My deep breath in gives me my words, "All that has happened throughout this investigation will probably remain classified, but we need to understand..." I can't finish.

Bob takes over the mike, "That is all for now."

The room breaks into all clapping their hands as we leave the room.

I stop in the back room. My anger is raging. My fist picks a target, through the drywall it travels to rectify my feelings, "A lot of people died today. All they can see is us *taking the lead*."

Bob grabs my arm, "They saw more than that. They saw two people who made a difference. Today we crushed the leadership. Now we need to get what is left. You and Jill are responsible for stopping what could have destroyed our country!"

I just want to get back to Jill.

Chapter Seventeen

One month later

Given time back at our ranch provided Jill and I with adequate time to heal. Our ranch is surrounded by the military, giving us protection during this time before our transition to witness protection. Whether we like it or not, we are retired to a life of different people.

Tomorrow, Bob and us are flying to Washington to receive a medal at the White House. Our notoriety will be buried with our identities after that.

Jill's shoulder is far from fully healed, she is now the patient and I the care giver. A position I am honored to fulfill.

The rustle of wind through the wind chimes on the deck provides us a moment of musical interlude as we sit having a cold beer on the deck.

"Let's go into town for a coffee." I am going stir crazy.

Jill responds, "Okey dokey."

As we make our way to the shiny new truck given us, I pause, "I miss the old girl."

Jill responds again, "Maybe we could sneak this one into the barn and rework it a little."

The thought did cross my mind.

The café in which started all this had framed portions of the newspapers covering the walls, that of the 'Knight Horse'. It has become our haven to visit our departed friend.

We both sit in silence as though planning our next adventure, although such activity is out of the question. Anonymity will be our last name soon.

In from the street two young lads and the father from my past enter after clearance from our bodyguards. They approach, glowing with the opportunity. In their hands are copies of a new comic book called Knight Horse. This also brought to mind the dime novel that the reporter was interviewing Longhorn and great-granddad about.

The cheek to cheek smile on Jill's face expresses how she feels about the two young boys approaching us as if they were meeting their super heroes.

Their arms reach forward with their comics in hand, their voices broken as they spoke in unison, "Could we get your autographs?"

It is for this reason we did what we did. Not for the glory or reward, but for the belief that there are now two more young boys that want what we fought for: Justice.

Missing from our days is Longhorn. Since the news conference, there have been no appearances. Although my meds are being reduced to the minimum, I am hoping that he is not just a delusion or a figment of my imagination. He is my friend.

After our two young friends leave, I had to ask, "Jill... remember back at the mountain when you saw Longhorn... you haven't said anything about that since. Did you actually see him or were you just going by what I had been saying?

"What I saw may have just been my mind playing with me in all the excitement. I just don't know. I just don't know." She takes a large gulp of coffee.

*   *   *

The flight to Washington means we will never see our ranch again. Fortunately, Image and Moon will be making the transition with us. To leave them behind just wouldn't work.

The White House is fluttering with activity prior to the ceremony. Our escorted walk down to the presentation is met with reporters and pictures being taken.

I just want this over. My body and mind are not making our change well. I am in conflict. The thought of hiding from the bad guys is compounding the stress of the day. The heart of the beast has been tore out, but the residual survivors of the New Confederacy will probably begin its rebirth one way or another.

A twinge in my leg causes me to waver in my step. The pain is brief but hard.

Jill picks up on it and tightens her grip on my arm. She whispers in my ear, "Are you okay?"

"Ya...just the stress."

Up on the stage before the crowd of dignitaries and media cameras, we sit with the command group from the assault at the park along with Bob. After the debriefing following the battle, Bob struck Brett from our undercover team. Officially, the NSA has buried his history in the hole it belongs.

The speaker brings our attention to the entrance of the President of the United States.

He begins his address, "Our country overcame a battle for our freedom in 1776. It has fought brother against brother during our Civil War. We have arisen out of the ashes of battle through two World Wars and sustained relative peace in Korea. We the people, of this great country of ours, fight to keep peace at the cost of many. Freedom is a way of life that is a cherished possession that our country holds with great passion.

"Amongst us are men and women that work hidden unceremoniously within the corrupt enemy of all of us. They are our fearless warriors that keep us protected from the forces of evil that attempt to undermine that freedom.

"Today, we have two people that fought far beyond their call of duty with personal sacrifice that gave this country a new step forward. I had the privilege of speaking with these two heroes of ours, and from our conversation I gained a humble understanding that they did not seek glory for their actions, but pursued with vigilance, justice for all.

"I see in them what has made our country, a country of compassion, honor and fortitude.

"After learning about the demanding extent these two people tempered a critical threat, we as a country owe them great gratitude.

"Would US Marshal William Harden and Jill Harden please step forward."

After that speech my legs feel like jelly, but my lady leads me forward.

He spoke as he presented, "Mr. William Harden. On behalf of the People of the United States, I present you with The Congressional Medal Of Honor for your dedication and bravery in the face of insurmountable odds. We thank you." The President shakes my hand after presenting me with the medal.

He moves to Jill and smiles, "Mrs. Jill Harden. This is an experience as a President, that humbles me in your presence. It is a person of your commitment that I am honored to present to you, for your bravery and ingenuity, this Congressional Medal of Honor."

I see the glow in her eyes as he presents the medal.

He continues, "The US Marshal Service asked me to present you with a special honor."

Bob joins him with a framed document and a US Marshal Badge, handing it to the President.

"It is also my honor to present you with this award of heroism, and a US Marshal Badge. Congratulations, US Marshal Jill Harden." He shakes her hand.

The room rises with hands together.

Bob asks us to step up to the podium to say something.

Jill whispers to me to speak for the both of us.

"Thank you Mr. President. On behalf of my beautiful wife and I, thank you for this honor bestowed upon us. We accept these medals on behalf of *all* those that were a part of this investigation, including those that gave their lives and the loved ones they left behind. Thank you."

***

We have entered our new life. But escaping into obscurity is difficult to maintain with national press coverage.

It is decided to return to our home ranch and face whatever or whoever is stupid enough to attempt retaliation from the New Confederacy.

Jill has developed a new line of residential protection gizmos to keep the bad guys at bay and would make them wish they had taken up a different line of work. She calls her security company *'I hope this house isn't protected by Jill Security'*. Rather long, but she doesn't conform to the usual.

The comics are doing well and have even produced action figures.

Jill and I finished the book. It is dedicated to my great-grandfather and Longhorn.

Chapter Eighteen

As a year passes in history, I miss the action. My adrenaline addiction is pushing me to do something a little out of the ordinary, and with Jill contributing to my delinquency, there is going to be trouble in these here parts.

Jill has said many times that cops don't retire, they just tire. I can't argue that, so now completed is *'Knight Horse 2'*. We acquired a 1994 Chevy Suburban. Painted satin black with new and improved gizmos... the 'Knights' shall terrorize the bad guys once again. This time we won't be so subtle in our approach.

Our first mission is to retrieve that artifact we almost forgot about in the locker. I figure it will take a few days to get there so we can create some havoc on the way with any felon that is in the wrong place at the right time.

Jill needs to watch that she doesn't outstretch the use of her arm. Her shoulder has restricted use but is managing very well.

K Horse 2 provides much more space for extra equipment and a handy dandy area for sleeping while the other is driving.

We have traveled several days and only minutes from reaching our hiding place for the artifact of gold. We encounter no opportunity to test our equipment. It seems crime is taking shelter on our route, or we are just too preoccupied with our new toy?

It is approaching noon as we park near the locker area. It has been a long time since we were in the heart of action when we left this place last, empty handed. We considered just leaving it *hidden*, but figured we should just donate the gold to a charity.

The lock clicks open. Nestled as before, I pull the heavy object from its confines. We scoot out to the truck to expose what may be the rarest artifact of North American history.

The sound of the bag zipper irritates my ears, but as we open the bag the irritation turns to shock. Atop the artifact lies a large brown envelope addressed to 'The Hardens'.

There are many times that surprises are welcome to encourage us to be wary, but this isn't one of them. I check the bag to make sure it isn't booby trapped and is clear.

Tearing it open, there is enclosed a typed note, it reads:

To my friends the Hardens;

Our last visit was rather exciting to say the least. Unfortunately, the damage you two caused us made me somewhat upset. But everything happens for a reason. Don't you think?

Anyway, aside from what has been and what is now, we need to push forward to continue where we left off. Which brings to mind my incredible desire to possess what you stole from me in the beginning. The papers and maps I mean. You see, I lied to you about their importance. It seems to keep our organization healthy, we do require you to hand over the documents.

Now we can draw this out with a lot of bloodshed. Or you can comply, at which time we will fade away out of your life. We wouldn't want to see any harm come to your parents, now would we.

Enclosed is a phone number to give me a ring. Oh, by the way; your parents say hi.

Your friend

Fredric Hitler

My hands begin to shake. My body trembles. I hand the letter to Jill for her to read.

I thought we killed that creature at the mountain!

A voice from the back seat startles us both causing us to grab our shoulder-holstered guns.

"I just can't leave you two alone for two minutes without me having to volunteer my services again." Longhorn struggles to sit in the confined seat, "These carriages don't give you room to stretch out the legs, do they? Rather sit my butt in a saddle, it's more natural."

Jill's jaw expresses her disbelief.

Longhorn cracks a smug grin, "Well, Jill, are you going to say you missed me or are you going to shoot me? Mind you, you would be wastin' a bullet."

I interject my opinion, "We need a holiday from our hobby!" I caught what is left of my breath, "Good to see you, partner."

Jill adds, "Ahhya... good to see... you... ahhya."

"We have a dilemma, partner. Fredric is still alive, and he has our parents." It is a relief sharing with Longhorn.

He still struggling to get comfortable, "So I see. Guess we had better get a move on then, hey?"

On the back of the envelope, a number is written in felt pen, Jill dials it.

"Hello my friends. Long-time no see. Have you got my papers?" Fredric's tone would scare the hell out of Satan.

Jill tries to sound strong, but breaks her words, "Do you have our parents?"

"Oh, most certainly. Would you like to speak with them?" There is a short pause then dad comes on the line, "Jill, we are okay."

Fredric grabs the conversation back, "Make your way to Fort Sumter, South Carolina. We will track you the whole route, so don't even think of calling in the cowboys, or your family will pay. Do you understand? Oh, I should mention that I made the mistake of underestimating you both the last time. That mistake will not happen again. See you soon." The dial tone sounds.

I need out of the truck to vent.

There must be purpose to this nightmare, but Hitler's legacy has stretched too far in this world. There isn't a hell hot enough for this creature.

I feel strength pushing through my body hard. What developed after my attack is nothing compared to now. My fist thrusts forward at the brick wall with exploding force, crushing through it as if it were paper.

Jill intervenes before I demolish the rest of the building. She grabs my hand to see what damage I've done to myself.

"Well that's good, your hand only has powder burns from the pulverized brick. Shall we calm down a bit before things get worse?" Jill is much more stable than I am.

"I'm sorry. Let's just get on the road." The adrenaline coursing through my veins should have an off switch.

My jets cool enough to speak without fire spewing from my nostrils, "I don't know what we should do. We don't have what he wants anymore, and the fort is not a place to easily access. Why would he pick that place? Unless they have done something like the mountain. That would be his style to build an underground fortress right under a fortress. Jill, can you get on the computer and get some schematics of the known grounds, as well as the structures. I need to think."

***

Two days later

It is a bright sunny day. Plans have come and gone from my thoughts with no solution. As we stand looking across at the stronghold, I am at a loss.

"Jill. Tell me about the layout. How can we slip into this place without alerting them we have arrived? How do we get on an island full of tourists?" My mind must be tired!

Jill starts her virtual description of what is now a Historical park, "The Confederate Army took the fort at the beginning of the Civil War. It says that the first shots were fired at this location. The Confederate engineers fortified it to be a nightmare against the Union Army attempts to take it back. After the war ended, the fort was all but destroyed. It was designated a historic park and restoration work began, but faded out until the Spanish/American War, when they felt it was a strategic location. More restoration has been performed ever since.

This would be a perfect front if the New Confederacy was in fact doing major construction underneath. What's that old saying about hiding in plain sight? There is a ferry that transports tourists on a route around the fort harbor that lands on site."

"Okay. We are going to play tourist toward the end of the day. I'm going to contact Bob and fill him in on what is happening. He can coordinate a *SEAL* unit assault from the water while we breach the entrance. I need to know where the main entrance would be most strategically positioned. There will also be a secondary entrance / exit to the lower levels. With all that, we need to know if there is a mainland site that could be a tunnel location. Okay, you have an hour." I wasn't trying to be ignorant… I'm just anxious.

No matter how this all fits, it just doesn't settle in my head that Fredric would isolate himself on an island. As he said, he won't underestimate us again. What does he have planned? He wants to put us in this area for his good reason.

As a cop, we try to fill the boots of our hunted. We try to think like them to understand our first principles of investigation. Who, what, where, and most critically… why. Fredric won't be fooled again so now we are treading in unknown territory.

The island is an open site for observation by the enemy. Any assault would be hard to cover in a cloak of darkness.

"This is not where our parents are being held!" My voice startles Jill, "Like he said; he wouldn't underestimate us again. He is playing us."

Jill responds in desperation, "They must be here. Why would he bring us here if they weren't?"

"Phone him."

Jill fumbles with the cell phone, "It's ringing."

"Well, well, if it isn't the heroes of America. Mrs. Harden… you had better give the phone to your husband before you drop it." Fredric is feeding Jill's anxiety.

She passes it to me.

If my anger could reach through the phone, he would be dead. I needed pause to speak, "Just get to the point and stop playing games. Obviously you can see us so get on with where you really want us to meet… if you do anything to hurt our parents, I will make sure, by the time I get finished with you, you will beg to have me just finish you off." My hand is shaking bad.

"I know you would like to kill me… again. Too bad you only got my double that last time while *I* made my escape."

"It seems hiding as a coward runs in your family. None of you can come out in the open and fight like a man. You cowl behind someone to take your bullet for you. So why don't you crawl out from under that rock you slithered under to meet me one on one? If you beat me, you can have your papers, so there's no purpose holding our family. Just let them go, and I give my word I will stand in front of you." My heart is pounding hard against my ribs. It is a time to finish.

"I can see you two are alone. If any cops come out of the woodwork, my men will shoot your family. Do you understand? One on one… I am sporting enough for that. Just remember… no cops. I will be there shortly."

His voice forces my veins to bulge.

"Jill, I need you to trace that call. He will have our parents close."

Jill smiles, "I already did. It is a block from here."

"Okay. Slip out of here and go get eyes on the building so his men don't move our parents while he is down here... don't do anything until I get back to you! Now go!"

She takes off on a run to clear the area. My fingers caress the trigger on my Colt, fighting the urge to break my word.

A black SUV swings around the corner and comes to an abrupt halt just feet from me.

A mountain of a man bails out of the driver's seat with an automatic weapon poised for use. Fredric slowly swings the passenger door open to make his entrance.

He is having second thoughts about our agreement, I can see it in his eyes, "Where is Mrs. Harden, my friend?"

"You are not my friend. She has gone to grab me a coffee. Without my caffeine fix, I can get rather grouchy." I lay my gun down to my side on the concrete. "Come on, let's get this over with, I have dinner reservations with our parents."

Fredric unholsters his gun and does the same, walking toward me.

I give no pause, my fist clenches and thrusts forward to his mid mass. The sound of a crushing sternum was followed by Fredric collapsing to the ground. Blood gurgles from his mouth. His eyes will see no more.

With his dying breath he utters, "You didn't say go, you cheated."

The driver raises his weapon to shoot, but the snap of a gunshot stops his move.

Bob took him out, "Couldn't let him shoot an unarmed man, now could I?"

He was sitting surveillance in a cab nearby.

Picking up my gun, I went to K Horse. Swinging the rear doors open I begin to put on my tactical gear.

"Do you have enough for your commander, or are you going it alone to retrieve your family?"

I smile, "Plenty here, let's move!"

The rumble of K Horse comes to life and the squeal of rubber sounds our attack.

Bob is on the radio calling for backup, but I am in no mood to wait as we see Jill at our target.

I almost forgot to put the truck in park in my haste, "Jill, I need you here to advise the troops when they get here." My hands cradle her face, "We will get them back, I promise."

She kisses me, "Be careful."

Bob lets me take lead.

We have been on many sorties together. Him I trust to cover my back. At the ground level entrance doors into the lobby, we can see armed men sheltered behind the security desk and wall corners.

Our backs caress the walls on either side of the exterior.

Bob comments, "Do we have any idea about *where* in this large building they are keeping your parents?"

"Not a clue. I figure one of our armed buddies inside may enlighten us." I take a deep breath in, "I am going to head to the right, by the planter. Can you give me cover fire?"

"Go." Bob sprays the interior with lead providing me with a couple of seconds of travel time.

The sound of sirens reverberates in the front street.

My exchange of gunfire gives Bob time to slip low and to the left, making his way to the security desk. The gunmen behind the desk retreat to the elevator area. Their exposed line of fire proves fatal. The others have made their way to the stairway.

We move forward to the stair entrance.

I look over to Bob, "Shall we take the stairs or elevator?"

"Personally, I don't like being locked down in a cabled box. Gives the enemy too much advantage… don't you think. Besides, since I have been flying the desk, I haven't been getting much exercise."

"Okay stairway it is… on three…"

They have a tactical advantage over us, but I had an attitude… which is more dangerous.

Bullets sear from above with random abandon, and their ricocheting paths are also a threat.

Step by step we advance up to third level.

It is now time to alter our climb. We move into a hall in search of another way up.

Even with the ear protection I wore to muffle the blast of the gun fire, I can hear voices. I motion to Bob. Two, possibly three bogies, three o'clock. He goes left, I right. We move in for attack.

There were three. Two are raked by our automatic weapon fire, one wounded against the wall.

Bob secures the two dead, as I kneel in front of the soldier fighting for breath.

There is no compassion in my words, for there is no reason for their purpose. There is no patience in my spirit, for there is no justification to restrain my anger. This soul before me is tainted with destruction.

My eyes burn into his, "If you have any wish to remain alive, you will tell me where the old people are."

He takes shallow breaths and remains silent, glaring back at me, "Tell me where they are!"

He stops breathing.

I shake him violently, "Tell me where they are!"

Bob puts his hand on my shoulder, "He's dead, my friend. We need to move on."

I throw the man to the ground in frustration.

Our radio sounds, "This is command two to command one. Do you copy?"

Bob responds, "This is command one."

"We understand there are possible hostages, times four. Two friendly's?"

Again he responds, "That is affirmative."

"There are birds in the nest and ground hogs. Do you copy?"

"This is command one. We copy. Stand firm until advised."

"That's a roger, command one. Command two standing by."

Bob looks over to me, "There is no place for the enemy to go. The roof is secured and lower level is closed off. We just need to find our hostages."

My eyes affix to a spot on the floor. My nerves vibrate as the electrical impulses radiate around my body. This gig should be free from emotion, because emotions cloud the mind. But reason is marred by fear that four innocent people will perish by the hand of a lunatic; a dead lunatic.

Bob commands my post, "Bill, regroup; or I will be forced to order you to stand down."

"I'm okay... just worried. We need to find the needle in the midst of this hay barn." I throw another clip into my weapon. The click of loading had another background sound. I drop low, swinging toward the noise.

"Bill, there are times in my position when I feel totally useless." Longhorn stands prone to fight, but is unable, "If I can't fight, then I can at least find your family."

An overwhelming sense of peace comes over me. My person is back to settle this nightmare in a proper state.

Longhorn vanishes.

Bob and I move to the next stairway.

The radio comes alive, "Command one, do you copy. This is command two."

"This is command two."

"What is your status?"

"We are at level three. Move your units to this level and hold. Keep the birds in the nest. Secure all to this level."

"Copy that, command one."

The radio goes quiet again.

Bob throws the stairway door open, allowing my entry. A shot skins pass my shoulder exploding into the wall, "We have one hostile at one o'clock."

More blow into the wall. I lobbed a grenade up to the landing, "Bob. Fire in the hole!"

We slam back behind the door.

Smoke billows from the stairway after the explosion.

Waiting a minute for the stair to clear of smoke gives me the chance to hear what Longhorn has to say. He came into my vision once more, "Your parents are well. They are secured in an office at the far end, north side, level five." His smile is that of satisfaction, "Partner... if we had guns like this back in my time, we could have cleaned up the west before barbeque in the evening."

I tap Bob on the shoulder, "Level five, north end office."

Bob looks at me strange, "What?"

"You heard me."

"How would you know that?"

My face should have told the story but… "I have intel inside. Just trust me… I haven't lost it."

"Oh, you mean Jill has eyes on somehow?"

"Well… Ya. She has eyes on." Hate to tell him a lie, but if I told him the truth he would put me in a strait jacket.

"How did she call you?"

"I have an ear bug in my other ear. Let's get up there."

The smoke has cleared enough to proceed with no resistance.

At the fifth level, I crack the door and use a mirror to get a peek, "Four north side, three left. Four south end. We can't risk shooting north, we might hit the hostages."

Before Bob can answer, "I have a plan. Their outfits are similar to our tack. I will put a shirt on from one of our former adversaries. You fire some rounds in the stairway and I will back through the door into the hall. They will think I am one of them being pushed back. Good plan, hey?"

"Bill, I really worry about you sometimes. After this is all over, I need you to go see the shrink. K?"

It is difficult finding a suitable shirt, but now I am undercover.

Bob shoots off a burst of rounds and just as planned, I did my thing.

Fortunately, they believe my ruse and don't shoot me. I am bullet free! I back over to the north door where four stand, it gives me a tactical advantage.

On cue, Bob throws a stun grenade as a diversion. Gun blazing, he breaks through into the hall.

I take out the side guards before they know what is going on. The four at the door change their direction to deal with me, but I again beat the odds. They went down with few shots exchanged.

My shoulder hit the door hard blowing it off its hinges.

The room is empty except for four happy, but bound people.

I hear Bob give the order for full breach. He also advises that the four hostages are safe.

The radio transmission was received.

To see my and Jill's parents in this place, like this, shakes my soul. Having tape on their mouths qualified my destroying the creature that put them here.

Dad lifts as I free him, and just stands before me. I can see the look that Longhorn shared with me the moment he told me where they were.

Dad reaches out his hand to mine, "Thank you, son."

The radio is ablaze, as the tactical units clear their way to us. Jill's winded voice comes across. She seemed to be running as she talked, "I'm on my way!"

All became surreal. The room swayed in front of me. Motion slowed.

Mom cries out, "You're bleeding!"

My eyes fail to focus, but I can feel a soaking of my undershirt, and it isn't sweat. I have been hit. Down I drop.

The faint sound of a man yelling sounds in my ears, "Officer down! Officer down!"

There must come a time that I have to refrain from using a war wound as a sleeping pill.

Chapter Nineteen

My consciousness wavers in and out briefly, and Image is nudging me with her nose to get my attention. I have no idea how long I have been out, but she is with me. My wounds are now strangely numb, and my vision is double. The last I see is Image taking off at a full run.

***

The beeps and buzzing of medical equipment brings me to semi-consciousness. I crack my eyes slightly to the bright light in my hospital room and see my commander next to my bed talking with my ex-wife.

Strangely, I notice a large ornate wall clock, and my stare becomes fixated on the second hand as it precisely changes position in measured movements. The wall around the time piece is covered in get well cards and letters. I must have been here for a long time to have enough to wallpaper. The ticking of the second hand is distinct in my ears and is reminding me that every second counts as a life time. It reverberates its movement to my awakening.

Waking to a state of disorientation is a substantial waver from sanity and triggers my body to defend itself yet I am unable to physically move.

The tube down my throat has me on the brink of gagging. Aside from my mental convulsion I have no feeling in any other part of my body.

They are not aware that I can hear them as my commander explains that Image came back to the ranch without me, and since I didn't report in, a team was sent to investigate. Image led them to where I was.

The doctor comes in and joins the conversation. He begins to explain to them the extent of my injuries, "The gun shot to his shoulder is surgically repaired and he will have no permanent dysfunction of his arm. However, he received severe trauma to his frontal brain lobe, and had massive cranial bleeding with two skull fractures. Like I said, his shoulder will heal, but he has no nerve response to any locations from his neck down. At this point we cannot determine if his nerve damage is permanent or the full extent he has suffered as far as permanent brain damage. We will have to wait until he comes out of his coma. We are keeping him heavily sedated because of his brain injury." The doctor goes on about lengths of coma without recovery and Jill, my ex-wife, begins to weep.

I want in the worst way to let them know I am awake, but I am locked in my own world without a key.

As Jill breaks down in tears, my commander wraps his arms around her to give comfort.

I slip back into my darkness.

Two weeks later

I swing my head back and forth to shake the tube out of my throat as my eyes open to the blast of light. Jill was sitting next to my bed until my movement and goes calling for a nurse.

A rush of hospital staff barge in the room to my attendance. With them is the surgeon that I saw when I last woke. He told tells them to take the breathing tube out of my throat and barks out more medical orders. The flurry of activity around my bed is making me unsettled. My mind has been in darkness and the activity shoots me with anger. Lost in a world isolated by my silence.

The doctor comes to my bedside and asks me some stupid questions; like if I know where I am, and what my name is. Of course I know! As he waits for my response, all I can do is mumble some unintelligible words. My lips can't form the words! No matter how hard I try I can't say the words! I am in here. I can see you, but why is it what I am thinking not transforming into speech? I can remember my life, I have memory. This should mean something! But I can't tell them! God! I can't feel my body! I can't move my body!

The doctor orders something for the nurse to give me and the shot slows my anxiety, but the anger is raging in my spirit. This is not like me to be so angry, but I have no control.

After the flurry of activity Jill moves her chair next to my bed and cradles my hand in hers. I can see her hold my hand, but there is no feeling.

Jill has warmth in her eyes, and that is all I can feel. I look into hers, but I can't say anything to her except a jumbled bunch of noises.

As I look at her, I can't see how our relationship ended in divorce. She is a good woman, but I neglected her to my mistress; my work. She didn't deserve what I gave her in return for her years of love and devotion. Now here she is sitting next to a vegetable and I can't tell her I am sorry. I close my eyes to darkness again.

***

The warmth of sunshine on my face raises my head upwards out of slumber. My eyes look about the room to gain awareness. I am home and looking out of my living room window! Of this I have no memory, coming home to be in this chair, in this spot. I last felt Jill's hand in mine in the hospital. All since has been blank.

A nurse is in the kitchen and sees me awake. Her smiling face welcomes me to the new morning and asks if I am ready for breakfast.

The last I remember is being in the hospital with Jill, and now this. I want to *say* yes to the breakfast, but all that I can do is shake my head up and down. Understanding my emergence back into this world without memory evades me.

Any semblance of my time home is vacant. What a horrible isolation!

She comes over to me with a warm face cloth and wipes the drool from my chin.

As I look down I can see I rest in a wheelchair with a blanket covering my legs. My arms are cradled on the chair rails and as I attempt to move my arms, they lift only slightly. My fingers twitch, and the harder I try, the more I can lift my arms. It's hard to describe how elated I am to just twitch my fingers. There is pain in my shoulder and I have a brutal headache, but the sun is shining.

Out front a car pulls up and out jumps Jill. As she comes to my side I get a hug and kiss on the cheek. She kneels in front of me and sees the tears in my eyes as I struggle again to raise my arms.

My eyes refocus on the barn and Image comes to mind. I try to talk, but give it up for a point with my finger toward the barn.

Jill says, "Oh, so you want to go see Image do you? Okay, let's go see her." She scoots around and wheels me toward the barn.

As we are approaching Jill tells me that Image came home and led the search party to where I was. She saved my life because I was on the brink of death when they got to me.

***

This day I have woken with a clouded mind, that all has been; my dream vanished. In my absence from reality my true life has returned. I don't understand! I have been here before. I have traveled this road… or have my thoughts been only that… a dream world within my unconscious delusion. I am still a cripple in a damaged body unable to function. My life is nothing anymore. To awake to this is worse than death.

We stop several yards back from the barn door.

Jill goes up to the broad doors and opens them to give me sight of Image. As the sunlight fills the now lit cavern, the front of Knight Horse glows in all her beauty, although ravaged by combat. Next to her, is Longhorn mounted on *Horse.*

Jill went inside to bring Image out to me. She appears to not be aware that our metal steed is still with us.

Longhorn and his mount step forward to me and stop. He throws a small book that lands on my lap.

As I peer down at it, I can see the cover quite clearly. There is Longhorn on *Horse,* with my great-grandfather saddled next to him on a horse twin to Image. The bold letters spell out the name of the dime novel: *Guardian Angels.*

It is my time to weep. Words cannot be spoken from my lips. To see the deep compassion in Longhorn's face gives me an understanding that the mind adjusts itself to cope in strange ways.

Longhorn vanishes from sight. My reality vanishes with him.

Jill leads Image out to me past where only moments ago Knight Horse *was,* and unaware of Longhorn. Further my mind twists me to a lower place. I am broken in body and spirit.

Image's nostrils flare as she nuzzles her head to mine. She is my partner and savior. To be blessed with life, but tortured in this world seems just too unfair.

As Jill approaches, she shifts to her left as if dodging an obstacle. Her head turns from side to side, "Did you feel that cold breeze? Strange to have cold in this heat."

She comes before me, "What is that on your lap?" Her eyes peer to identify my new acquisition.

As my crooked fingers caress the cover, I raise my eyes to her. If only I could speak. I am now at peace, for my life will be spoken aloud.

To dream gives one purpose. To wake gives one life. There are no endings; Just new beginnings.

*****

Also by Bryce Baker

*****

Ghosts of Time

In a dynamic story of action, adventure, danger, suspense and romance, Andrew, a not-your-average paranormal psychology professor, is hired by a bewitching heiress to research and investigate her quest for answers concerning the incomprehensible mystery of her missing uncle. Her uncle was researching some mysterious supernatural events, and as the story grows, so does the adventure to the mystical realm of the unknown and the unnatural. The saga is a mesmerizing, unearthly, sometimes humorous, action-packed journey into the paranormal to solve an old mystery. Not only does Andrew find more action and adventure than he expected, he found romance and love in the most unusual manner. Exciting thriller from the author of best seller, *Shield and Sword – The Kabe Legacy.*

Shield and Sword – the Kabe Legacy

THE BEGINNING

The odor of the pews and raw wood penetrated my sinuses with a scent reminiscent of the farmhouse. The year is 1869 and with all that has transpired since the war my heart has hardened, leaving a gaping hollow hole inside. Sanctuary in this old church provides me a temporary reprieve and further prepares me for a visit to my mom's grave, the first in over a year.

Footsteps break my solace and I swing around with Colt in hand. The dark-cloaked Pastor seems unprovoked by my action and raises his hand out to me as a sign of welcome.

"Joshua, is that you? It's okay; you are in the house of the Lord and weapons of destruction are unnecessary here." His voice echoed off the walls, but was at once both calming and was peaceful. "How have you been since last we spoke?"

Without saying a word, I'm sure he could see by my leather cladding and well-worn gun holster that the hunter was also the hunted. There was a long silence before I could swallow the lump embedded in my throat, and reply. "My hunt for my mother's killer's has lead me across several states, but as of yet I'm no closer than the day I started." I bowed my head in sheer exhaustion. "I owe it to her to bring them to justice."

"Joshua, your mother's death was not your fault." He put his hand on my shoulder and continued. "If you were there at the time you would be in a grave as well. The guilt you feel is normal, but in the eyes of the Lord the guilty will be punished. Whether He brings down the killers by your hand or by some other means is not your decision. This guilt you feel will continue to consume you day by day and will be relentless unless you release it."

When a man makes a living bounty hunting, even words of wisdom tend to fall on deaf ears. It's like knowing one shouldn't step off a cliff but ignoring all sense of rational thinking. One's focus is so self determined that the quest seems unstoppable. Even without another word the Pastor could read my face.

"When was the last time you saw your fiancé?"

"I haven't seen her since the war and I'm sure she's moved on."

"Josh you need to settle down in some place. Get married. Start a family." Pastor Kenny seemed almost demanding. "Get a job as the local sheriff and start a new life. It has been many years and the grieving could end. Revenge is not an option. You've got to get your life turned around." Pastor Kenny paused as he pondered his next words. "Josh, there is a barn dance tonight. There will be lots of food and good times. Why don't you take some time to be around people and start digging yourself out of the pit you're in?"

Pastor Kenny is a man my age. He was born and raised here. I remember times as kids when we'd swim down at the river, torment the girls with slimy things and laugh endlessly. It was a time of innocence that we should cherish forever. Out of those memories I answered. "Alright!"

***

It was a bright and sunny day as I rode toward town. The smell of wild flowers and lilac was a welcome break from old blankets and Jake's 'scent de horse'. Jake, if you haven't guessed, is my horse, an Indian pony with an attitude.

We entered town with busy streets and no one seemed to notice the stranger. The town boasted a small population of about three hundred. My dusty throat called for a stop at the saloon and a quick beer before locating a bathhouse and maybe some clean clothes.

Before I pushed open the saloon doors the rumble of conversations from within had already reached my ears. Inside was a full house of wranglers, gamblers and dance hall girls. Behind the bar was an old friend, 'Will'. He recognized me straight away. His loud deep voice hammered over the crowd. "Josh, is that you under that road dirt?" Before I could approach any further he was over the bar, shaking my hand. "Go sit at a table, I'll bring us a bottle."

Will pushed two patrons from a table and offered me one of their spaces. "I'll fetch us a bottle of the good stuff and be right back."

Returning from the bar, with bottle and glasses in hand he sat with me.

"I thought me eyes were playing games when you walked through the door. Heard tell uv'e bin huntin' fer the 'Rebs'." Will poured while he talked.

Before I could respond we downed a shot and he poured another. "Ya, seems that's the story."

"Betchas perty excitin' bein' a bounty hunter, hey?" Will never did make it to school!

Will may not have been well-educated but if you didn't have a loaf of bread to eat, he'd give you a meal. Over the course of the bottle we reminisced and shared 'the good old times'. It was great sitting with an old friend but it was time to clean up and get to the dance.

*****